I0619416

Soul of Asimina

Kristi Strong

Soul of Asimina

©2013 by Kristi Strong. All Rights Reserved
Edited by Kristina Circelli – Red Road Editing
Cover Art by Once Upon a Time Covers

No part of this document may be reproduced or transmitted in any form or by any means, electronic, mechanical, photocopying, recording, or otherwise, without prior written permission of Kristi Strong. Permission may be obtained by contacting Kristi Strong through her email, StrongNovels@live.com.

This is a work of fiction. Names, characters, places, events, and incidents are either the products of the author's imagination or used in a fictitious manner. Any resemblance to actual persons, living or dead, or actual events is purely coincidental.

ISBN 10: 0615938957
ISBN 13: 978-0615938950

Acknowledgments

Soul of Asimina is so much more than just words on a page, and the people who have helped in its creation so much more than their titles.

The fabulously amazing Kristina Circelli, not only a talented editor who forgives my consistent errors and embarrassing typos, but also an incredible friend who has helped me through so much in life.

Stephanie with Once Upon a Time Covers, the mastermind behind the exquisite cover of Soul of Asimina, who is so talented that she was able to perfectly create Sabina before the character even existed.

Roger and Jackie Grondin, my sounding board for characters, events, and the constant supporters of my "imaginary friends".

Scott and Kaylee, for living with a wife and mother stuck in her head, who randomly jumps up to furiously type on the keyboard or scribble a note in the middle of a game.

I would also like to thank the incredible group of ladies in Story for Story, for helping with word selections, descriptions, and motivation through writer's block.

Enjoy!

Character Descriptions

Court of Kaldalangra

/'Kal-da-' lahn-gra/

Rowan de Nespa: Known as the Grand Duke of Kaldalangra; Rowan is married to Rhea, and father to Sabina, Aaron, and Katrina

Rhea Aralia: Known as the Duchess of Kaldalangra and Lady of Steinbrekka; Rhea is married to Rowan, and mother to Sabina, Aaron, and Katrina

Lianna de Dhome: Once a Mercene of the court, Lianna now helps her husband, Savin, rule the village of Vestona

Savin de Caislean: Once a Komisar for Rhea, Savin now rules the village of Vestona

Nyssa de DamaTalous: Known as the Queen of Kaldalangra; Nyssa accepted the throne upon Rowan's abdication. She is married to Sebast, and mother to Alcine and Josef

Sebast de Asimina: Known as the Duke of Kaldalangra; Sebast resides at court with his wife, Nyssa. Their son, Alcine, now rules the village of Asimina in his stead

King Verikhan: The tyrannical former King of Kaldalangra and father to Rowan and Nyssa

Queen Sula: The former Queen of Kaldalangra, wife to Verikhan, mother to Rowan and Nyssa

Mateo Verikh de Kalda: The former High Prince of Kaldalangra, also known as Matt

Agrafina: The former consort of the High Prince, Agrafina is now married to Brokkan and mother to Rafael

Kylassame

(Kil-ah-sah-may)

Nastasio: After his mother's death, Nastasio moved from the court to Kylassame

Liam: The Governor of Kylassame, husband to Cassie and father to Mya

Cassie: Rhea's best friend and Mya's mother

Lily: Rhea's best friend and Arielle's mother

Chapter 1

Asimina

The man crept along the bushes, his taut abdomen brushing against the top of the dewy grass, the moisture soaking through his cotton T-shirt and raising goose bumps on his skin. His deep blue eyes, the hue of the open ocean, scanned the open spaces between the leaves, searching through the twigs and the thorns that kept him slowly creeping through the dense undergrowth, when all he wanted was to burst through the vegetation.

Sharp rocks dug into his knees through his thick denim jeans, and he paused in his motion to sit back for a moment's rest. A tanned, calloused hand brushed through the tangled dirty-blonde hair and the man winced at a thorn that had become embedded in a knot. It had grown unruly in the past week, unwashed and uncombed since his arrival in this world.

The sound of laughter reached his ears, and he dropped back to his belly, muscular arms and legs propelling him forward in a military crawl until he was fully buried under the shrubbery. Beyond that line of shrubs laid the outskirts of the village, his first destination, his first option. He smelled the aroma of dinner in the muggy air, heard children screaming in play, and saw adults in the distance talking animatedly. Smoke curled lazily from a cooking fire near a

1

cluster of huts, spiraling into the sky, blending in with the purple and blue hues that signaled the impending night.

The man found a break in the thorny ring of bushes and slowly eased through, keeping his body low, silently watching the village, looking at the people moving between the small, one-story woven houses, looking for *her*.

She has to be here, he thought. *I know I heard her voice in the night. I can practically feel her here, practically smell her. She has to be here. If I am still enough, quiet enough, I can feel her heart beating.*

A cool autumn breeze drifted over his still form, giving temporary relief to the muggy heat that had been his only companion during the daylight hours. Sweat trickled down his dusty neck as he began to move, low and silent, along the wood's edge to an orchard of fruit trees nearby.

He had spent months trying to get to this place, months of searching, and swearing, and doubting his own sanity. His single focus, his sole purpose for breathing, was to get back to *her*, to get *her* back. Friends thought he was crazy, that he was under the influence of drugs, or alcohol, or both. Some thought he was grief stricken, his mind lost in the haze of loss when she disappeared. His parents sent him to therapy, to medical doctors, even to a holistic healer trying to help him "get back to reality," or so they said.

They don't understand what happened. What we went through. What could have been. What should have been. They don't understand how much I love her, or how she loves me. They don't understand what she went through to save me. How could I just leave her? How could I not at least try.

She was right there, in his mind, the entire time. He would crawl into bed at night, exhausted from days of searching, and smell her on his pillow. Her beautiful, rich auburn hair and the way it felt when it trailed through his fingers, was always there on the surface. He could feel those deep, wise, hazel eyes boring into his soul, seeing his pain in a way no one else could. That memory guided him to the abandoned warehouse, convinced him to jump into the dark pit where the floor used to be, celebrated as his feet once again touched the realm of Kaldalangra.

As he pushed through the forest surrounding the village, he could feel her. His blood, his breath, his soul pulsed with the beat of her heart. She was there, in every tree, in every creature. When the wind trailed through the trees he could smell her, the scented lavender soap that she always used teasing him as he ran along the path.

There, again! His breath quickened as the sounds of female shrieks, joyful and carefree, dissolved into laughter. The sound was moving toward him, and his heart began to race as he recognized that laugh, the inflections, that beautiful voice.

He crouched under the apple tree as the group of people darted into the orchard, two young men being chased by three women. They did not notice him, intent on their path. The women's small feet danced over the tree roots as they gained on the men, their taller, larger frames hampered by the low-lying branches.

There! He felt pressure around his head, his blood heating at his good fortune, at months of pain and anguish coming to an end.

She was just as he imagined. Her long, brown hair was tied into a loose braid, and trailed behind her as she ran, chestnut strands catching the sun as it bounced. Stray locks had fallen from the braid and danced in the air as she jumped, twirled, and danced around the orchard. Her skin was tanner than he remembered, but then, the last time he saw her had been in deep winter. Her laugh bounced through the orchard, the action slowing her motions until her companions were far ahead.

"Oh, go on, then!" she called out, and her voice was like liquid heaven as it sang upon his ears.

Her! He thought fiercely as another rush of adrenaline coursed through his body. *I finally found her. I can finally save her!*

He stood up slowly, and a branch cracked under his feet. She was only ten feet away, almost close enough to touch. She heard him. She turned. But her eyes showed fear instead of happiness. She looked around furtively, and then focused her attention on him again.

"I'm here," he said, his voice cracking from both disuse and emotion. "I came back to save you. I'm here."

She just looked at him with wide eyes, all the while slowly backing away.

So young, he thought, *too young. It was her, it had to be. Why does she look so young?*

~ * ~ * ~

Sabina stood in the orchard, as frozen as a rabbit caught in the sight of one of her father's hunting hounds, and quickly ticked off her options.

Too close for me to run, she calculated. The stranger was over a foot taller than her, and looked to be athletic enough to overtake her before she escaped the orchard. Her friends had turned and were coming back, but too slowly, not realizing the danger. She could yell, but there was no assurance that help would come quickly enough.

She looked into his glassy eyes and saw a feverish hope there, a longing so intense that it raised the tiny hairs on her arms. He was covered in dust and mud, and his shaggy hair was tangled with twigs and thorns.

"Hello. Are you lost?" she asked, carefully backing up as she spoke, aware that he moved closer with every step.

"I'm here. Don't you recognize me? I'm here." The man stretched out a hand toward her face, the movement smooth and unthreatening.

"I'm sorry, but I don't. Are you from the court? Are you from the other world?" Sabina glanced to her right, saw her friends approaching, and saw the shift from carefree friends to young warriors as the men approached. Above them, her faithful avian companion, Faulks, began a dive from the sky, angling toward her position in the orchard.

"It's me. I came back to save you. I came back to help you. Now we can find our way back again, together." His eyes were glistening with unshed tears of relief that he had finally found her.

"Why don't you come back to the village with me? We can get you some food, some clean clothes, and then we can talk." Sabina slowly reached out a hand for the man, heart pounding in her chest, carefully tracking her friend, Nastasio, as he moved behind the stranger.

"We should leave now, before they trap you again." He stepped forward to grab her hand, preparing to flee with her into the woods.

5

Nastasio moved as soon as the stranger's hand touched his friend, and a quick elbow to the temple sent the man crumpling to the floor. Only a second later, Faulks landed heavily on Sabina's shoulder, talons digging into the thick shoulder pad she always wore when taking the hawk into the field.

Sabina glared at her friend as she absent-mindedly stroked Faulk's head feathers. "Overreact much?"

Nastasio raised an eyebrow in disbelief before dropping his gaze to the man. "You heard him, Seb. The man is clearly delusional and who knows how dangerous." His eyes rolled in annoyance as she dropped down to inspect the man. "Besides, I just grazed him."

Faulks lifted off her shoulder, agitated at the rapid shift in position and perched on a nearby branch, keeping one eye on the stranger. Sabina lightly placed her fingers on the man's throat to confirm that his heart still beat and then sat back on her heels to look at the stranger.

He was a tall man, and she supposed he would be handsome once some of the muck was cleaned off. Clothing hung from his body as tattered rags, and his shoulder-length, dirt-covered hair was strewn with twigs, leaves, and forest debris.

Though his skin was taut from serious dehydration, she could see that starvation had begun withering the muscles below. While she had no idea what his frame was like prior to this encounter, it seemed that he had possessed a toned, athletic build before becoming lost in woods surrounding the village. His skin blanched under her careful touch, and she suspected that beneath the brown, dusty film was skin that was viciously sunburned.

6

Nastasio squatted down beside him and patted the man's pockets, searching for weapons. "Doesn't seem to be armed, or have any provisions. How long do you think he's been out here?"

She shook her head and shrugged before glancing at her other friend, Henri. "Mid-twenties for age?"

Henri studied the man intently from his position a few feet away. Even in his youth, he had always been a good judge of age. After becoming an adult, he was frequently brought to the nearby court of Kaldalangra or the village of Kylassame to help identify individuals found wandering the land.

The job duty kept him busy, as people frequently fell into the realm of Kaldalangra, his homeland. Ever increasing in amount over the last five years, Queen Nyssa, the official ruler of the realm, had specially created refugee sanctuaries to accommodate the extra needs of the booming population. He and Sabina frequently volunteered their time at the sanctuaries, helping the newcomers adapt to the ways of their new world.

He squatted down beside the man and studied the face carefully before nodding in agreement. "Twenty-five, maybe twenty-seven?"

Sabina gently moved a lock of dusty hair that had fallen over one eye and gazed down at his face thoughtfully. "He doesn't seem dangerous. He acted like he knew me. Maybe the sunburn and the dehydration were causing him to hallucinate."

Nastasio relaxed as several men armed with clubs and swords approached the group's position in the orchard. Weapons were lowered as they realized the threat had been neutralized, but they still moved at a quick clip toward the group.

"Hallucination or not, he had plans to abduct you." Nastasio kept his voice low, aware of how well sound traveled in the fall air.

Sabina huffed. "Well, obviously that didn't work out for him." She chewed her lip thoughtfully before adding, "I think we should take him to Mom. She's good at calming down the lost people."

Henri gave a dry laugh. "I think we send him straight to the nearest camp and let them sort him out." His suggestion fell on deaf ears, so, with a shrug, he turned toward the group of men to brief them on the strange encounter.

"No," Sabina tilted her head slightly as her finger traced the man's jawline. "I think we'll keep him right here."

Chapter 2

Asimina

"Seb, wake up." Aaron shook his older sister's shoulder softly in the darkness of their hut.

Sabina blinked as the pre-dawn glow came in through the smoke-hole in the top of the hut and rubbed a hand over her eyes. "What's wrong, Aaron?"

"It's the guy. He's awake and keeps asking for you. Henri and Cole had to tie him up because he kept trying to leave the hut and find you."

That information had Sabina quickly throwing a light, calf-length jacket over her nightclothes and moving out the door. "What were you doing there this early? You know that Dad wouldn't want you hanging around a stranger. We don't know if he's dangerous or not."

He rolled his eyes but gave no answer as he followed her from their family hut and walked beside her across the village.

A hiss of frustration seeped through Sabina's lips and her eyes narrowed in annoyance. "I knew I should have left you in Kylassame. You promised me that you would behave!"

Her brother was only fifteen, and fond of going on wild adventures that caused their parents to perpetually fear for his safety. Sabina had begged her parents to keep him at their home in Kylassame during her visit to Asimina, but they caved to his pleas since he rarely was afforded the chance to spend time in the small village. *He would be good,* he had insisted. He would stay close to his older sister and Nastasio, a family friend. There would be no wild antics or needless risks.

Sabina wrapped her coat tighter around her body and leaves crunched under her feet as she approached the large hut where the stranger was temporarily housed. "Go home, Aaron. Now."

The teenager just gave her a sideways glance and kept walking. "I was safe, and technically I was following the rules. Nasta is in there along with Cole. I just kept them company while the stranger slept. There was hardly any danger with the guy asleep and tied up."

"You are going to be the death of me," Sabina grumbled as she pushed open the door created of firmly lashed branches.

The sight of the stranger had her stopping dead in the doorway, and she barely noticed as Aaron, not paying attention, smacked into her back with a mumbled curse.

The man kneeled on a woven blanket in a back corner of the hut, hands and feet tied behind his body and a length of cord wrapped around his arms, pinning his elbows to his torso. His downcast eyes were glazed with fever and shudders wracked his body as he used all of his energy to keep from falling over.

"Seriously?" Sabina strode across the small space, glaring at Nastasio and Cole.

She untied the clean cloth they had wrapped around the strangers mouth and he sucked in a raspy breath of morning air. "I'm pretty sure that gagging the man was overkill."

Cole just glanced at Nastasio, uncertain and anxious. He was only a year older than Aaron and had been living in Asimina for several months at his parents' request. Torn between his lifelong loyalty to Sabina, his near-cousin, and his want for acceptance among the men, his voice remained silent as he watched the adults.

Nastasio met Sabina's piercing eyes with a calmness that infuriated her. "If you want to go snap at someone, go speak with Alcine. He's the one who gave the orders."

Her brow furrowed as Sabina processed this additional news. Alcine was her cousin, older by a year, and the future leader of Asimina. As such, his word was law, and he rarely showed poor judgment while dealing with people in the village.

"Why?" she asked, divided between her desire to help the stranger and show deference to her cousin.

Cole licked his lips nervously and he glanced at Nastasio for reassurance. "He kept talking about taking you away, to the other world; kept saying that he needed to save you. Take you home, away from us."

Sabina let out a long breath and then squatted in front of the man. "What is your name?" It was an effort to keep her voice soft and even with the turmoil that swirled in her stomach.

He pressed his cracked lips together and shook his head, refusing to meet her eyes.

Nastasio leaned against a support post. "He won't tell us anything, Seb. No name, no location, not even how he got here. All he

11

says is that he needs to find *her* and rescue *her*. When we asked who she was, he said-"

"The woman from the orchard," the stranger whispered, eyes staring at Sabina "I need to save her. I love her. I won't hurt her ever again. I promise."

Another long breath, then Sabina gently said, "We've never met before. I think you are confusing me with someone else."

His sapphire eyes never left hers. "No. No, it's you. I finally found you. But I don't know who these people are, or why you seem so young."

"Do you remember who you are?" Sabina asked cautiously. It was not uncommon for strangers to the realm to forget who they were.

He nodded his head in confirmation, eyes never leaving Sabina's face.

"Can you tell me who you are?" Sabina gently laid a hand on his shoulder.

The stranger shook his head vehemently, twigs and dust scattering into the air. "They all hate me. That's why we had to leave. But they wouldn't let you leave. We have to leave before they want to hurt you too," he whispered, glancing fearfully at the young men in the hut.

Sabina carefully ran a hand over his matted hair. "Aaron, go get me some water, please."

"Here." Cole handed her a small wooden cup filled with drinking water from the hut's water jar.

12

She placed the cup against the stranger's lips, encouraged as he gulped down the water. "Drink this down. It will help with the fever." She straightened and said, "I'm going to go talk to Alcine. Aaron, go back to our hut."

Sabina walked out of the hut without looking to see if her brother had followed her orders. He never did, so there was no use in thinking that he would this time. At least she could tell her parents that she tried. She rolled her shoulders to ease some of the tension that had begun to build when she saw the strange man in the orchard.

Try to be understanding to Aaron. He only has freedom for one more year. Let him have his adventures, she reminded herself. They all knew that, as the first-born female of the family, Sabina had a freedom that her brother, the only boy, would never have. Their youngest sister, Katrina, had the best position of the family. Five years younger than Sabina, Katrina spent most of her time at the Court of Kaldalangra, enjoying the feel of silk upon her skin and luxuriating in her undying love of idle pastimes.

Sabina and her brother spent most of their time at Kylassame, learning the various trades and helping their parents with the daily happenings of the only village modeled after the other world. Aaron spent the remainder of the year at the Kaldalangran Court with Katrina, learning the proper ways of conduct in that setting, while Sabina generally toured the many villages of the realm.

The sun had just peeked over the horizon as she walked around the hut that belonged to Alcine, after knocking at the door and receiving no answer. She stopped as she rounded the final wall and took a breath to steady the onslaught of nerves as she watched her cousin move through his morning exercise.

At twenty, Alcine had already unofficially ruled Asimina for several years. Unwed, he was a man to be wanted by women and envied by men. Shirtless and wearing only light cotton trousers, he moved through his morning exercise fluidly, sword in hand. His skin was still deeply tanned from the summer sun and his hair just beginning to grow out from the short style he preferred during the summer heat. His constant drive to improve the village, better the fields, and care for the orchards kept his body lean, and his demeanor somber.

Though he was not born of this realm, Alcine took to Asimina with all of his heart and soul. His love for the land, the village, and her people made the established population accept him without hesitation. His forgiving, companionable, and steady personality made them love him.

The routine ended in a graceful spin, the sword raised high and then slashing lightning-fast toward the earth. It hovered, just touching the soft sand of his practice space as he stayed frozen in a deep crouch, eyes fixed on the white, just-risen sun.

Sabina cautiously cleared her throat, uncertain if she would be addressing Alcine, her loving cousin, or Alcine, the leader of Asimina.

Dark brown eyes locked onto her face as he slowly rose from his crouched position. The trance was broken as he blinked, ran a hand over his short black hair, and then smiled at his cousin.

"Seb. I thought you would have been here long before now."

Relieved that she was dealing with her loving cousin, Sabina allowed her temper to slip. "One - what the hell was my brother doing in the same hut as a stranger?" She raised her hand to stop the answer as she continued. "And two," she paused, collecting her emotions. "A gag? Really? The man is so feverish he can barely stand, and yet he's trussed up like a chicken and gagged?"

Alcine calmly rubbed a towel over his shoulders to collect the sweat that beaded up on his skin. "One - you will have to take up with your brother. I told him that he was to obey everything you said while in this village. The last thing I want is the wrath of your father descending upon me, or your constant pestering."

He gave his cousin a scathing look that halted her snappish response. "And two, who do you think you are telling me how to conduct business in my village?"

Sabina swallowed hard, breaking his intense gaze by grabbing the jar of drinking water and handing it to him. "He's not well, Alcine. He's feverish, and hallucinating. He's obviously been in the wild for some time. I'm not trying to tell you how to run the village. I would never do that. But I'm not sure that you are handling this particular case in the correct manner."

"He wanted to kidnap you. How did you think the men of your family would react?"

"Not me. Not really." She twirled the end of her braid around her finger distractedly. "I think he's caught in some memory. He just needs a little time to realize where he is."

"Seb." He shook his head and then glanced up at her with the sheep-dog grin that usually melted a female's heart. "You know I love you, but you are really naïve sometimes."

She stood open-mouthed as he walked by her. "I am not!" she finally stammered out.

Chocolate brown eyes twinkled as he chuckled. "Tell you what; I'll make you a deal. You can interact with this guy under the condition that Nastasio or I are in the room with you." Alcine jerked his head toward the river path. "Have Nasta take him down to the river. I'll meet you down there as soon as I get cleaned up."

Chapter 3

Asimina

Sabina glanced up the pathway to the village before wading into the bathing section of the stream. Long ago the women of Asimina had used large river-rocks to create this pool, effectively damming a small portion of the stream that was the lifeblood of the village. In doing so they were able to create a cool, safe, and communal area for bathing and swimming.

Henri and Nastasio were already in the pool, carefully walking down the steps where the water deepened to their hips. An adjoining section went deeper, up to the average villager's neck, but the two men had determined that would be too risky, that the chance of the man escaping, or drowning, would be too high.

Cole and Aaron stood on the grassy shore, tossing a soft leather ball back and forth as they stood guard over the older men's weapons. Too young to be in the water with a strange man, as water hampered defensive movement, they had been banished to the shore before Sabina arrived, something she silently thanked Nastasio for as she stepped into the cool water.

Nastasio was the older brother that she always wished for, although she did wish he was slightly less strict around her. Ten years her elder, he had first come to Kylassame when he was only eight years old and quickly adjusted to the new lifestyle. Sabina knew that

17

he had been born in the shadow of the castle and once had family there, but in the nineteen years of her life she had never been able to convince him to share stories of that time. He would simply give a sad smile, shake his head, and tell her that his life began in Kylassame.

The stranger balanced carefully in the slowly moving water, his legs free to walk but his hands still bound behind his back. The aqua water was deep enough here that a fall would plunge him under the surface, and he was not confident that the men holding him steady would rescue him.

Sabina stepped up to him, her bathing supplies in a specially-designed mesh pouch tied to her belt. She had shed her traditional woven tunic for a blue cotton tank top that she had brought from Kylassame, and, as her skin prickled, gave her body a moment to adjust to the cool water.

Her pouch contained a wide-toothed comb made of bone and a small bar of soap, scented with lavender. The stranger looked at her oddly as she approached, and she slowed her steps until the wild look receded from his eyes.

The men gestured for him to dunk his body under the water, and, after a moment's hesitation, the man did so, the first layer of dust, dirt, and blood from his journey in the undergrowth washing away. A second dunking removed the next layer, and revealed the bare skin, now exposed to the mid-day sun.

A small gasp of horror escaped from Sabina's mouth and she shook herself to keep her eyes from welling with useless tears. The man had obviously been tortured, scars that looked just months old stood out as bright white streaks against the sunburned skin and cascaded down his shoulders, chest, and back. Sabina had seen old injuries, whip-lashes and battle scars, on the bodies of her family and the elders, but these took her breath away. It was as if someone had tried to rip the man's flesh from his body, to skin him alive.

She dunked herself under the water to give her mind time to settle, then shook the water droplets from her braided hair and approached the man.

"I'm going to use this soap to wash you, alright?"

He nodded, his muscles tight enough to snap as she rubbed the soap between her hands to create lavender suds, and then gently ran her hands over his shoulders and chest. She felt the shudder that coursed through his body as her hands drifted over the scars, and carefully moved down his back, then his chest, the soap removing the final layer of grime.

Henri glanced at the man, eyes widening in reluctant admission that, based on the scars, this man was a fighter, and tougher than he had seemed. "What did this guy go through to get those?"

Nastasio stared at the scars, a memory of an event nagging at him, but never coming to the surface. "I can't imagine what could even cause those kinds of scars. Torture, maybe?" His grip on the man, still firm, gentled slightly as he felt sympathy for a man who had not had an easy life. He stared at the scars on a body slightly shorter than his own, and, while muscular, weak in comparison.

"How old are you? Can you tell us that?" Nastasio took a water jug from Sabina and carefully poured it over the stranger, the suds swirling around them before the current swept them away.

The stranger hesitated, swallowed hard, and then hoarsely responded, "Twenty-five, give or take a few months."

Sabina looked up into his eyes in surprise, slightly frightened at the way her heart beat faster at the sound of his voice. "What happened to you? How did-" she trailed off as her finger passed over the large, parallel lines that covered his upper chest, and felt his skin quivered under her touch.

Those deep blue eyes swung to her face, and he whispered, "Punishment. Atonement. Retribution for something I never realized I did."

She bit her lower lip nervously. "Are you tall enough to kneel in the water? I'd like to try to get your hair a little tidier. It will make you feel better."

He nodded and the men slowly helped him to kneel on the muddy river bottom, the water taking most of his weight as his body sank below the surface. He felt her move around behind him, her body warming the water against his back.

Gentle hands rubbed the lavender soap into his hair, and she spent time using a combination of the wide-toothed comb and her fingers to slowly un-matte the tangled mess. As the debris floated away, strands of blonde began to emerge, the hair curling slightly in response to the freedom.

Sabina moved back around to the front of the man and moved a stray lock from in front of his eyes. "All done with the hair. Just the face left."

The men rose from the water and she used a soft cotton square to delicately remove the last of debris and blood from the stranger's face. "We'll get some clean clothes for you when we get to the hut. You should be able to fit into some of my father's clothes. Come on."

Chapter 4

Asimina

Not her. He realized as his body stopped shivering and the warmth of the small fire began to seep into his muscles. *Not her, but ... almost.* He shifted uncomfortably, his arms still bound behind his back and his feet hobbled together. He was able to move around the hut, somewhat, by carefully shuffling, but unable to escape.

The men who captured him were not unkind, but he knew that they would not hesitate to rip him to shreds if he attempted to escape, or tried to touch the woman to prove to himself that she was not the one for whom he had searched so long.

She was kind to him, her gentle voice soothing as she rubbed a gel over his skin, the burning sensation from the sunburn calming from a searing pain to an itching annoyance. She was watchful as the men retied his bonds, using a softer rope this time, and a kinder touch.

The woman was beautiful, and so close to the woman he dreamed about, the woman he had searched for such a long time. Her dark chestnut hair, unbound after coming up from the stream, hung in long waves, streaked with red highlights that shimmered in the sunlight as they had moved up the path. Her face was kind, but tough; the high cheekbones and full lips gave the image of a woman who knew what she wanted, and would stop at nothing to obtain it.

Her touch in the stream thrilled him, and terrified him. When her fingers fell upon his scars he felt an immediate sense of shame, waited for her to recoil from him, or worse, recognize him. Yet, her touch only contained a quiet strength as she moved over his body, and her eyes grew more puzzled as he refused to tell his story.

~ * ~ * ~

"Is he still asleep?" Sabina asked quietly, ducking her head into the small hut where the stranger lay.

Nastasio nodded. "The aloe mixture helped. I also mixed some herbs with the tea you had him drink to help him rest." He hesitated before adding, "There is something about him I don't like, something … off, almost threatening."

She raised her eyebrow and bit back the laugh. "It's hard to be threatening when you are tied up."

He stirred the fire with a hardened stick. "I'm serious, Seb. I can't put my finger on it but it's there." He paused before changing the subject. "When are you going back to Kylassame?"

"Not for another few weeks," she replied, wrinkling her nose. "I need to head out in a few days for my time at court."

"You sound thrilled."

Sabina sighed and sat silently for a moment, her eyes falling on the sleeping man in the corner. "Court has become … I don't feel comfortable there. It's too formal, too orchestrated." She shook her head, reluctant to admit the real reason she had started hating her court visits in the past few years.

"And?" Nastasio glanced up at her before turning his attention back to the embers.

"And … I'm not smart enough to compete with the people there. I'm not witty enough, or charming enough, or pretty enough. They expect me to be perfect, because of who I am, but I'm just … not good enough."

"Meaning, you aren't fake enough to suit them?"

"Nasta!" She clamped a hand over her mouth to muffle the outburst. "That's not very nice."

He shrugged. "Neither are the people at court."

It was a truth that she hated to admit, especially because her family had roots, had its very beginning, in the Court of Kaldalangra. Yet even those roots were not enough for her to ever feel comfortable in the large, stone castle. The people were of a different temperament there, sharper, saccharine, and she often questioned anyone's sincerity.

The only person that she ever felt safe around at the court was her friend Bryan, who was in training to take over the stables from his mentor, Aleksei. Bryan never cared if she had dirt on her shoes or a dreamy look in her eyes. He understood her need for fresh air, and was always honest with her, never afraid of her reaction if he disagreed with her stance.

She carefully moved over to where the stranger lay sleeping, and pulled the blanket higher on his chest. "I just wish I knew who he was, his name at least, before I leave."

Nastasio jumped to his feet as the stranger opened his eyes and sat up quickly, both motions causing Sabina to scurry back in alarm.

The stranger looked at the woman and spoke, his voice rough with disuse. "Eric. My name is Eric. Please don't leave."

Chapter 5

Asimina

Sabina rolled her stiff shoulders as she stepped through the door of her hut, letting the thick tapestry that served as a door sway behind her. A messenger had arrived the night before, and informed her that her request to delay her visit to court was denied, and she had been summoned by the queen.

She plucked at the finely sewn lace that brushed her fingertips, embellishments attached to the long-sleeved silk dress that had been crafted so well that no stitches could be detected. The deep plum color of the dress set off the red hues in her hair, and the bodice hugged her trim figure. Her hips formed a flare at the beginning of the long skirt, which split in the center to allow the wearer an easier time in the saddle, and revealed black cotton trousers that gracefully flared over polished riding boots.

Her only consolation was that Alcine had also been called back to court, and his irritation eased the annoyance she felt at their positions.

Alcine tightened his leather wrist guards before swinging onto his mount, mouth set in a hard line. "Come on, Seb. Let's go get this over with."

She followed suit, taking a moment to settle her long riding skirt evenly across her gelding's back. "I don't see what you're so grumpy about. You had to realize by now that being the queen's son means spending time at court."

His brows raised but a trace of a smile crossed his face. He gently urged his mount forward, calling back, "I could say the same for you."

Sabina huffed and urged her gelding forward, slowing when she was riding beside Alcine. He had also dressed for court, with just as many grumbles and sighs as she had given. He looked like a prince in the perfectly tailored purple doublet, dyed to show his status as a member of the DamaTalous, the royal family. His brown pants were tucked into knee-high black leather boots covered with gold embellishments.

He shifted uncomfortably in the stiff saddle, and sighed once again. "Have I ever mentioned that I despise this saddle?"

Sabina's body shook with silent laughter as she murmured her sympathy. The saddles used by the people of Asimina were simple in nature, as was the very nature of Asimina. A thick, specially shaped blanket woven of wool designed to provide comfort for both the horse and rider. The rider could easily feel the intent of the animal below, while the horse carried little extra weight and could respond to the lightest of commands. Carefully braided straps created stirrups and several sturdy metal rings were added to allow for baggage and storage while traveling.

In contrast, the saddles used by the court were heavy, thick, and unwieldy. Though stunning in design and covered with gleaming gems, they were uncomfortable for both the horse and rider. They were made for short trips where display took precedence over functionality, and not for trips that involved a pace faster than a walk, or any uneven terrain.

Alcine's saddle was created out of thick leather molded around a wooden internal structure, the blackened leather exquisitely tooled and gilded with designs associated with the royal family. A thick pommel, covered in gold and precious gems, rose in the front of the saddle, causing constant annoyance any time he tried to bend forward to look at a dip in the path or his mount's footing. Gem-studded flaps of thick leather lay between his knees and his horse's barrel, limiting his ability to communicate through the subtle shifts of the thigh and calf muscles.

Their horses tossed their heads as they loped down the well-traveled road that would return them to the court of Kaldalangra. Even the horses disliked the outer embellishments and decorative pieces that came with a visit to court. Their bridles were created of stiff leather, beautifully tooled and embedded with precious gems. Tassels swayed from the buckles and trailed down the length of the reins, causing the horses to startle when a bright flash unexpectedly appeared into their vision.

Sabina began to chuckle as they rode, receiving a glare from Alcine, whose mood had grown darker every step closer to the court.

"I'm sorry, Alcine. I was just remembering the first time that we put these stupid bridles on our mounts."

The man cracked a smile and began to chuckle as well, rubbing his mare affectionately on the neck, even though the pommel placed uncomfortable pressure on his hip.

They had received the horses as gifts during the summer following their sixteenth birthdays. The geldings had been trained by the men of Kylassame, and that village was known for their horses.

The young animals had responded and warmed to their new riders immediately, only occasionally giving in to the skittish and sometimes erratic behavior customary for an inexperienced mount.

Then the horses had been introduced to their court gear, and it was all that the two humans could do to keep them from panicking. The heavy weight of the saddles caused them to stumble and jump around, certain that there was a dangerous predator on their backs. The red and gold tassels that swayed along the reins randomly blinked into the eyesight, causing them to dance in circles, trying to get away from the threat that was always there.

It took the cousins over a month before the animals would accept the impractical and fear-inducing equipment, and no attempt at diplomacy could convince the queen that the traditional tack was unnecessary and should be replaced by the simpler gear of Asimina.

She's had a hard time the last decade, Sabina mused as they slowed their horses to a walk, moving over the wide wooden bridge that separated the outlying settlements of the court from the rest of the realm.

Queen Nyssa had taken over the court when her own father had been killed, years before Sabina's birth. The stories of the man's rage and vileness had faded into legend as time passed, the people of Sabina's generation having lived only in peace through their lives.

"I would have gone mad if I were in the court twenty years ago," she said, startling when Alcine responded in the affirmation, unaware that she had spoken aloud.

The court was better now, or so said the long-standing residents who had been there during the time of King Verikhan. During his rule, thousands had died, mostly the people of Asimina and Albadarl, but also those of lower status in the court system. The people of the court were given volumes of books in proper protocol, and one day, as a young teenager, Sabina had succumbed to boredom and read through a dust-covered copy she found in one of her mother's old trunks.

How did anyone survive, she had wondered, *when every rule seemed to contradict itself?* The only rule she understood easily was: *The king's will is law, and must be obeyed at all times.*

She had questioned her parents about that rule after reading it, and had been shaken by their response. Her father's body, muscled and hardened from a lifetime of travel between his villages, had gone tight as a bow-string, his eyes turning dark and angry. Her mother drew a shuddery breath as her tan face instantly paled and she sat down rapidly as if her legs lost their strength.

"Be glad you were born in a time of peace," was their only response, and Sabina did not push for more information, terrified at the sight of her unflappable parents' immediate reactions.

"Here we go," Alcine grumbled as they approached the protective walls surrounding the castle. Within those walls lived the people of the court, high-born and low, loyal and deceitful, and all of the politics that came with them.

Sabina took a deep breath alongside him, both making the intentional emotional shift to being members of the DamaTalous. His face grew even more somber as he became Lord Alcine, son of Queen Nyssa de Verikh. Jaw set and shoulders pulled back, she once more was Dauphine Sabina, daughter of the Grand Duke Rowan de Nespa.

Chapter 6

The Court

Citrus and vanilla scents filled the air of the room, and Sabina took a careful breath to quell her annoyance as feminine peals of laughter bounced off the walls around her.

She loved her sister, Katrina, but loved her more when they were not together at the court of Kaldalangra.

The woman beside her leaned over and smiled, wheat-blonde hair falling delicately over her shoulder. "It is good that you have returned to us from those dusty outliers, Dauphine. It has been too long since you have graced us with your presence."

Katrina, seated across from her older sister, lifted the delicate silk fan to cover the smirk that had begun to form. Peers of the court only used Sabina's official title of Dauphine when they wished to get in her good graces, though the attempts were usually futile. "How was your time at the village of Asimina, sister?"

Sabina forced a smile on her face and tilted her head, emulating the motions of the other women in the room. "It was pleasant, although, there was a small disturbance that required my attentions and those of Alcine, thus delaying our return to the court."

"Oh, you are so lucky to have had an entire journey with Lord Alcine," another woman sighed dreamily, running delicate fingers through goldenrod-hued locks. She had been infatuated with the man, or rather, her visions of becoming a member of the DamaTalous, for years.

"Yes, Irena, it was quite a pleasant journey." This time Sabina fought to keep an amused smile from forming, an action which would surely give offense.

Irena had made her intentions known to Alcine eight years prior; before he had left the court to establish his home in the village of Asimina. She had been drawn to the man's darkness, his non-conventional appearance combined with his status giving him a touch of the exotic that the women of the court fawned over.

"Lady Sabina, could I implore upon you to mention my name to him in conversation? I find his presence so very divine, yet he seems to be avoiding me as of late." Irena fixed her brown eyes onto Sabina's, blinking rapidly as they began to moisten with emotion.

Sabina forced a friendly expression upon her face and politely replied, "Of course, Irena. I will be sure to do so, next time I speak with him."

The avoidance had been intentional on Alcine's part and prudent after Irena had tried to coerce him into bed many years ago. The woman had been sure that he would have been unable to resist her charms, but Alcine was well aware of the ramifications of taking a Patron's daughter into the bedroom and quickly removed himself from the situation. He had been groomed for leadership from a young age, and warned of the dangers and pitfalls that he would encounter because of his place in the realm.

The second woman, Caela, placed a hand on Sabina's knee, her fingertips cold through the thin fabric of the dress. "Lady Sabina, do you know of the events that are scheduled to occur after the dinner hour? Katrina keeps hinting at something spectacular, but refuses to give any details!"

Hazel eyes fixed onto gray as Sabina looked at her little sister, disquiet growing in her gut at Katrina's attempt at avoidance and sudden discomfort. "No, I have yet to speak with my aunt, the queen, and be briefed. Katrina, is there something we need to discuss?"

The fourteen-year-old licked her lips nervously. "I apologize, but I am unable to divulge the information at this time. The information will be formally shared in just a few hours." She quickly stood up, and then took a long moment to smooth her long, silk skirt and adjust her dark-brown curls. "I am feeling a bit peaked. I will see all of you at dinner. Please, excuse me and enjoy yourselves."

Sabina warily rose from her seat, casting an apologetic glance to the small gathering of young women. "Please, excuse me as well. I have just only arrived at court and believe it is prudent that I speak with my sister on this matter. Have a good afternoon, ladies."

She caught up with Katrina down the hallway and clapped a firm hand onto the girl's shoulder before leading her into a nearby private room. Katrina looked close to tears, an unusual state of being for who sister, who was usually self-assured to the point of narcissism.

Katrina walked into the room, slippers swishing across the plush carpet, and collapsed onto a low couch just as she burst into tears. "I am sorry, Sabina. I did not mean to almost tell them the secret, but I was so excited for Josef that I almost revealed everything. Mother would have been so angry, and Aunt Nyssa would have never forgiven me."

32

Sabina sat down on the couch and gently stroked her sister's dark hair. "What secret, Katrina? I was not lying when I said that I had not had a chance to visit with Nyssa yet or be caught up with the current politics."

Katrina sniffed, looking so lost and confused that Sabina embraced her and reminded herself that Katrina was caught in the tumultuous time when a girl became a woman. Her sister had always been in control of her emotions and her companions, while at court, and Katrina took any failure of composure to heart.

"Josef is sixteen now, and ready to start his training." Katrina gripped her sister's hand tightly. "I was so excited for Josef that I forgot to realize what was going to happen to Alcine. I completely forgot about it, until Irena mentioned him."

Sabina waited patiently as Katrina rubbed the tears from her cheeks. Her voice meek and shaky, Katina continued. "Tonight they are going to announce that Josef is going to be next-in-line for the throne, and will begin his training as heir. They are all going to question me about why it is not Alcine. What do I do? I do not want Alcine to hate me! What do I tell them all?"

Katrina collapsed into sobs again, burying her head in Sabina's lap and letting the uncertainty flow from her heart.

Sabina gently stroked her hair and murmured soothingly to help the younger girl settle her emotion. She had noticed that Katrina seemed more high-strung, jumpier than she usually was around the court, and had avoided Alcine when they first rode into the courtyard.

It was a well-kept family secret that Alcine was not going to be heir to the throne, and he had been made well aware of that when he reached his teenage years and had begun training as the sovereign ruler of Asimina. They had all ignored, or denied, the fact that one day their secret would need to be revealed to the people of the realm.

The family had made the decision to keep Alcine's past, and his birth record, away from the prying eyes and ears of the court. He had been raised from an infant as the son of Nyssa and Sebast, and if that was true in heart but not by blood, none had spoken of it. The public never questioned why Josef carried the title of Dauphin, and Alcine the simpler title of Lord Prince. The traditional hereditary title of High Prince had been abolished when Nyssa accepted the crown, as no living person wanted to be associated with the person who once held that position.

It had caused great tension in the family before the birth of their second son, Josef. The appointment of sovereignty went through the bloodline of the DamaTalous, and would have passed to Sabina herself, had Josef not been born. Though she was technically the heir to the realm, as the oldest child, all agreed that a child of Nyssa's would be more widely accepted than any child of Rowan's. It was a relief when Josef was born, a healthy boy who would stand to inherit the realm, should Sabina chose to abdicate the throne.

Sabina had no intent of ruling the realm, preferring her life of travel and good works, and was more than happy to pass her birthright to her oldest cousin by blood, the son of the current ruling queen.

She gently wiped away the tears from Katrina's face as her younger sister sat up, still miserable with guilt and worry, all amplified by teenage hormones.

"Katrina, it is okay to be happy for Josef. This is going to be a big day for him, one of the biggest of his life. Alcine has known from day one that he was never going to be in line for the throne, and has never wanted to be the heir to begin with. His soul belongs in Asimina, not in the court."

Katrina sniffed and took a shaky breath. "What do I tell my friends, though?"

Sabina hugged her, pulling her sister tightly to her. "You just tell them that it is a family decision, and if they want any more information they must ask the queen herself."

Chapter 7

The Court

They stood, shoulder to shoulder, gazing out at the happy Patrons who danced and gossiped around the dance floor. The Great Room of the castle had been decked out in royal glory, the crest of the DamaTalous painstakingly embroidered onto great lengths of cloth that draped from the ceiling to graze the floor. The marble floor had been cleaned and polished until it shone so brightly that the white stone reflected the colors of the brilliant dresses as women spun and dipped with their partners.

The Patrons of the court still enjoyed their opulence, although there was a greater deal of variety now that the court events had been opened up to all castes of the realm. The wealthy women wore great gowns of silk, the sumptuous fabric tailored for flare, and for notice. Hair was pulled up with glittering combs and bejeweled pins, and faces carefully painted to enhance their features.

Men of the court dressed in a simpler manner, yet opulent nonetheless. Black suits worn with spotless white silk shirts were most commonly seen, with an occasional brown trouser worn by a lower caste member. Rings on fingers flashed as their hands moved, the gold bands and precious gemstones worth a lifetime of toil for those who had not been born into wealth.

Sabina looked over as Alcine shifted his weight, causing his shoulder to brush against hers. "Are you ready for tonight?" she asked in a low tone.

He shrugged, his usual expression one of boredom and nonchalance. This was the face he wore while at court, indifference perfected over his lifetime.

"Irena told me to give her a good word. I see her over there, looking for you, wanting you."

His lips tugged into a frown before he realized his cousin was being facetious. "Since when have you started to speak for Irena?"

This time is was Sabina who shrugged, before smiling to Irena, still across the room. Pitching her tone so that it would be unheard by any around them, she replied, "She is a petty little bitch who wants the status that she would get, or rather, thinks she would get, by joining with you. But the less she knows about how I feel, the more her tongue wags about how she feels, and that information can be quite useful, don't you agree?"

"The status she thinks she would get?" His eyes grew dark for a moment as he looked over to where his brother, younger by four years, stood next to their mother. "Her affections will not be a problem for long then."

Sabina followed his eyes and gave a small smile as she took in Josef. The boy was going to have a hard time convincing the people of the court that he was a king in the making. He had recently turned sixteen, and was at the stage of transformation from boy to man when nothing was correctly proportioned.

He was tall, already greater in height than his mother, though he had several years of growing left to do. His frame was lean and lanky, his muscles still developing as he grew into manhood. The colts in the stables had a similar look, their bodies awkwardly holding the deep wells of power and confidence that would soon allow them to grow into powerful stallions. Dark blonde hair had been combed back into a neat knot at the nape of his neck, and his clothes had been pressed to perfection.

Josef wore the ceremonial clothes well, despite his changing body, and with an ease that Alcine had never been able to accomplish. A deep red vest embellished with the gold crest of the DamaTalous was tailored to fit his wide shoulders impeccably. Black pants clad his legs, the material tucked into knee-high black leather boots, gilded and bejeweled. His expression did not give away the nerves, the reservations he had about this day, the day he would be named the official successor to the queen and future ruler of the realm. All people who looked at him saw the confidence, the peace of a person who knew exactly where he belonged; even if they did not yet know the whole truth about how truly he belonged in this role.

Compared to the rest of the court, he looks the part, she thought. *Compared to Alcine ...* she sighed. While Alcine may not feel or look as at ease in the formal trappings of royalty, his tall, athletic body meant that all eyes went to his person when he entered the room. The deep, rich voice held the attention of any within earshot, and people followed his command without question.

A quick snapping of Alcine's fingers abruptly brought her out of her thoughts, and he quietly murmured, "Look lively," as a man approached them.

"Dauphine Sabina," the man said as he smoothly bowed in front of them. "Lord Prince Alcine," he added with a small bow to the man before turning back to Sabina. "May I ask the Dauphine to grace me with a dance?"

Sabina swallowed her anxieties and smiled. "Of course, Lord Brendan. I would be delighted."

She placed her hand gently on his and allowed him to lead her onto the dance floor.

"The queen does the realm proud with this celebration." He spoke softly as they joined the couples maneuvering the steps of a slower-paced court dance. "It is only moments now until she makes the grand announcement that is being foretold. Based on her generosity, it must be a momentous one indeed."

Her head dipped to indicate agreement, and Sabina tried to enjoy the dance, ignoring that the man's hand had slid slightly lower on her hips than was custom.

He's not a bad person to have as a suitor, she thought as they executed a slow spin on the dance floor. He was a handsome man, with the light blonde hair that was once the only acceptable coloring of the court. His cognac brown eyes twinkled as they glanced at her face, before once again looking downward to focus on the steps of the dance.

Women in the room sighed in envy as the couple swept by, for Brendan belonged to old blood, his parents rising to one of the highest Patron castes before Queen Nyssa erased the official classification lists.

Yet, as they flowed gracefully around the room, her thoughts could not help but be drawn back to the man lying in the hut of Asimina, with scars on his body, and unfeigned adoration in his eyes.

Brendan's hand tightened slightly on Sabina's hip, drawing her attention back onto the dance floor. "Lady Sabina, do you have knowledge of what this announcement will be about? There is some rumor it regards your claim to the crown."

She gave a smile and lied. "I have not a clue, my Lord. I too can surmise its importance only by the grandeur provided this night. Ah, here we are, back where we began."

He leaned forward and kissed her, once on each cheek, in farewell. She managed to keep a straight face until he was across the room and out of sight. Then she allowed herself one huff of frustration before lightly hitting Alcine's arm for laughing at her plight.

"It is not funny, Alcine."

Alcine glanced over at her and composed himself. "Of course not. Love is never funny."

She stammered a rebuttal before narrowing her eyes. "I will go get Irena this instant, Lord Prince Alcine de DamaTalous."

His gaze shifted to behind her shoulder and his eyes grew dark. The stoic expression fell into place once again, as if a curtain had snapped shut. "It is time."

Sabina turned to follow his gaze and took a deep breath as she saw her aunt, uncle, and younger cousin step up to the raised platform set at the end of the room. She let it out slowly as Nyssa sat upon her throne, her husband, Sebast, standing one side of her, and her son on the other.

The din of the crowd tapered out as Patron after Patron saw the queen seated on her throne, and turned to hear the grand announcement that they had been promised.

Only Sabina saw hesitation in her aunt's face as Queen Nyssa stood up, resplendent in her golden silk gown, the fabric shining on her body as if the sun itself had been woven into the strands. Her hair had been carefully coiled upon her head, strands of curls escaping to tumble gracefully onto her pale neck and artfully cascade over the delicately crafted crown of office.

Sabina reached over and took Alcine's hand as his eyes met those of his mother, and he dipped his head once to accept the unspoken apology that those blue eyes conveyed to him and him alone.

Her voice rang out, clear and melodically over the assembly, as Josef stood by her throne, silent and tense

"Good people of Kaldalangra, beloved of this land and of this court. I thank you for joining us on this eve, this time of great change, and great joy. Tonight, you will all bear witness to an event that was previously held in secret and in terror."

She drew a deep breath. "Tonight, in the view of the members of this court, and the good people of Kaldalangra, I wish to formally announce and present my heir, the man who will become King of Kaldalangra after my soul has passed from this earth."

Patron after Patron turned to look at Alcine, some with great joy in anticipation of his assumed rule becoming official, some in jealousy and denial that one who had such dark features could be so named.

"I present to you, good people of Kaldalangra, the lawful heir to the throne of the DamaTalous, the son of my blood and future King, Dauphin Josef de DamaTalous."

There was a moment of awful, stunned silence as the crowd took in the news, realizing that Alcine, so long believed to have been the intended heir due to his status as oldest son of the queen, would be passed up for his younger brother.

A tentative voice called out, "And what of the Dauphine Sabina?"

Sabina felt heat slowly fill her body as her angry, glittering green eyes searched the crowd for the speaker. Alcine's hand tightened on hers, as his personal anger had been replaced with worry for his cousin and his brother.

The crowd murmured, the doubt beginning to fester as they realized that none had witnessed the birth of the princess, the event having happened in the village of Kylassame. They had all spent the last twenty years believing that Alcine would be heir, or possibly the Dauphine Sabina. She was the daughter of the oldest child of King Verikhan and Queen Sula, and her absence in line to the throne was a strike into their hearts.

Queen Nyssa raised one hand, her blue eyes hard as she addressed the crowd. "The Dauphine's position to the throne is not up for discussion."

"Why not? Are they both so unsuitable to be rulers that you go straight to the third born? Is Sabina really some whore's unwanted get?" a second voice called out harshly.

A third interjected, "Let the Dauphine or her parents speak, I am sure there is a good reason for this," in a kind but firm manner.

Sabina drew in a breath and steadied herself, aware of the way the crowd melted away as she moved toward the dais, Alcine one step behind. She gave a curtsy to the queen, and Nyssa granted permission for Sabina to step upon the platform.

Murmurs filled the crowd below as her parents moved to her side in support. Nyssa lightly touched Rowan's shoulder and then carefully handed him a light object wrapped in pure white silk.

Sabina could barely hear her aunt's voice as Nyssa murmured, "You were wise to prepare for this, brother," to Rowan.

He tilted his head in acknowledgment and turned to the crowd, his rich voice flowing so that all could hear, his anger concealed through a lifetime of training.

"Good people of the court, hear my words. It is for the best interest of the court, and of the realm, that Queen Nyssa rose to power in my stead, even though she is not the first-born child of the previous ruler. As you know, the line of power must be unbroken, passed by blood and relinquished willfully when taken out of turn."

Rowan continued, his eyes taking in the crowd, his voice clear over the murmurs of the crowd. "Most of you were not witness to the punishment that befell the High Prince Mateo for stepping out of this decreed order, but we were, and believe me when I say, none want to repeat that horror."

His hand moved in a flourish, carefully sliding away the white silk cloth to reveal an exquisitely crafted crown of gold, delicate whorls and curves set with a large emerald jewel and a band of smaller onyx chips. The crowd sucked in their breath, tears welling in the eyes of the oldest patrons, those who were suddenly assailed with memories of the last queen to wear that crown.

"This is the crown of my mother, the wise and revered, late Queen Sula." Rowan held it gently, and the lights from the lanterns that lined the hall glinted from the polished gold. The crown had been placed into his care by Nyssa, a symbolic gesture in two ways. The first, that she would wear the crown of their father, an effort to validate her rule by the unhappy members of court. The second, as assurance that Rowan's children would hold equal claim to the throne when the time came to announce an heir.

Sabina's breathing hitched as her father turned, the crown held carefully before him.

"Daughter, you are the true heir to the realm, the oldest born child of the oldest born reagent. As the first-born child of the Grand Duke Rowan de Nespa, protector of Kylassame and defender of the realm, and the Duchess Rhea Aralia de Nespa, Lady of Steinbrekka, this crown is yours to claim, if you so desire."

He placed the crown on her trembling, outstretched hands reverently, and with a small smile. His lips gently touched her forehead in benediction and he whispered, "The choice is yours, sweetheart. We will support you no matter what you decide," before taking a step back.

Sabina took a moment to look at the crown, and felt the pull of power. As queen, she would have the power to make the changes needed for the outlying villages. She would have nearly unlimited funds at her disposal to improve the villages, and the ability to demand changes in the court.

Her vision blurred, and she saw the court crumbling, the people rising to overthrow her. Sabina was the first to admit that she held no love for the court, or the people who lived within the castle walls. Her dislike for the court way of life would constantly chip away at her happiness, leaching into the peace of the realm as would an infectious disease.

She licked her lips and swallowed, then lifted her eyes to the crowd. "Good people of the court, I ask you to bear witness to this day."

Two steps took her to where Josef stood, chin high in the face of public scrutiny and eyes calm. Sabina gave a low curtsy, crown extended before her.

"I give to you the crown of Sula as a gesture of my goodwill, and my blessing. I rescind my claim to the throne while you draw breath, and fully support that my cousin, Dauphin Josef de DamaTalous, son of Nyssa, be declared as heir to the realm."

Josef reverently took the crown and gave his cousin a kiss on the cheek. The action hid his nervous, whispered assurance, "I will place this in a safe place until you or Aaron have children, at which time it will be restored to the de Nespa line. I will never forget this, Seb."

He turned to the crowd and lifted the crown high. "I accept the role as heir-apparent, and the responsibilities it entails. Let no one speak ill of my family, and let the realm of Kaldalangra continue to live in peace."

Sabina stepped off the dais, once again standing next to Alcine as an eruption of cheers and well-wishes for the new heir to the throne filled the room, ringing through the hallways of the castle. Their superficial loyalty to their once heir-apparent and the challenge to Sabina's heritage were quickly forgotten in the clamor to forge alliances within the new court.

Alcine looked over at Sabina, a slight shimmer in his dark eyes the only betrayal of emotion behind the stoic façade. "Well. It is done, then."

~ * ~ * ~

She found him several hours later, when the sun had set and darkness filled the spaces between the candles and torches of the castle. Alcine had given his swearing of loyalty to the declared heir, and then surreptitiously exited from the party that still continued long into the night. There had been some speculative glances, some murmurs that the man must have been disappointed in the announcement, and rumors of why he had been removed from the line of power had begun to circulate.

Josef, aware of the rumors and anxious about his brother's rapid exit, had approached Sabina and asked her to find him, and to make sure that he was well.

Sabina almost missed him, a dark shadow lying on the grass in the middle of a large garden that was tucked onto the side of the castle and unknown to all but family. They had come to this garden often as children and ran to the clearing where her mother would point out clouds, and name the shapes that floated across the blue sky.

Alcine lay on his back on the grass, his palms forming a pillow for his head, and eyes staring at the moon. "I didn't think it would hurt, you know?" He gave a small laugh. "I've known about this day, anticipated this day, my entire life, and never cared a bit, never wanted the position. So why does it still hurt?"

She settled beside him, sitting in the cool grass and pulling her knees to her chest. "It is still a shock, for it to be final. You left quickly. Josef is worried about you."

His voice was hoarse as he replied, "I could see it in their eyes; the questions, the speculation. They never knew that I wasn't of Nyssa's blood, they never would have known. All assumed I received my dark features from Sebast. Now? Now they wonder why I was passed up, deemed unworthy. How do I handle that? What do I do now?"

"Now, we go back home, to Asimina. I have some obligations tomorrow, and you really do need to spend time with Josef so he knows that you don't blame him. The morning after tomorrow, first thing, we will go back to Asimina and away from here, just as we always intended."

Chapter 8

The Court

"Bryan!" Sabina called out as she entered the stable and smiled as the young man stuck his head out of a stall.

"Hey-a, Seb! About time you made it in here." He gestured for her to join him in the stall, and then ducked his head back out of sight.

She hurried down the aisle, casting her veil aside and feeling the stress of the past day rolling off her shoulders with each step. "You would not believe all the crap that I have been dealing with after last night. Every time I step foot out of my room it's 'Sabina this' and 'Sabina that.' I can't wait to get out of here."

"You would leave me so soon?" His brown eyes looked over at her with a woeful and hurt expression. "But I even have a present for you."

"A present?" Sabina looked at him suspiciously, and then laughed at his expression. "Oh, stop it with the woe-is-me look, Bryan."

He shook his head in mock sadness. "Alas, the lady of the castle has no time for poor Bryan, the lonely stable hand who toils and works his fingers to the bone. She is so consumed by the people of the court that she even forgets how to properly greet her friend, who she has not seen in such a long, horribly long time."

Sabina laughed then and wrapped her arms around his neck, giving him a friendly kiss. "There, happy now?"

There had always been an easy relationship between the two of them, if a socially unacceptable one. Sabina knew that her parents' status meant that she had to be careful with romance, and with any dalliances. With Bryan, she could have the bit of fun from a playful romance, without fear that it was politically related, either to increase his status or to sabotage her own. He accepted her even with dirt under her fingernails and tears in her eyes, an anchor in her ever-changing world.

A man cleared his throat behind them and she rapidly pulled away. Bryan quickly swung between her and the sound, placing her closest to the door that led to the pasture in case a quick escape was necessary.

"Now how would it be spoken of if a Patron had found you two?" Aleksei, Bryan's mentor and a family friend of Sabina's, leaned against the edge of the door.

Bryan glanced at Sabina before answering. "It was just a hello, Aleksei. No harm meant."

"Do you know about any presents?" Sabina asked the older man, an attempt at diverting the conversation.

Aleksei smiled and winked at them. "As a matter of fact, I do. But I will let Bryan show it to you, seeing as how he received such an enthusiastic greeting while I just get glares."

Sabina laughed and stepped forward then to hug Aleksei, the man squeezing her tightly in return. "Thank you for being you, Aleksei."

"Uh-huh. You mean, thank you for not telling your mother?" he teased.

"More like my father," she replied.

Bryan's face lost all color as he stammered, "You would not actually tell him, would you?"

Aleksei laughed and walked down the aisle, shaking his head at the impetuousness of youth, unwilling to ruin the happy relationship that the two had formed, even though it toed the line between both castes and seriousness.

Sabina turned around and put her hand on Bryan's shoulder when the man simply stared down the aisle. "You okay?"

He looked at her, and she sensed him withdrawing even though he did not move. "I just, you know that we, I mean … " He blushed.

She smiled then, understanding. "Bryan, you are my best friend, sometimes my only friend in this place. We have always had an understanding, right?"

He blushed again. "Yes, we have, but I know who you are, and who I am. I never thought about how others might perceive that until now, and worry that I may have been giving you the wrong impression."

She laughed and took his hand. "You know who you are? You are a man who is going to show me this damn present before I have to shake it out of you myself!"

50

He joined in her laughter then, and led her through the door that led to the sunlit pasture.

Shielding her eyes from the sun, Sabina gasped in surprise and pleasure as she saw the small filly peeking out from behind her dame, a gray mare who was the grand-foal of her mother's beloved mare, Kalar.

"Oh, Bryan! She is beautiful!"

The filly poked her head out farther, her coat a pattern of mottled gray and black on a white background. With an encouraging nudge from her mother, she walked out farther, four legs nothing but spindles that she still was learning to control.

Her body was the same tri-color as her head, a white base with large black patches ringed with gray fur. Her mane, short and stiff as young horses tend to be, was black at her ears, slowly fading into gray, and then into white as it touched her withers.

"She is adorable! Oh, look at her run!" Sabina grabbed Bryan's arm in excitement as the filly began to run, slowly gaining speed as her four legs determined how they needed to fall in order to go faster.

Her uncle's voice sounded softly behind her. "She certainly is a beauty. I cannot wait for your mother to come out and see her. I am amazed she is not out here already. She has been worried about the mare for months now."

Sabina smiled at Sebast, her only uncle and the man who had been the leader of Asimina until he began handing over the duties to Alcine. "She should be out shortly. She is still inside with Nyssa, figuring out how to handle the court's reaction to Josef's sudden rise in status, and Alcine's frustrations."

The man's lips tightened as he asked, "And how is Alcine?"

51

Sabina watched the filly for a moment, letting the innocence of her exploits around the pasture calm her mind. She chuckled as the filly investigated a butterfly with her small nose, leaping into the air in fright as the butterfly took wing.

"He is hurt, and surprised that he is reacting to the decision so strongly." She laced her fingers together to keep from fidgeting, a nervous habit she had developed over the years. "He has never wanted to rule in court, and has always thought he was prepared for this day. He loves, and belongs, in Asimina."

"But?" Sebast prompted.

"But," she continued reluctantly, unsure of how much information Alcine would want shared. "He still lost status today, a lot of status. The fall out is beginning to break through his indifference and he is having trouble accepting the change."

Sebast opened his mouth to reply, but was silenced by the sound of angry voices in the courtyard of the castle grounds. "What is going on over there?"

Sabina listened a moment, then picked up the familiar voices of her cousins. "It is Alcine and Josef." She paused as she evaluated the third voice. "And Cademar?"

The trio quickly jumped the pasture gate and moved toward the sound of male voices rising in anger. Sabina viewed Aleksei moving toward the commotion from his position in the stable as her father stepped out of the wide front doors that led from the castle to the courtyard.

They arrived to hear Cademar shouting as the crowd grew around the conflict. "Now you are nothing but the bastard we always suspected you were! Nothing but a -" his words were halted by

Alcine's heavy fist upon his lips, the blow knocking the breath from Cademar's chest.

Cademar staggered backward with the blow, tripping slightly on the cobblestones below. While he was older than Alcine by several years, he had never left the court, finding excuses to avoid the customary trips to Asimina that had been implemented and eschewing physical activities at every chance. His dark hair and brown eyes stood in contrast to his high-status birth, and his parents related stories of, what they considered, the glorious time of Patronage during the reign of King Verikhan, when the whims of the high-born were catered without question.

Alcine stood in front of the taller, but weaker man. "Say that again," he growled, the sound carrying over the crowd that had circled the men.

Cademar simply smiled, brushing the back of his hand against his lip, split open from the punch. "You heard me, bastard. You are nothing but a Skov's unwanted parasite, an orphan of a broken mother who decided to dive off the northern tower rather than stay with her child."

Everyone in the courtyard stood silent, and for several long moments the only sound that could be heard was the soft swish of fabrics that swayed in the light breeze. No one had dared to use the word Skov in Queen Nyssa's time. It was a term for an outsider, a sub-human, which was commonly used in the time of King Verikhan, usually before a decree for that person's death.

Then Alcine moved, and Cademar was flat on his back, gasping for air. Alcine had an arm over Cademar's throat, and his eyes glittered black with rage. "I may not be heir-apparent, but I am still the son of Queen Nyssa and Duke Sebast, and I am still, and will always be, a prince of this realm. Do not think that you can use such lies to displace me, Cademar, or I will destroy you."

Josef had seen the trio's arrival and moved next to Sabina, unsure how to respond to the situation in a manner that would not further endanger their family. His body was tense, poised to act if his brother should lose his grip and become the defender.

Sebast stepped forward before Josef could interfere, drawing Alcine's attention, and his son released his hold on Cademar out of respect for his father.

"Alcine, Josef, you will remain here." Sebast fixed his eyes on Cademar, still on the ground, his eyes bright with tears born of fear and lack of oxygen. "Cademar, go home. We will be requiring your presence in the throne room tomorrow at noon, with your parents."

"He is the one who assaulted me!" Cademar sputtered out, awkwardly getting to his feet and straightening his shirt.

"You instigated conflict with a member of the DamaTalous, in front of witnesses, and in front of your future king. That is not to be permitted. Noon, Cademar." Sebast nodded toward the man's father, who had seen the episode occur, as the man led his son away with a cuff to the back of the head.

Sebast looked at the remaining members of the court and castle workers who had remained, eager to hear the end to the drama. "You are all dismissed. Return to your labors and your leisure. Let this be a lesson that any hostility toward the DamaTalous will not be tolerated. Any person living in the land of Kaldalangra is free to request an audience if there is need for resolution, or suspicions of misconduct by any member of the realm."

Rowan moved forward and jerked his head toward the castle doors. "Come on, let us go convene indoors and you can tell us what this was about. No," he interrupted Josef, who had begun to protest. "No, this needs to be done in private, and away from gossiping tongues."

Sabina gave a quick smile of parting to Bryan as he and Aleksei left the group and went back to the stable, aware of the need for privacy when the members of the royal family had discussions. She followed a few steps behind her father, who walked behind Sebast and his sons.

Her father slowed his pace a step and offered his arm in escort. "Sabina, is Alcine truly accepting of last night's decision?"

She linked her arm through his, grateful for the solid sense of safety that always seemed to gather around the man. "Yes, he just needs time to adjust to it being official." She sighed and ran her free fingers through her hair. "Dad, this has been a long time coming, this conflict with Cademar. That man has been waiting his entire life for an opportunity like this. His life's dream was to find a chink in the armor we have built around our family, a way to get under our skin and sow discontent."

He nodded thoughtfully, but remained silent, giving her a small smile of encouragement as they entered the private room where the family held meetings.

There was an eerie silence in the room, no one willing to start the discussion until Queen Nyssa or Lady Rhea arrived. Sabina perched on the edge of the chair arm, positioned between her father and Alcine.

Her cousin sat stiffly on the chair, emotions temporarily checked and with a face of stone. His black hair remained tousled from the fight but he had brushed the dust from his pants. Dark eyes revealed nothing of his thoughts, and he stood ready for judgment for his actions, as assaulting a standing member of the court was no small transgression.

In contrast to Alcine's calmness, his brother Josef paced the room, fidgeting and sputtering, torn between wanting to speak for his brother and obeying his father's wordless order for silence.

Sebast was a model of calmness, a mirror to Rowan. He stood at the door with a slight smile on his face as he and his brother-by-marriage seemed to communicate without words. There was an almost inaudible shifting of fabric outside of the room and he swung the door open, allowing Nyssa and Rhea to enter.

The two women entered and stood by their husbands. Nyssa had been dressed for court business, a gown of deep crimson edged with white ribbons, the hem gracefully trailing behind her as she took her place on the high-backed, plush chair beside Sebast.

Rhea was dressed in a simpler manner, in a long gray dress that brushed the floor, with a belt of woven strands that shimmered green and gold as she moved. Her hair had been pulled back into a long plait that hung over her shoulder, bound at the end with a simple green ribbon. Shadows darkened the skin under her eyes, and Sabina wondered if her mother had been called out of another nightmare to come to this meeting.

The door to the room had barely closed before Josef broke the silence, unable to contain his emotions any further. "He is not a Skov, and was never unwanted!" His eyes flashed with anger as his voice rose. "And his mother did not dive off the tower rather than be with him. He is my brother. Our mother is sitting right there."

Rhea sucked in a breath, and Sabina glanced over with concern as Rowan wrapped his arm around his wife's waist for support. Her eyes filled with tears and she waved off the looks of concern around the room. "I'm fine, just dark memories."

Nyssa licked her lips, then sighed and leaned forward in the chair. "Half-truths, but not entire truths." She glanced at Josef and then at Alcine. "It seems that our attempts to keep the darker reasons for your adoption into the DamaTalous are not as secret as we had hoped. Josef, Sabina, could you leave us?"

Sabina began to straighten, but jerked to a stop as Alcine's hand came down firmly on her wrist, locking her in place beside him. His other hand moved to rest on his brother's chest, halting his indignant exit of the room.

"Whatever you need to say to me, is better said with them present as well. There have been, it appears, too many secrets kept in this family already." His voice was steady, deep with resolve, though his heartbeat visibly pulsed on his neck.

Nyssa nodded her head in agreement, and took a deep breath before beginning.

"Alcine, ever since you were six months old, you were the son of my heart, if not my womb. Your mother came to us from the other world, from Rhea's world, but many thousands of years after Rhea's time. Your father, Arden, was a great man, a protector of his people. He was killed by evil people intent on bringing destruction to the area. Mairi protected you as best she could by allowing you both to be marked by the Oprimata, but was nearly killed as well, only saved by stumbling into our world."

Alcine jerked slightly, his hand still gripping Sabina, his only reaction to hearing his birth parents' names for the first time in his life. Sabina found herself glancing to the strange tattoo that had always been on the back of Alcine's neck, a circle encompassing a sunburst, with a series of vertical lines on the bottom half of the circle.

"When we found her, and you, you were both starved, and days away from death. Your mother was frightened and desperate, having found herself in a world where she knew nothing, and no one spoke her language."

"She could not feed you, could not give you the life-giving nourishment that you so desperately needed, so we asked a woman of Asimina who had recently given birth to act as a wet nurse until you were old enough to receive additional food."

Rhea shuddered, and then quietly spoke. "Your mother loved you, Alcine, more than you can possibly know. It killed the part of her that creates the will to live when she could not take care of you, could not feed you or protect you from harm. It is a horrible feeling to know, to even think, that you have failed your child when he has barely begun to live."

Rowan gently kissed his wife on the temple before picking up the history. "One day, a few weeks after you had come to the realm, she gave up. You were healthy, growing, and beloved by all who resided in the court. She kissed you, told you she loved you, and then walked up to the north tower to end the pain. It was after that when Nyssa decided to take you as her son, and raise you as a member of the DamaTalous."

Nyssa stood up then, and gently placed her trembling hands on Alcine's cheeks, looking up at her son with clear blue eyes that sparkled with incoming tears. "You are so loved, Alcine, by so many. Never forget that. Blood or not, you are my son, and no one will ever take that away from us."

Chapter 9

Asimina

The man called Eric rolled over, staring at the figure standing over his cot who had gently shaken him awake.

Nastasio took a step back as Eric opened his eyes, giving him space to sit up and swing his legs over the edge. Alcine had returned the day before, and ordered the stranger's bonds to be severed, and to begin the physical rehabilitation needed for the man to regain his strength.

"Come on. Time for a walk around the village. We have to get some strength back into your legs if you want to become part of Asimina." Nastasio held out a hand for support, which Eric took as he stood up, his legs shaking with the effort.

They had come back yesterday, the woman and the fearsome leader of this village. Both had seemed troubled, quiet, and shared secretive glances as they spoke in hushed tones outside the door to the hut. Then Alcine came in, cut the bonds that had been around his wrists and ankles, and ordered him to begin healing.

Sabina looked at him with those beautiful eyes, and gave a small smile as he rolled off the cot and stood, unhobbled, for the first time in weeks.

It hurt to stand, gravity setting his nerves on fire as his legs strained to hold his weight, though he had grown dangerously lean since he had woken up in the woods surrounding Asimina. When he moved he did so slowly, carefully, afraid that if he fell, he would lack the strength or will to stand again.

With Nastasio's guidance and encouragement, he made a circuit around the perimeter of the village, stopping frequently to rest and catch his breath. On several occasions one of the young women would bring him a cup of water, or a soft piece of cotton, which he would use to wipe the dripping sweat from his face. They had grown curious, and fond of the stranger who had been detained, who had been nothing but courteous and polite whenever they brought him food to eat or changes of clothing.

They pity me, he thought grimly. *What a twist of fate, a piece of perfect irony, that they pity me and offer me assistance. I, who once was so capable, so self-assured, and a man feared by all.*

He waved Nastasio to a stop again and kneeled down on the leaves that covered the edge of the village. They had all fallen from the trees after turning beautiful hues of red and yellow. Eric took a few deep breaths and wiped his forehead with his arm.

"I don't think I can go anymore."

Nastasio squatted down beside him and grinned. "That was two circuits! You could barely do half of one when we released you yesterday. We will get you back up to normal in no time at this pace."

Eric chuckled; it was hard not to get caught up in the man's enthusiasm. It seemed that Nastasio was fond of taking care of the injured, though most of his charges were small birds and mammals. He had shown a few to Eric to pass the time after Alcine had departed.

He glanced toward the edge of the village, where Sabina stood talking to a man with dark brown hair and a lean, muscular body. Eric felt fear rush through his body at the sight of him, and struggled to get his breathing steady and even, focusing on the rock by his feet.

"You okay, man? I did not mean to push you so badly." Nastasio helped him to his feet and they began to slowly move back toward the village.

"I will be fine." Eric whispered out, too aware that every step closer to the hut where he had resided was one step closer to the man next to Sabina.

Then she turned and smiled at him, and he swallowed down his fear. "Hello, Sabina. I am very sorry that I frightened you when I first came to this place. I was not … myself."

Hazel eyes stared up into his blue and she placed her hand on his elbow before introducing him to the man. "Papa, this is Eric, the man I was telling you about who came from the other world. Eric, this is my father, Grand Duke Rowan de Nespa, co-reagent to the realm of Kaldalangra, the realm that encompasses Asimina."

Rowan held out a hand and shook Eric's, his grip strong and firm. "Welcome to Asimina, Eric. I trust that you have been well taken care of during your stay here?"

"Yes, sir." His voice cracked on the words and he hated how noticeably his hand was shaking.

Sabina's eyes narrowed and she quickly slipped her arm around his waist, taking much of the weight off of his taxed limbs. "Come on, now, back to your hut we go. We can finish proper introductions later, right now you need rest."

His right arm draped over her back, lightly resting on her shoulder as they walked, step by shaking step, back to his hut. Her body felt comforting where it pressed against his, warm and friendly, a solid strength in feminine form.

When they arrived at the hut he hesitated, hating to go back into the darkness after so long without the sun's touch. "Sabina, I don't suppose we could sit out here, could we?"

She smiled and nodded, removing her arm from his waist to duck into the hut, then returning outside with a pile of thick blankets. After folding them neatly and placing them on the ground as cushions, she helped Eric to sink down onto the seating and lean back against a support pole of the hut.

"Sabina," he began, her name rolling off his tongue like a prayer. "Did you have a good time, where you went?"

She sighed and for a moment he felt alarmed at the response, forcing himself to breathe deeply once more. "It was fine. I just hate visiting the court. It is very tense, and everything is political, and it is exhausting to always be on guard with your emotions."

"What is court like?" He gave a small wave as a group of young children ran past, chasing a bouncing ball across the ground. They had come to visit him often, once Nastasio and Cole had decided he was too weak to be a threat and welcomed the company.

Sabina closed her eyes and laid her head back against the sun-warmed, woven tapestry wall of the hut. "Most people are in awe of it. The castle is, well, a castle. It is beautiful, with walls and floors made of polished marble, so well-kept that it reflects all the colors that move by its surface. There are also tapestries, beautiful weavings on huge bolts of cloth that flutter in the breeze, and depict all the important historical events of the court."

"And the queen? What is she like?"

"Nyssa? Oh, she is wonderful. Granted, she is my aunt so I am rather biased, but she has always been a fair ruler. She is gentle but firm, strict but forgiving. We hear stories, sometimes, of the rulers before her, the King and the High Prince, and everyone who was around back then always say they are grateful for Queen Nyssa."

He glanced at her, took in her closed eyes, long black lashes laying across the tops of her cheeks as she breathed in deeply, taking in the peace of the morning. Her legs, bare below the hemline of her knee-length skirt were smooth and well-shaped. The light-green cotton tunic flowed in the breeze that curled around the sides of the hut, giving him a glimpse of her collar bone, her neck, the top of her shoulder.

Eric shook his head to clear the thoughts that began to form. She was not the one he sought, though he felt a strong connection with her. He shuddered at night at the feel of her hands from his first time in the stream, her fingers gently passing over his scars without judgment or accusation.

"Eric? Did you hear me?" Sabina had opened her eyes and was staring at his quizzically.

"Sorry, my mind wandered."

"Would you like to meet my mother? She was from your world, originally. I think that she might be able to help explain a few things to you, help you adjust."

He nodded, and then felt his heart begin to race in his chest as Sabina waved toward a woman across the village, still wearing her riding cloak after her recent arrival to the village.

The woman approached, small hands gracefully sliding the hood of the cloak from her head. Her auburn hair shone in the sun, the hue blending in with the brightly colored autumn leaves. Green-tinted hazel eyes looked up on him affectionately, and she smiled as she approached her daughter and the man.

"Hello, Eric. I am Sabina's mother. My name is Rhea. Shall we talk?"

~ * ~ * ~

Eric lay on his back in the hut, stretched out on the cot after speaking for hours with Rhea and Sabina. He had finally pleaded exhaustion, and both women helped him inside, lowering his body onto the bed and covering him with the cotton blanket.

Tears pressed against his eyes as he lay there, staring at the bunched thatch and small twigs that made up the roof of the house. Mother and daughter were so alike, their hair color, their eyes, the composition of their faces. They could have been sisters, for all their twenty years of difference.

He let out a small laugh of futility. Twenty years of difference. Sabina's mother, Rhea, was a woman in her forties; though her smooth skin and youthful energy would fool a man into thinking she was much younger. She had smelled of lavender, and the skin of her palm felt smooth and cool as she checked for a fever, alarmed at the paleness of his skin.

Months had passed in his world as he searched for his friend, for his love. He had thought it a short amount of time in hindsight, having put all of his energy and yearning into the search.

Twenty-three years had passed in hers, years that rendered him forgotten, a distant memory and a ghost of her past.

He carefully turned onto his side, taking shelter in the closeness of the wall that hung just beyond his cot. His body shivered with a suppressed sob, and he allowed himself one tear to fall, one tear for everything that had happened, and the death of his dream.

Then he sucked in his breath, rolled over, and stared at the ceiling once more, thinking.

I am here now, forever. I lost my chance at returning to my home, I gave it away like a sigh in the wind. From now on I am Eric, from Indiana. Eric, who came into the world searching for his sister, a girl who had been kidnapped many years ago, and had chestnut hair and hazel eyes. Eric, who is going to pour his body and soul into helping the village of Asimina, and hold the tenuous friendships that are starting to form. Eric, who will fall in love with the daughter, and forget the mother. Eric, who has never harmed a fly and never had an ill thought, or committed a crime.

He shuddered and whispered to the darkness inside the hut. "I am Eric now, only Eric, and both Matt and Mateo are dead."

Chapter 10

Asimina

"It's only for a short time, probably a month at the most, which will fly by," Sabina repeated nervously as she folded the clothes lying scattered on her grass-filled mattress. She then carefully arranged them in the saddlebags Eric held open, aware of the small distance between their hands.

Eric smiled and shifted the bag so that the clothes inside settled, making room for the remaining articles to be packed. "You have already said that, several times."

She bit her lip and gave him a shy glance. "I know, I just … I guess I don't want you to feel alone here."

Laughter fell from his lips and he placed the saddlebag down onto a low wooden table. "Seb, I will be fine. It has been months since I came here and I feel almost normal. Thanks to you and Nastasio, I know my way around the village as well as most of the population."

"I know, it's just …" she hesitated.

He reached forward and gently cupped her cheek in his hand. "What are you so worried about, Sabina?"

She gazed up at him, feeling a little fluttering in her stomach at the soft touch of his hand on her cheek. "I'll just miss you." She blushed bright red at the confession and quickly added, "Okay, that sounded juvenile. I had better head over to the bathing house so that I am clean for the journey."

Eric leaned down and gently kissed her on the forehead before releasing his gentle grip. "I'll come with you. After the workout Alcine put me through, I could use a dip myself."

Sabina chuckled then, the memory of her cousin working the newest member of Asimina helping to settle her nerves. She had walked over to Alcine's home to see if he needed any messages taken to the refugee camps, or items brought to Asimina upon their return, and found both men outside going through the paces.

The two men worked well together as they went through the practice forms, and then worked through the slow sparring routines that Alcine practiced tirelessly. Her cousin was taller and stronger, but Eric had begun to rebuild his body in the time that he spent in Asimina, his muscles beginning to strengthen and grow under Alcine's guidance. It was hard to see when they were not sparring, as most of the people of Asimina had begun to don their winter clothes, the thick cottons and furs morphing them into shapeless creatures that darted between houses to escape the chill in the air.

Alcine had never minded the cold, and even in the bitterest winter would conduct his morning exercises wearing only a pair of trousers, his chest and arms exposed to the environments. Not one to be outdone and beginning to show a bit of a competitive streak, Eric had also removed his layers, and Sabina had felt uncomfortable at the warmth that filled her body watching the man go through his movements.

"Well," she said, snapping herself back to the present after noticing a slight smirk on his face, "we had better head over there before it gets too busy."

They walked across the village to the bathing house that had been built beside the river. The building had been Eric's idea, after he heard several women complaining about having to pour hot water into the small bathing tubs or having an ice bath. He had sketched it out with paper and pencils procured from Alcine's house, and the men of the village watched intently and made suggestions as he drew.

The finished product had taken a month to complete, but the village had echoed with cheers at its opening, just as the winter snows began to fall. This would allow the people of Asimina to bathe in comfort, with a steamy interior and water pools of various temperatures that soothed and cleansed. The large structure also served as a new gathering point for the village and people regularly met to socialize in the warmth of the waters.

Sabina ducked into the small, chilly addition that served as a changing area for the women, while Eric disappeared into the adjacent section set aside for the men. She quickly shed her winter layers and slipped into the dark green bikini, one of the suits that had arrived in a shipment from Kylassame at the beginning of the summer. The people of Asimina loved the bathing suits, and reveled in the freedom of being among the opposite sex while in the water.

She stepped into the large room and let out a sigh of relief as the warmth from the fire pits seeped into her bones. The room had been built wide, but with low ceilings to keep the warmth from rising above where people could feel it. Small fire pits were maintained by youths in the village and kept to low burning embers, emitting heat but without the smoke and risk that a larger fire would have caused.

There were three large pools that had been dug into the earth of the structure, tiered to create a waterfall effect. Water that was redirected from the river flowed into the top tier, forming a pool of chilly water where the children of the village flocked, splashing and shrieking in joy.

The middle tier was where most of the adults of the village spent their time, the water a mixture of temperatures. Warmer water pooled in the deeper areas and central section of the large pool, while the chilly run-off from the cold pool above created a flowing current along the side.

While Asimina did not have an elderly population, not after the decimation of King Verikhan's reign, Rowan and Rhea's generation enjoyed the lower tier, which sat slightly off to the side of the other two. In this pool the water remained hot, and helped to soothe aching joints and ease the chill from sore, tired muscles.

Sabina looked around the room, dark compared to the twilight outside. A soft red glow bounced off the walls from the embers that burned low and shimmered across the water's surface. For once, the bath house stood empty, the majority of visitors having already retreated into their houses and huddled down for the night.

She saw Eric standing waist-deep on the steps of the middle pool and blushed as he turned to watch her walk toward the edge. Sabina had spent most of her youth and teenage years in Asimina clad in as little as possible, reveling in the feel of sunlight on her skin and free of the tug and pull of cloth hampering her movements. Summers in Asimina were carefree for those who were not in committed relationships, the youth of the village celebrating freedom to run in shorts or sleeveless tops without constant fear of degradation for the first time in decades.

But now, she felt exposed and shy as Eric's eyes widened at the sight of her bikini-clad body, and uneasy that she cared how he viewed her. That was a new feeling for her, and one that she did not particularly relish. No man had ever interested her enough to cause her to wonder how they saw her, and though Bryan came close, he enjoyed her company the most when they were both covered in dust and hay.

Eric held out a hand in support as she carefully made her way down the stone steps into the pool. They had been carefully constructed of flat river stones, the surfaces strategically pounded with rounded hammer-stones to create a myriad of small bumps that allowed the foot to easily grip the surface.

"It would appear that we are the only ones still up." Sabina's voice held a slight, nervous wobble as she stepped into the waters, moving toward the deeper end where the stream flowed by, rinsing the dirt and grime off into a separate furrow to be taken away from the pools.

"It would appear that way." Eric followed her, ducking below the water and then shaking his head when he rose, flinging water from his hair.

Sabina laughed as the water pelted her face and shoulders, and responded by splashing him in return with a wide sweep of her arm. A shriek of joy sounded from her throat as he retaliated, then she gasped in surprise when he dropped below the dark waters, coming up suddenly behind her.

His sudden appearance startled her, and Sabina spun around quickly, her foot losing its grip on the river-stones that made up the pool floor. He immediately reached out and wrapped his arms around her waist, stopping her fall just before her head went under, and pulling her close to his body in the process.

"That was a close one," he murmured, looking down at her face, taking in the small drops of water that formed on her eyelashes.

"Yes, it was, wasn't it?" she replied, aware that now their bodies were touching in the warm water, his arms still wrapped around her waist. The heat of his body competed with that of the pool, and she could feel his skin, firm and smooth above the well-formed muscles, against her bare stomach.

"It would have been a shame to let you go under, when I am right here to help." Eric's arms tightened slightly around her waist, pulling her closer to him, his pulse racing.

Her arms moved of their own accord, wrapping around his strong shoulders, her body rising onto her toes to move her lips closer to his. "Very kind of you to save me. How can I make it up to you?"

His eyes glowed with desire, reflecting the embers burning at the edges of the pool. "I could think of a few ways." He lowered his lips to hers then, feeling her respond to the kiss as her body pressed closer.

The sound of a throat clearing caused them to jump apart, water splashing as their hands hit the surface. Sabina's foot slipped once again as she turned, this time successfully dunking herself into the pool. She rose and turned multiple shades of red as she saw her father, dressed in his own bathing shorts, standing at the doorway to the bathing house.

Rowan gave a reserved smile as he moved toward the pool. "I can come back later, if I am interrupting. I had just thought to take a quick dip tonight since I will have nothing but a small bathing tub once we leave."

Eric had slid a foot away from Sabina, and glanced at her nervously as her father stood, waiting for an answer. "No, sir. Please come and join us. We were just … ah …"

"Talking," Sabina chimed in, giving her father her most innocent smile. "Just talking."

His eyes sparkled as Rowan looked at his daughter, rarely having the opportunity to see her unnerved. He had begun to worry about her, and her future. Most of the young women had already experienced love, in some form, by the time that they were his daughter's age, yet Sabina held herself apart from the courtship dance, from any physical affection. He knew why and accepted the distance, having held himself back from any feelings that would complicate the politics of court, or the daily flow of life in the other villages, but his wife had been of another mind.

She had questioned him often on his involvement in Sabina's lack of a love life, wanting to know if he was using his status as co-reagent, and formidable history as a guard, as barriers. Rhea was concerned that their daughter was shut off from the world, and was taking her future role in the realm too seriously, causing her to miss a vital part of being a young adult.

So he kept his voice teasing as he stepped into the pool. "Talking very quietly it would seem."

His daughter flushed again and sunk down in the water to regain composure. A moment later, Sabina rose gracefully and looked between the two men. "Well, I had better go and see if mom needs any help packing. You two just … um …" She shook her head for lack of words and began to walk out of the pool.

Eric gently reached forward as she moved away and brushed his fingers against her arm. "I'll come see you off tomorrow."

Sabina gave him a soft smile and nodded, then quickly exited the bathing house.

Rowan dunked himself in the cold current to rinse off, then rose and eyed Eric. "I think I will go into the hot pool. Care to join me?"

Eric nodded, cautiously following Rowan to the other pool, then sliding down to his neck in the hot, dark waters. "Is it a long journey to Kylassame?"

The older man shrugged. "A few days of moderate riding, but normally not too bad. The recent snow storms make it more difficult, but should not add too much time." He closed his eyes and rested the back of his head against the edge of the pool, letting the waters relax him.

"Is it a direct journey?" Eric asked carefully, feeling his guard slightly relax.

Rowan chuckled, the action causing the water to ripple around him. "It used to be, back twenty years ago. Now we will make several stops to check on the refugee camps and see if they need anything from the other villages."

Eric idly moved his hand on the surface of the pool, creating tiny waves. "Refugee camps? I don't remember those."

Rowan's eyes opened to slits, noticing the touch of confusion in the man's tone. "Remember?"

"When I fell into this world, I mean. I spent a good amount of time wandering around in the wilderness and they seem like something I would have stumbled into." Eric sank down further in the water, his strong chin just touching the surface and darkening the tips of his already dark-blonde hair with fresh moisture.

"Ah," Rowan responded, closing his eyes once more. "The closest one is a day's ride from Asimina, so you may not have been far enough. A person can travel between Asimina and the Court within a day, so when the first villages went up, they were formed further out."

"What are they for, the villages?"

Rowan smiled and gave the obvious answer. "The refugees, of course." He opened his eyes and immediately felt contrite at the look of confusion on Eric's face. "About five years ago people from the outside world began appearing in larger and larger numbers. Most were already starved, and their bodies broken in various ways. We were unable to bring them to established villages because of the numbers, but could hardly leave them to fend for themselves in the wilderness outside the established villages."

Eric nodded thoughtfully. "So small villages were created around the different groups. Logical."

"Yes. It was Rhea's idea, initially. They are places where people can go to heal, as well as places where the current residents of the realm can receive training in medicine, survival, and diplomacy."

"Then, the newcomers are not taken to Steinbrekka anymore?" Eric said quietly, speaking to himself as he became lost in memories.

Rowan felt a hard knot in his stomach form at the mention of Steinbrekka, the area where most people met their death in the previous reign. It once was a desolate, rocky area and home to an assortment of terrifying and deadly creatures. His wife had changed that, when she went there and first met the Magi, Ayewoke, and the small but vicious foxlike creatures known as the Ellyn. She had not only survived at Steinbrekka, but had proven to be the woman the creatures had been waiting for, their new Lady.

"No, Steinbrekka is now a region of peace, and has flourished under Rhea's guidance. People go there still, on occasion, for the creatures do not always choose to act peacefully, but no one is sent there to die."

"That is good, then. It is good that there has been that change." Eric moved an arm out of the water and rested it on the edge of pool.

A small ember flared up behind the man as Rowan looked his way, and accented the pale lines of Eric's scars that ran down his shoulders to disappear in the water. Those scars pushed at him, pecked at the back of his mind as they sat in a moment of companionable silence.

He stood behind Rhea in the dining chamber, furious at the abuse that she had suffered at the hands of the High Prince Mateo, the feeling of futility at her refusal to flee to the protection of Kylassame. There had been tears in her eyes when she told him that she had to stay at court, had to protect the people of the court from the King and his heir.

Then the door crashed open, and the High Prince Mateo walked in, with the dark, angry creature, the Gormellyn, upon his shoulder. The creature was there to extract vengeance and retribution for all the wrongs that had been done to Rhea, the Lady of Steinbrekka, and the rightful heir to the throne, Rowan de Nespa.

The High Prince wavered on his feet from blood loss, his shirt ripped to shreds from the Gormellyn's razor-sharp claws. As they watched in horror, the creature continued to tear into the man's shoulder and chest, blood running in rivers to pool on the marble floor below.

She stopped the creature, with her love for the man Mateo once was driving her to act. Rhea stepped forward, and then Rowan offered his own throat to save her. That was how it began, the end of the reign of Verikhan.

75

Mateo was taken away to be healed, and through the magic of Risalka and her magical powers his memories of his old life returned, and he was Matt once again. A short time later, he stepped through the shining portal and back to the other world.

Rowan stared as the man shifted again in contentment, felt the pain and rage grow as Eric's upper chest rose out of the water, revealing more scars, scars that were created by vengeance for a lifetime of wrongdoing.

"You bastard," Rowan growled as he launched himself across the pool and grabbed the man's shoulders, swinging him to the center of pool where Eric lost his footing and went under.

Rowan took two steps forward, his fingers grabbing Eric's blonde hair in a fist and jerking him up. "Who are you?"

Eric sputtered and coughed, dazed and confused by the quick attack. "My name is Eric."

Rowan shoved him under the water, and then pulled the man back up. "Try again. Why are you here?"

Gasping for air, Eric tried to move away, unwilling to engage in an altercation with the man who was Sabina's father. "What did I do, sir? I fell into this world. I'm here because it's the closest vil -"

He was shoved under again, but this time Rowan released his grip on the blonde hair. Eric rose and coughed, then saw that the entrance of a small boy who had come to check the fires had loosened the older man's hold.

Rowan smiled at the boy before turning his eyes to Eric, rage turning their usual green color into a glittering black. "Follow me." He stepped out of the pool and walked toward the dressing area, not bothering to see if Eric followed, knowing he would.

Eric coughed again and took a deep breath before following Rowan out of the pool. Eric's eyes focused on the older man who moved in front of him, his back crossed with pale scars from whiplashes, injuries from decades past. A buzzing sound filled his head, and he stopped, momentarily dizzy, as his vision blurred.

He stood in front of a gathered crowd, cold and furious. He looked at the man in front of him, the disowned son of the queen, a man who could never be allowed to take the throne. This was the man whose very existence threatened his own status as future king, and who was winning the heart of the beautiful stranger, Rhea Aralia, a woman whose spirit he would enjoy breaking.

The man jerked beneath the whip, and for a second Rowan's green eyes focused on Mateo's, glittering with dark rage. Then they shifted, and Mateo noticed with increasing interest how they traveled to Rhea, the woman that Rowan had been charged to guard with his life.

Ah yes, he had thought. This would make it all the sweeter. She would come to him now on her own accord, and walk into his lair of pain and humiliation willingly. The whip continued to fly, yet the man never cried out in pain, never yielded. Mateo closed his eyes and took a deep breath, the smell of blood and fear on the air exciting him like nothing else could. Soon, he would have it all, and Rowan would be a corpse given to the vultures.

Eric jerked out of the memory and violently trembled as he realized the reason for Rowan's rage, and the knowledge that the older man could easily kill him without question.

He stepped into the changing area and was instantly shoved to the side, his bare back slamming into a wooden support post.

"Let us try this again, and this time I want the truth. Why are you back?" Rowan had already changed into his inner layer of clothes, and the knife he carried on his waist glimmered in the near darkness.

Eric kept his hands down, resisting the will to fight back and protect himself, refusing to cause more pain to this man, or his family. "I wanted to know that she was okay, that she would be fine. After I got back to our old world, I didn't want to live in a world without Rhea." He kept his eyes on Rowan's, praying that the man would accept the near truth.

"And so you came back to a realm that you had destroyed, to a village that you, *personally*, had decimated, and thought to freely live among the people you once tried to wipe out of existence?"

Rowan kept his voice low, aware of how well sound traveled in the winter nights of Asimina. "Why Sabina?" His voice took on a feral, dangerous quality. "You nearly killed my wife once, and now you think to toy with my daughter?"

His stomach heaved and Eric felt his legs trembling with fear. He had never been a fighter, not as Matt, and not as Eric. The training with Alcine had helped him regain his strength, but his instincts had never tended toward violence.

"Rowan, I would never harm Sabina. I didn't know so much time had passed. I didn't know that she was your daughter. I only knew that she saved me." He leaned toward Rowan, ignoring the increased pressure on his sternum. "I am sorry for every pain I have caused you, I truly am. Please, you must believe me."

A voice called from the darkness outside. "Rowan? Are you still in there? We need to get some sleep." His wife, come to bring her husband home to get rest before their morning journey. The pressure on Eric's chest was released as Rowan stepped back, eyes slowly returning to a glittering, sharp green.

Rowan turned and looked at Eric before carefully putting on his outer layer of clothing. "Listen to me now, Eric, once Matt, once

Mateo. I will let you live, for now. I am not blind to the good that you have been doing in this village, or the love that the villagers have toward you, although I suspect that would change in an instant were they to know what you did. But if you touch Sabina in any way, any way at all, that causes her pain, I will destroy you. If you harm any person of this realm in any way, I will take you to the court and let the older generation who were abused under your reign of terror rip you to shreds. Is this understood?"

Eric could only nod, shivering in the cold as Rowan opened the door and walked into the night. A shuddering breath fled from his lungs as he quietly repeated, "I am Eric now, only Eric."

Chapter 11

Vestona

Snow swirled around the thick canvas tent as Sabina shrugged off her thick fur coat with a soft grunt. It had taken them longer than planned to reach the refugee camp that lay between Asimina and Kylassame, the village that had been named Vestona by the permanent residents.

The travelling party, comprised of Sabina, her parents, Henri, and a few other men of Asimina, had ridden in silence, concentrating only on the movement of their horses and keeping their direction through the tall snow drifts that mocked their ability to navigate. Winter had fallen upon the realm fast and hard, and the wind blew sharp enough to bite, forcing the travelers to wrap thick scarves around their faces and pull their fur-lined hoods down low on their heads.

Rhea sat down on the low wooden bed-frame with a thump and a groan. "I'm getting too old for this."

Sabina chuckled as she bent over to remove her leather boots, sodden with snow melt. She hopped around wildly on one foot for a moment, trying to remove the boot before it finally released her foot.

"Oh, Mom. You're not getting old. Even I felt that journey." She removed her other boot and wiggled her toes, grateful as the warmth from the large fire in the stone hearth seeped into her frozen flesh.

Their living area at Vestona was rough by court standards, but Sabina loved it for its rawness and unapologetic nature. A thick canvas tent that had been strategically cut and draped over poles provided the roof and walls of the structure. There was a large central area with wooden benches, a cooking fire that also provided warmth in the winter, and crude shelves to hold the items needed for their visits to the camp.

Around the edge of the central area were beds - raised frameworks of sticks and cut branches topped with cotton mattresses created with grasses and lavender leaves. The children of the family all had single beds, built to the length of a single adult. Rowan and Rhea's bed was wide enough for both to sleep comfortably, though they rarely slept in it at the same time while in the camp.

Supplies of cut wood surrounded the beds, forming a layer of insulation and protection for the inhabitants of the house. They had learned that not all newcomers could be trusted in the early days, when a man with a knife had cut his own entrance into the house, intending to snatch Sabina.

Rowan had met the man with deadly efficiency, the first time that eight-year-old Sabina had seen that side of her father. She had been shocked by how easy he slipped into a killing violence, and avoided him for weeks. It was her mother who had finally sat her down and explained about her father's past, and the skills he possessed but refused to use unless someone he loved was under threat.

She had only seen that violence rise in her father a few more times, and it no longer frightened her that one day he might turn on the family. Her mother was the wisest woman that she knew, and if Rhea was unafraid, she would be as well.

"Mom," she said, quietly and afraid to provoke her other parent's temper. "Do you know why Dad looked so angry when Eric came to see me off?"

They had left first thing in the morning, just before the sun had risen. Eric had been out with Alcine, going through the morning exercises. He had a straight line of bruised and scratched skin on his back, and she had asked him if something had happened after they parted company.

He had denied it, saying only that he missed a step and fell hard into one of the support beams. Steam rose from his hot skin into the cold winter morning, and Sabina found her eyes focused on his lips, and wanting him to kiss her.

Eric might have, if Alcine had not taken that moment to toss a towel at him before walking inside, breaking the tension. Seconds later she could hear her father calling, ready to leave. Eric had looked up to where her father was standing, staring down at the couple with a strange hardness in his expression that Sabina rarely saw.

He had let her go with nothing more than a smile, and a promise to be in Asimina when she returned in a month's time.

Rhea looked at her daughter and gestured for her to sit on the soft dirt in front of the bed. "Come here and let me comb your hair."

She did, recognizing the pattern that she and her mother had created over the years for conversations that may get difficult. Some things were easier to hear when the people talking stared in the same direction, and hands were kept busy.

Her mother began to run a wide-toothed comb through Sabina's tangled locks. "You know how fathers can be, when a man shows interest in their daughter. It is especially difficult when it is an older man."

Sabina rolled her eyes but held still, the methodical pull of the comb against her hair soothing. "I guess Dad told you about the bath house, huh? Beside, he's not that much older, no more than you and Dad were when you met."

Rhea smiled. "Yes, yes he did. And while your father is reserved and a bit scared of the implications, I am cautiously thrilled for you."

"Thrilled?"

"Sabina," Rhea paused in consideration, then continued. "I have been worried about you. I would have thought that by now you would have found someone who piqued your interest, some suitor who would give you flowers and make you smile."

Sabina snorted. "I have plenty of suitors, Mom. Just look around court and you can find twenty men who would be more than happy to vie for my hand." Her voice deepened, mocking the men.

"Dear, beautiful, wonderful Dauphine Sabina! It would bring me such great pleasure to have a person of your brilliance in my company as we dine on this fair eve. Please, will you give me the honor of escorting you across this treacherous marble hall, which you have crossed millions of time in your life without incident?"

Her mother laughed at the impersonation and placed her hand on Sabina's shoulder. "Oh, sweetheart. Is that what you think courtship is? Haven't you had any good experiences?"

Sabina thought hard. "I guess the closest to a real court suitor would be Brendan. He's nice enough, and does seem to genuinely enjoy my company. I know Kat would love for me to end up marrying him, and creating children to fill the castle."

"But?"

"He doesn't make my heart flutter." Sabina felt tears fill her eyes and angrily dashed them away. She had never cared that she had no love interest before, and was not about to begin now. None of the children of the court did, anyway. Alcine had shut himself off when Irena tried to force his hand, and that event had always been in the back of the minds of the children and young adults of the DamaTalous.

Rhea paused in her brushing and leaned close to her daughter to whisper, "Does Bryan make your heart flutter?"

Sabina jumped. "Mom! How did you know about that?" She turned around quickly so that she was facing her mother, though still on her knees. "It was my idea, not his. We just were both lonely and thought we would have a little fun. Nothing has ever happened but kissing, and we were always really careful to make sure that no one in the court saw or knew about anything. Please don't tell Dad. It will get Bryan in so much trouble. Please!"

Her mother just chuckled and smiled at her daughter. "I know, sweetheart. Bryan is a good man, a trustworthy one, and if I thought the court would not ostracize both of you for such a union I would push for it to become more than kisses. Your secret is safe with me."

Sabina settled back down and laid her head upon her mother's knee. "What did you think of the injured man at Asimina?"

Rhea's lips twitched but she kept her voice steady. "I think that my interactions with him have shown a very nice and respectful young man. He actually reminds me quite a bit of my best friend from back when I was your age, although your father seems to think otherwise of Eric's character, for some reason."

A frown tugged at her lips as Rhea remembered her husband's return the night before. He had been shaking with rage and spent the long hours of the night staring at the door, jumping at each small noise as if there were a deadly predator roaming the night.

Sabina fiddled with a small piece of her mother's dress, rolling the cotton between her thumb and index finger. "I don't understand why he was so angry. I mean, I know it was probably a bit of a jolt for him, to walk in on your daughter and a man ... you know ... kissing. But when I left, the two of them seemed okay."

"Well, he will tell us in his own time I'm sure, so don't worry about it." Rhea stroked her daughter's hair thoughtfully. "He does it, doesn't he, make your stomach flutter?"

Sabina nodded, the butterflies in her stomach dancing as she remembered the feel of Eric's hands on her bare skin.

Rhea sighed. "I'll deal with your father, then. You just enjoy the ride."

Chapter 12

Vestona

Henri stood beside Sabina and let out a low whistle of anxiety. "There are certainly a lot of them this time."

She nodded silently, standing next to her friend at the top of a tall hill as she drank her cup of hot tea and took in the morning view of the refugee camp as they began their day.

The camp was set up as two distinct sections. The first section, where Sabina's family resided, was known as Vestona and was the area established by the permanent residents. Their homes, made of the same thick canvas as Sabina's, formed giant domes with small paths cleared in between, temporary walkways created since the recent snowfall. The village was protected from the worst of the elements by its positioning, with a thick forest on one side and a large cliff on the other.

In front of Vestona was the area known as Novost. Here, there was little privacy, and the canvassed tents stood out starkly against the horizon. There were two halls, long and narrow, that served as sleeping chambers for the refugees, the people who had stumbled into this world. The males all slept in one, while the women slept in the other. Any children who were found typically slept within the women's chambers, although many times a permanent resident would foster them and take them into their home almost immediately.

Close to the sleeping barracks were the feasting hall and an infirmary. The feasting hall was the center of the refugee community and, during harsh weather, a place for tentative socialization. Tables were lined up, end on end, with benches and chairs for the use of the refugees and volunteers from the community. Fire pits had been dug after every three tables, allowing warmth to be evenly distributed throughout the hall, and providing light in addition to the lanterns hung upon the thick center poles.

The infirmary consisted of a large, circular dome with small, low beds lined up in rows. Small curtains had been erected around the edges of the space to afford the semblance of privacy for some of the bigger injuries, or give the mortally wounded a place of respect as they drew their last breath. This was where Sabina spent most of her time while at the various camps, helping her mother and her Aunt Lianna tend to the injured.

Her uncle, Savin, stepped up to the couple; a giant compared to her, and sipped his own cup of hot brew. "You came at a good time, Sabina. Lianna could use another set of hands."

Savin and Lianna were not related to Sabina by blood, but through their deep love for her parents and her family. They had acted as a second set of guardians as she grew through childhood and into adulthood, and she thought of them as family. They were close-lipped about the events that occurred before her birth, but Sabina knew they had a friendship that had lived through blood and tears, and would never be broken.

Henri puffed out a breath of cold air. "How many since last time we were here?"

"Twenty or so," Savin replied wearily. He and Lianna had taken on the refugee camp and the village that grew from the dust as their own, guiding the people through the necessary changes to a new life.

"That many?" Sabina wondered. The camp had begun when she was a little girl, and then had only consisted of a few family groups. Now there were over fifty permanent residents, and almost one hundred newcomers.

Savin nodded and led them back down the hill. "Something bad seems to be happening in the other world, something that is driving people into the in-between spaces where they normally would not go." He automatically reached out a hand to steady Sabina as she tripped in the snow. "Most talk about running into caves, or jumping into deep holes to escape capture, then falling and waking up here. The newer ones are having a harder time adjusting. They are deeply distrusting that the residents of the village will not cause them harm and want to set up their own group. We have about twenty-five, not including the newest refugees, who petitioned for a new, permanent settlement to be made."

"Demographics of the most recent?" Henri asked, already planning on how to situate those who wished to stay, and move those who would fit in well with already established villages.

The three walked up to the entrance of the camp. "Five men, five women, ten adolescents. They were found just before you got here, and all but three men are in the infirmary." He glanced at Sabina. "They are in bad shape, Seb. Lianna wanted me to warn you. Henri, I would like for you to go with Sabina to help out this morning."

The young man began to protest, his mind focused on the duties he regularly performed, but thought better of it. If Savin required him to accompany Sabina, it was not for his healing abilities, which were nothing notable, but for security.

Warmth thawed Sabina's skin as Savin opened the thick wooden door to the infirmary and they stepped into the dim interior. Her aunt had built the fire in the stone hearth to burn hot, allowing the people inside the structure to be comfortable in only the barest of clothing. Women and children were given thin cotton tunics and pants to wear, clothing which covered them modestly but allowed for easy access for any required medical procedures. Men wore loose trousers, or if their injury required, a knee-length piece of cotton cloth that gave them privacy but left easy access to their legs.

Gabriella, Lianna's daughter and Cole's twin sister, waved from the back of the room where she had a pot of boiling water going. "You guys made it! Backup has finally arrived."

Sabina immediately crossed the room and embraced her friend, having missed her company for almost half the year. "What do we have here, Gab? We were just passing through but your mom asked us to stay a few days to give you extra hands."

The younger woman hefted a basket of cloths that had been soaked in hot water onto her hip, signaling for Henri and Sabina to do the same. "The children came in together. Seven are covered in minor burns, and three have deep lacerations on the arms along with more severe burns."

Gabriella took a shuddering breath before continuing. "The oldest of the children is ten. He told me that the others were trapped in their school when it was set on fire. He had gone to visit his sister, who is six, and found the doors locked and barricaded, and flames shooting up the walls.

"He and his friends, the two older girls with the cuts, broke the basement windows and crawled in that way. They got the children down into the basement, and then realized they were trapped, the windows having been boarded up behind them by scouts hidden in the woods. The others, they say there were fifteen more, panicked and ran back upstairs and into the flames."

Sabina sniffed, pushing back the tears that would not aid anyone in this room. "How did it end? How did they get here?"

"The littlest girl went to follow them upstairs and tripped. When the oldest went to pick her up he found a handle to a trap door that never existed before. He lifted it and they all jumped. They woke up just outside the entrance gate to Novost and were found about an hour ago by the scouts."

Henri shook his head as he placed the basket of linens on the small work table by the cots. "Who would do such a thing, and to children?"

Lianna stood up from where she had been gently stitching a large gash on a child's arm, a little girl of just nine-years-old who was trying very hard not to cry as the needle pierced her skin and closed the wound.

"Sabina, I am so glad you were able to come. The children speak our language, or close enough, but they are so frightened …"

Her aunt looked exhausted and in low spirits, her heart heavy from the senseless violence done to the children.

Sabina sat down on a cot beside one of the children and gently applied a burn salve to the blisters. "Go get some rest, Aunt. Gabby and I will take care of the children." She turned to the child and softly introduced herself as her aunt walked out, taking the opportunity to rest and to cry.

The small girl looked up at her with eyes as wide as saucers and filled with fear. "We not bad, I promise."

"I am sure you are not bad at all," Sabina responded gently. "No one here will hurt you. You are safe now."

She shook her head, matted brown hair moving stiffly with the motion, ash rising into the air. "Never safe, never. They find us. The Oprimata find us!" Her voice rose to a panicked cry, and the oldest of the boys quickly came and sat beside her with a look of protectiveness that bordered on hostile.

A man in the corner lifted his head sharply at the child's cries, the movement drawing Sabina's attention. He was seated on a low cot that had been pushed against the corner, one leg drawn to his chest, the other extended in front of his body. His short hair, so dark brown it was nearly black, was plastered to his skull with grime and sweat. Blood from an arrow wound trickled down his chest, the shaft still protruding from his skin. Strong black lines had been inked into his chest, the design beginning at his neck, extending to fully surround his left shoulder, and then snaking down to cover the left side of his torso, dipping below the waistband of his pants. Strong arms bore a series of long lacerations, each weeping fluids, but the blood had clotted on its own accord

Sabina felt her head spin as she looked into his eyes, a deep purple hue that she had never seen before, and realized the agony he must be enveloped within as he sat, untended, on the cot.

Gabriella followed her gaze. "Oh, him. Every time I try to get near him he just hisses at me, and backs away. It was causing more harm than good for me to even try."

Henri gave the man an assessing look. "With those wounds, he'll hold steady for another hour, two at the most. Is he dangerous?"

She snorted in response. "Hardly. The man can barely sit up in this condition. I think he came from the same time as the children, but different region. Their clothing is similar, and so is their accent, though his is thicker. Somehow, they know enough of our language to communicate, but I'm not sure if he truly doesn't know it, or just doesn't want to talk."

Sabina turned her attention back to the children, carefully helping to tend to the wounds as she tried to lift their spirits. A soft cradle song began to flow from her lips, one that her mother had sung to her as a small child when she was afraid during stormy weather.

One of the children smiled at her, and then slowly moved the few feet needed to crawl onto Sabina's lap. She continued singing as she gently wrapped her arms around the child and rocked slowly in time to the melody. Within moments, the child had fallen into a deep sleep, the first sleep tolerated since the harrowing time in the school.

She carefully laid the child down on the cot and covered her in a soft blanket, still humming the tune. The rest of the children soon followed, curling up around the smallest child like a litter of puppies, their courage growing in the nurturing presence of Sabina and Gabriella.

After the last child began to take the breaths of deep sleep, Sabina took a deep breath and accepted the cup of cold water offered by Henri. "I need some air. Watch over Gab for me?"

The winter air bit into her skin as she stepped outside the door, unprotected from the elements in her cotton trousers and tunic. Sabina ignored the painful touch and took several gulps of air, clearing her mind from the horror that the children must have felt in those moments before they stumbled into this world.

A high-pitched screech behind her was followed by a loud thump and low groan. Sabina spun around to fling open the door, cursing the few seconds it took for her eyes to adjust to the dimness within the structure.

Henri stood, knife in hand, between Gabriella and the stranger with the purple eyes. The man was on his knees, unarmed, one hand pressing around the arrow shaft in his chest while the other supported his weight. The children remained asleep; their bodies past the point of arousal, and the other occupants of the infirmary looked too tired and hurt to care about the movement.

"Henri, what happened?" Sabina took the few steps needed to cross to her friend, who had already begun sheathing his still-clean knife.

"He cried out when you left, and made to follow you. Gabriella shrieked a warning." He gave his head a frustrated shake. "I shouldn't have pulled the knife, him being injured like he was. He didn't even make three steps before his legs gave out. It startled me, though." Henri's eyes never left the injured man, who was now staring intently at Sabina from his position on the ground.

"He was fast, so fast," Gabriella said softly from her position by the children. "With as much blood loss as he's had, and his injuries, he should not have been able to move that quickly. It scared me."

Sabina stared at him a moment, before carefully walking forward. She approached him as she would an injured wild animal, slowly, calmly, keeping her eyes fixed on his face and shoulders, aware of every slight motion.

"My name is Sabina. Do you understand our language?"

The man kneeled on the ground, breath coming hard, the arrow shaft rising and falling as new blood trickled around the smooth wood. His eyes narrowed in concentration, and then he shook his head.

She sucked in her breath as his head dipped down in exhaustion, the action revealing his neck, and a black circle with a jagged sunburst and series of lines. Though it was sharper and darker, it was an exact replica of the curious marking on Alcine's neck. On a hunch, she tried the language that her mother had taught her as a learning game, the language that her mother had started to learn from Alcine's mother, Mairi.

"We are friends. We mean you no harm. You are safe here."

At that, his head shot up, his taxed muscles shaking from the quick movement. "How do you know to speak Zajedica?"

Cold seeped through her trousers as Sabina kneeled on the wooden plank floor, ignoring the quiet warning sounds from Henri. "My mother learned it from a friend, and taught it to me. Others have come here who have spoken it before. What is your name?"

He looked toward the sleeping children. "Names are dangerous. You are already in danger by having me, and them, in this room. I do not wish to further the danger to you. People have been killed for harboring my kind. It is better that you let me leave, now, before my presence is discovered."

She shook her head in disagreement, though unclear of the accuracy of her translation as he spoke quickly and with unknown words. "There is no more danger here. My father and my aunt rule this land. It is a different place than the one from whence you came.

The men you and the children speak of, the Oprimata, do not exist here."

A brief flitter of happiness flashed in the man's eyes. "If they do not have a hold here, there is hope. My name is Darian. Thank you for your help. Be sure to guard the children."

Sabina and Henri lunged forward as the man fell, managing to push his body away from the arrow shaft at the last moment. Sabina hurriedly felt for a pulse, relieved when the gently thumping vein in his wrist confirmed life, if not consciousness.

"Come on. Let's get him up on the bed. We might as well get this arrow out while he can't feel it or protest."

It took a combined effort by the three to get Darian onto the low bed platform. The man was covered in strong muscles, and even with Henri's strength, it was difficult to move him across the floor without causing further injury. They gently laid him on the bed, head cushioned by a thin pillow.

Gabriella nodded to Sabina, then quickly and smoothly grasped the arrow shaft in her hand and pulled. Both women released sighs of relief that the tip of the projectile was smooth, and not barbed. The arrow had missed vital organs, and the tunnel formed by the sharp point was free of further damage. Sabina quickly placed clean, astringent-soaked cotton squares on the injury, pressing down until the blood-flow slowed, replacing them with a thick cloth before wrapping the injury tightly with linens.

Henri gave a low whistle of admiration as the two women quietly murmured an assessment of the man's wounds as they tended to him. Several lacerations on the arms needed to be stitched, which Gabriella did efficiently with her tiny needle and thread. His arms also contained several large burn marks and puncture wounds, all which were well cleaned, covered in a salve to prevent infection, and tightly bandaged.

His chest was a series of deep lacerations along with puncture wounds, and Gabriella once again plied her strong needle to the task. Both women stared for long moments at the tattooed markings, which flowed around the side of his torso and continued to wrap around the left side of his back. His back and shoulders showed large white lines, both jagged and straight, scars from past abuse. Large bruises covered his lower ribcage, various shades of angry purples and blacks.

Satisfied that he still slept, the women quickly slit the legs of his trousers to assess the damage done to his legs, opening the fabric from ankle to thigh to expose the skin below. It took long hours to pull out the tiny pieces of metal and glass with their small bone tweezers, the worst located in the skin and muscle of his lower legs. The man's muscular thighs contained a series of linear marks, old scars mixing with new lash marks, all crisscrossed by a myriad of smaller scratches.

Henri shook his head as he watched the process, keeping one eye on the other adults in the room who had visibly relaxed after the man's conversation with Sabina. "What did this man go through? What version of the other world did he come from?"

Sabina gave a moment of consideration as she remembered where she heard the term "Oprimata" in the past. It was the story that her aunt had told of Alcine's birth father, a man who had a cruel death at the hands of a group called the Oprimata. "A man who has been through hell and back, I think. We will have to treat him gently, for who knows what he has seen."

Gabriella gave her friend a subtle nudge and both women turned to look at the group of children, the oldest of which had opened his eyes and was staring with the adoration at the man. "You will help the Saverlen?" he asked in Zajedica. "You will not kill him? We did not dare ask you before in case you were the enemy."

Their eyes filled with tears at the child's tentative hope and Gabriella answered the child. "Yes, we will help him. We will help all of you."

Chapter 13

Vestona

"Miss Sabina," ten-year-old Basu called as he hesitantly approached. "Miss Sabina, I was wondering if I could speak with you a minute?"

Sabina paused just inside the door to the infirmary and turned around, smiling at the boy. "Yes, Basu?"

He glanced at the children, then toward Darian. "Not in here, is there any place that we could speak privately?"

She followed his glance, her eyes meeting those of the man. He had woken up twenty-four hours after his collapse and remained sullen and quiet. The only move he made was his eyes, shifting from Sabina to the children, or an occasion grimace as he shifted his body to inspect his wounds.

"Of course. Here." She handed the young boy a thick cloak before they stepped out into the daylight. There was no conversation as they followed the pathways cut through the thick snow, for the ground was slick beneath their feet. Both gave sighs of relief as they stepped into the eating hall and found a warm, quiet corner where they could talk in peace.

Basu fiddled with the edges of the cloak, watching the snow that had collected on the hem melt and drip to the floor. "It's the man,

Darian. I just thought you should know, he's a good man, or at least, he should be a good man, his kind always are." His big blue eyes stared up at her, and she saw the innocence he should have held had been scarred forever by the events in the school.

"He has yet to show any indication otherwise. Is there something that I need to know about him?" Sabina watched the movements of the eating hall while they spoke, carefully noting the groups that formed and silently calculating which people would go on to Kylassame when they left in a few days' time.

"Do you know about the Saverlen? I heard you speaking the language and thought, well, that you might understand." Basu frowned at the dirt floor in concentration, caught between wanting to protect the man and protect the other children.

Sabina thought back to the conversations she had with her mother, and with her aunt Nyssa. "I don't think that I do. I have a - friend - who originally came from Zajed Seganu. His mother friended mine, and my mother taught me the language, along with several others who came from that place. We know very little about the place though, the mother died shortly after arriving here and we never asked the others."

"Is he branded?" The boy's voice was barely louder than a whisper.

"Well, I'm not sure if it was a brand, but he does have a black marking on his neck, yes."

Blue eyes turned and regarded her carefully, as if the answer to his next question would mean life or death. "Does it look like this?" He tugged down the collar of the borrowed cloak and warm cotton shirt underneath, revealing a tattoo on his neck, a black circle with a jagged sunburst at the top, and a series of triangles below.

"No," Sabina murmured as she studied the design. "Not quite like that. He has the sunburst within the circle, but there are lines below, not triangles."

Tears filled Basu's eyes before he dashed them away. "Not my brother, then. He disappeared a few months before the fire. I had hoped maybe he had come here too."

Sabina reached out her hand and gently took his frail fingers in hers. "Just because this man is not him, does not mean he is not here. I will make sure that everyone keeps an eye out for any others with the markings."

She hesitated a moment, unwilling to make any demands of a young person who had seen so much evil, before deciding to get an answer to a question that had plagued her for years. "Basu, can you explain the marking to me? My friend does not know what it means and we have always wondered."

"Back home, we call it a branding. The circle with the sun on the inside means that the person belongs to the Oprimata. They came when I was just born, so my mom said. They brand everyone and rule over us like we are just slaves for them." His voice grew angry and loud, and he took a deep breath when a few heads turned their directions.

"The triangles, and in your friend's case, the lines, are the village or town where they occupied," he continued. "Everyone is marked in this way, getting the mark whenever their village is taken, or when they turn five, if the village had already been occupied before their birth."

Sabina tilted her head sideways in thought. "The man in the infirmary, Darian, had the same marking as my friend, exactly the same. Only my friend's is a bit blurry around the markings, not quite as sharp."

He nodded in understanding. "When a person is branded as a baby or very young child it will do that as they grow. Most who have that are rebranded when they reach my age, and then at adulthood." He paused as he thought of the implications. "Does he have the mark of the Saverlen too?" Basu asked.

"Are those the markings on the man's torso? No," Sabina answered. "What are the Saverlen?"

Basu looked around the hall again, and then started drawing small designs in the dirt as he spoke, mimicking the whorls and spirals of the tattoo. "The Saverlen are the saviors of the region. Before the Oprimata came, they were the group who would help deliver justice, rebuild houses, clear areas, whatever was needed. Sometimes they stayed in one place, but mostly they traveled around doing whatever needed to be done. Then, they became the ones who fought against the Oprimata and started to help the people who are hurt by them. The Oprimata usually take anything they can get their hands on, like food and supplies, the girls and women, and the Saverlen try to keep them from doing that."

Pride shown on his face for a moment before it snuffed out. "I was in training to become a Saverlen, just the initial training. You can start when you are nine, but you are not allowed to begin the marking until you are sixteen."

She glanced around the room, trying to discern if any other inhabitants had similar markings, trying to remember if any others who had come before were marked. People came into the realm in all races and from various cultures, and she never realized the markings could have given such an important message. "Do you know the Saverlen in the infirmary?"

He shook his head. "No, he is not from my village. I just know that the marks are the same for all of them. The whorls, the spiral things, in the design stand for Oprimata killed. He has too many to count! Most only get up to five kills before they are caught or killed themselves. It does not count if you use any ancient weapons either, like guns or anything. They have to be current weapons, like the Oprimata have, crossbows and knives and spears and stuff. He must be very skilled at weapons and evasion to have such a big marking!"

Sabina felt her throat dry up as she tried to continue talking, her mind suddenly blank. The stranger had seemed so weak and helpless when she was helping Gabriella with his healing. *Once he is healed, he will not be weak anymore.* She nodded her head absent-mindedly as Basu continued to speak of his old world. *I will have to tell this to Henri so we can keep an eye on him. This man could be a danger to us all.*

Chapter 14

Vestona

Rhea glanced over at her daughter as they both sat on the ground, legs comfortably tucked under their bodies, in front of the imposing man.

Rowan had agreed to this meeting only on the condition that he and Henri were to be in the room with the women during the discussion. Savin stood just at the doorway, one eye on the proceedings and one watching the shadows that moved outside the canvas.

They had pulled a privacy curtain in one large room of the infirmary, for Sabina wanted to get more information from him in order to decide where he, and the children, should go. She was adamant that they could not stay here, that their fear and the chance of running into one of the Oprimata, should one stumble into the world, was too great. The children refused to leave the corner of the infirmary, visibly terrified of every new person who walked in with an injury. Darian refused to leave the building as well, citing he was unwilling to risk the entire village if his presence was discovered.

He sat quietly on the floor, legs crossed and hands resting lightly on his knees. He had been dressed in a long tunic that wrapped around his body, allowing easy removal for the women to check on his wounds, which were improving. His legs were clad in light cotton trousers, any heavier fabric rubbing the dozens of shallow raw and postponing the healing.

"Thank you for this meeting," he said hesitantly, uncertain of why he was called, or who these people were. *These are important people,* he guessed. *But why are they important? Where am I?*

Sabina smiled in encouragement and gestured as she went around the room with the introductions. "Darian is a man who has come from the other world. Darian, this is my father, Rowan, the co-reagent of this realm. This is his wife, my mother, Rhea. She is the one who taught me Zajedica and once met a woman from your time."

"Those men are Henri, a friend, and Savin, my uncle. They are here to make sure that everyone in this room, including you, is safe." She gestured to Henri who stood behind Darian, and then to Savin at the door.

Darian nodded brusquely, still unconvinced that a member of the Oprimata was not going to slice through the canvas and destroy them all for harboring him. "I thank you, but while I do not wish to give insult by doubting the protective capabilities of these men, I still think that you should release me from this place."

That was the reason for this discussion. It had been several days since the man had collapsed, and his strength had returned enough for him to make slow walks around the camp and contemplate travel. The moment he was able to stand he had tried to walk out of the infirmary, Henri dragging him back into the canvassed dome.

Rhea looked at him calmly with her hazel eyes before speaking in a combination of English and Zajedica. "I think I understand your concern, somewhat. My friend, her name was Mairi, spoke of the Oprimata as well. Her husband was a member of the

Saverlen, and was killed by them. When she grieved over his ashes, she was hunted down as an enemy of the Oprimata, just for crying over someone they had deemed the enemy."

Darian nodded again, leaning forward toward Rhea slightly with suppressed excitement. "Mairi? Where is she? Can I speak with her?"

Rhea's eyes filled with tears and she took a moment to compose her emotions. "Mairi died, a long time ago." She shook herself and forced another smile. "But that is not why we are here."

Henri spoke then, his rich voice floating from behind Darian. "Let us speak truly and not waste time. Who are you, what are you, and can we trust you?"

The excitement slowly fell from Darian's eyes, though they still held a trace of unbridled hope. "My name is Darian, and I am from a place called Zajed Seganu. I am a member of the Saverlen, a group formed to protect the common people from any invaders or malevolent forces. By the time I joined, it served only to protect from the Oprimata who pushed against our borders."

"To the Oprimata, we are apostates, terrorists, people who refuse to accept progressive change. We work to stay one step ahead of them, to warn villages of their encroachment, and try to prevent the crimes for which they are so well known."

He glanced up at Sabina. "The children in the school … that is their first method of attack on most villages. It was their way of flushing those with the will to disobey from the herd. Any parents who had tried to save their children were cut down before they could reach the school, and those who stood by and watched until the school and its occupants turned to ash would take their own lives before the last ember cooled."

"Some, some let the darkness of the Oprimata seep into their own hearts, allowing the justifications to rape their souls, believing that their children were tainted, and the community cleansed by the pyre, or drowned, or similarly killed."

Rhea's hand moved to cover her mouth. She had not been in the infirmary to hear the story, but somewhere in her mind she felt a hint of familiarity. She shook her head slightly, a memory of children burning in a schoolhouse, windows barred by iron and a door by bricks, but unclear of when it occurred.

Darian cleared his throat nervously, glancing at the door. "You are good people, I saw that instantly. There is a light in your hearts and a kindness in your touch, your voice. I do not want to be the one to cause the Oprimata to destroy your village for harboring me."

Rowan's brows furrowed as he stared at the stranger. "You seem certain that the Oprimata will find you here, will try to seek vengeance. Why?"

He looked up at Rowan; his eyes filled with respect, and fear. "Because, sir, three of them tumbled through with me."

Chapter 15

Asimina

A light snow swirled around Eric's feet as he moved toward the central cistern to draw water. The cold breeze did not penetrate the thick fur coat that he wore, or the multi-layered cotton trousers, but his cheeks burned red below his fur-lined hood.

Alcine walked beside him, two empty water skins slung over his shoulder, boots crunching in the snow dusting. "I have a proposition for you, as presented to me by a member of the community."

Eric shifted his own water skin and looked curiously over at the man. "Oh? What would that be?"

"I am well aware of how uncomfortable it is for you to stay in the hut where we keep the injured, yet we do not have the resources to build a new one quite yet, nor have we discussed with you the option of moving here permanently."

He held up a hand to quell Eric's oncoming interruption. "We do not ask a newcomer to decide until they have an opportunity to visit many villages of the realm. Each has their own distinctive style and way of life and many will feel uncomfortable in one village, only to perfectly fit into another."

"What are the villages of the realm?" Eric used a small iron spike to break up the thin ice at the top of the cistern and then began to turn the large crank used to raise and lower the thick wooden bucket.

Alcine pulled the full bucket up and carefully poured the water into the first of the skins, propping the full container against the stone well. "Well, there is the Court of Kaldalangra, which is a few hours' ride to the east. It is ruled by Queen Nyssa and a place that fits well for people who like opulence and convenience. Meals are provided by staff, spacious rooms are provided, entertainment given, and more variety in goods."

"Yet, you do not sound excited to speak of it?"

He gave a grunt in response. "Yes, well, it has always been a difficult place for me. My mother and I were not born of this realm, and I was adopted by Nyssa when I was an infant. As such, I have always known that I would not stand to inherit the realm, and it would be passed either to my cousin Seb or to my younger brother, Josef."

"And?" Eric urged the story on.

Alcine sighed as he propped the second water skin against the stones. "And apparently none of the people of the court, other than my family, were aware of the adoption. My brother was formally declared as heir to the throne, per Nyssa and Rowan's combined wishes, and court has become, shall we say, difficult because of that."

Eric cranked the bucket once more, biting on his lip as he thought into the past. "Does Seb like the court?" He could vaguely remember the castle, though most of his vivid memories were only of the room where he had healed from a vicious attack, and the garden where he and Rhea had sat to discuss their future.

"Definitely not. The people are ... gilded, I suppose. They are beautiful in appearance but their smiles hide schemes, and their words are often riddles used to twist others for their own purpose. While there, Seb spends most of her time with the family, or with the staff, and avoids the rest of the people as much as possible."

"I know I'm in Asimina, but I was wondering, is there a story behind the village? I'm not familiar with other villages of the realm, but it seems like there is a lack of elders, and several generation gaps within the population."

The taller man winced. "Yes, well. Asimina has a bloody history. Before I was born, when the realm was ruled by my grandfather, Verikhan, Asimina was used as an outlet for his rage. He and his heir regularly kidnapped people and slaughtered them for entertainment, guised as sacrifices to the spirits. My Aunt Rhea changed all that, though not before entire generations were reduced to piles of corpses."

Eric felt his stomach twist in knots as strange, violent scenes suddenly flashing before his eyes and he had to pause to shake his head clear.

"You okay? We can rest if you need." Alcine put out a hand to steady Eric as he wavered a moment on his feet.

"Fine, just a little dizzy."

Alcine laughed and clapped a hand on his shoulder in companionship as they walked across the village. "I told you not to push yourself so hard this morning. Your body needs time."

Eric forced a laugh out, bile still rising at the images that flickered in his mind.

Him, astride on a great white horse, sword dripping with blood as he stood and surveyed a village built of twigs and moldy thatch.

Him, watching and grinning as soldiers tossed nets over the women of the village, violating them as others captured the men, hobbling their legs, tying their hands and watching them stumble behind the horses back to the castle.

Him, body flooding with an almost painfully intense level of joy as a man with sandy brown hair was beaten down and tied to the pommel of his saddle so that his unconscious body could be dragged from the village.

His stomach heaved and Eric stopped to bend over, hands braced on his knees, and gulped in deep breaths of the cold air. "Must have had something last night that disagreed with me," he panted.

"I guess so," Alcine responded, taking Eric's water skin and slinging it over his shoulder with the others. "Come on, let us go sit in my hut while we discuss one potential path of your future."

Eric nodded and followed Alcine on wobbly legs, grateful to sink down onto the fur-lined section of floor in Alcine's hut.

The hut was considerably homier than the one where he had resided during his stay in the village. A small central fire provided warmth and the ability for rudimentary cooking, and the embers were surrounded by an ankle-high wall of stone for safety. A ring of hard-packed dirt surrounded the stones, and then several layers of furs and thick cotton weavings had been placed for seated comfort.

A thin tapestry separated a section of the hut to create a sleeping quarters, the curtain currently pulled aside to reveal a low cot with a grass mattress and quilted blanket.

"Where else is there in the realm for people to go?" Eric asked, teeth clenched as his stomach reluctantly settled. He was not sure if the smell of the breakfast was helping or hindering his attempts at steadiness.

Alcine poked at the fire, small flames flickering up to boil a small kettle of water that set next to the cooking pan. "Well, there is Vestona. That is a small village that supports one of the refugee camps, called Novost. They live simply there, fairly rustic, but it is a good place for those who have difficulty adjusting to the rest of the realm. The people have created a community with a good blend of traditions and cultures.

"Kylassame is where most of the people from your world and time end up," he continued. "That village is a decent distance from here and takes several days on horseback to reach. It has grown into a fairly large community with running water and many of the conveniences found in the other world. Rowan is the leader of that village and that is where he resides for most of the year."

Eric let the soothing voice of Alcine ease away the feeling of unease as he talked of other villages, most relating to the refugee camps that had been created during the mass arrival of so many refugees from the other world.

His head snapped up as Alcine spoke of another village, Albadarl, which stood a few days ride from Asimina. "Who did you say was in charge of that village?"

Alcine stirred the oat and honey mixture and spooned out a portion for each of them. "Kibwe. He's a good leader, a fair one. It serves him well that Albadarl is small, and remains for the most part untouched. The woods protect their own and rarely do any incomers choose to visit or remain in Albadarl. It is also good that it is small because the man had his leg cut off when he was a young boy and still has difficulty traveling over wide tracts of land."

This time his stomach heaved violently and Eric barely made it outside of the hut before he was sick, his emptied stomach dry-heaving until his eyes stung.

Ever since he walked through that shimmering veil he had been haunted by the image of a small boy with one leg, a young boy who stood shorter than Eric's waist, with deep ebony skin and eyes white with fear. The boy had stood there, blood dripping from his stump of a leg, sorrow in his eyes as he repeated the question, "Why?"

Eric stumbled back in, muttering apologies and taking a careful sip of hot mint tea to settle his stomach and nerves.

Alcine watched as Eric, his skin clammy and damp, brought a shaky spoonful of oatmeal to his mouth. "It seems that my next request may be just in time. I am obviously not being observant enough in your health and apologize for that."

Eric swallowed the oats carefully, then took another tentative spoonful when his stomach did not react. "No, it's my fault. I'm sorry. I'm not normally this weak."

The firelight flickered as Alcine removed the pot of tea to pour a second cup. "I have an offer of hospitality for you, which was freely given. It would give you an opportunity to learn the ways of Asimina from the life of a community member, as opposed to a visitor, or a man healing from wounds."

"Who gave this offer?" Eric answered hesitantly, unsure of his expected role.

Alcine smiled, his straight, white teeth glinting in the firelight. "Come meet her."

Chapter 16

Vestona

Wind whistled through the trees at the edge of Vestona, blowing the snow from tree branches as the individuals in the traveling party mounted their horses, wool scarves wrapped around their exposed faces to keep out the worst of the cold. The sun had just crested the hill behind the village when the men and women had gathered, ready to depart at first light.

Darian stiffly mounted the blood-bay gelding, a reliable animal often used to transport people from one village to another and accustomed to green riders. He had ridden before, for all people from Zajed Seganu had lessons in horsemanship, the fastest and most efficient way to travel since the fall of the electric infrastructure, but had no horse of his own in the other world. The Saverlen relied on absolute control, stealth, and agility in order to stay alive, none of which were reliable with a horse.

Sabina eyed his movements for a minute before mounting her own gelding in a fluid motion, only slightly hampered by the thick layers that protected her from the cold. She edged the horse over to Darian's side.

"I am still not convinced you should be riding. You would be better off in a wagon so the jolts don't open up your wounds." Sabina saw the man's shoulders hunch and he shook his head.

"I will be fine. Let the children have the space. They will need it." He huddled in the borrowed outerwear that Savin had loaned him, as Rowan's clothes had been too tight for his larger frame.

Sabina gave a frustrated huff. "Will you at least agree to let me check on the wounds when we get there?"

He hesitated before giving a forced nod of agreement. Darian had pulled away from Sabina in the days after the family discussion of his past, afraid for her safety. All people, even the males, had been denied access to his body, something that they tolerated with the fear that any physical confrontation would be worse for the wounds than the lack of care.

Rowan raised his hand and swung his fist in a tight circle, the signal for the party to begin their travel. Sabina put a hand to the top of her hood, holding the fur-lined fabric in place as she tilted her head back and searched the skies.

A sharp whistle came from her pursed lips, then a large shadow in the white sky dove down, causing Darian to nearly jump from his horse as the large hawk dropped from the sky, wings flapping to achieve a light landing on Sabina's padded arm.

She stroked the raptor's feathers with her thick leather gloves and kissed his head, aware of the tension that every person around her felt as her face became dangerously close to the deadly beak. "His name is Faulks. He decided to become my protector when I was still in my mother's womb and has been by my side ever since."

Darian glanced at the hawk who sat calmly on the woman's arm, eyes closed in pleasure as she scratched its neck and brushed away the snow and ice from its feathers. "How old is he then? Sixteen?"

She bristled at his assumption and hunkered into her coat. "I am nineteen, for your information. Faulks is," she paused, doing the math. "Faulks is around forty years old. He was a gift to my father when both were young and then watched over my father until I was born, and now he watches over me."

The man gave a low whistle of admiration. "Forty? Do hawks even live that long?"

"None others to our knowledge. They usually live around twenty, maybe thirty years old? He is special though, like my mother's old horse."

"Old horse?"

"Her name was Kataolya. Everyone says that she was the most beautiful mare that existed, with jet-black fur, one blue eye and one brown, and a long flowing mane. She came to my grandmother, the Queen Sula when the queen was just a little girl and the filly had just been born. Kataolya died when my mom was pregnant with me, over thirty years later."

"Who are your parents? They seem … important."

Sabina snorted and then laughed, the sound carrying to the head of the party where her father rode. She waved her free hand to indicate there was no issue and for him to continue on. "I guess you could say that. My father is the Grand Duke of Kaldalangra, this realm. He is also the protector of the villages of Kylassame and Albadarl. My mother is known as the Lady of Steinbrekka, a region that was once used to brainwash and kill people who were brought, or fell, into this realm, like you. That changed once she was taken to Steinbrekka and befriended the creatures there, and then defeated the tyrant king, my father's father."

"Yet your father rides out here freely, without a guard, and allows you to help in an infirmary with total strangers?" Darian's voice held a touch of masked disapproval.

Sabina shrugged through her coat, the action slightly upsetting Faulks who had fallen into a doze on her arm. "It's his realm, after all; well, his and my aunt, Queen Nyssa. No one will attack them, especially out here. Besides, Savin is the best personal guard in the realm, and Henri is probably the second best. Between those two we are safe."

"And the queen, do her children walk among strangers with little protection?"

She gave him a sharp glance, offended on her father and aunt's behalf. "Yes, they do actually. We do know how to defend ourselves, and the people of the realm are loyal, and would never dare to harm us. Her youngest son is somewhat more defended as he resides at the court with her, and has a personal guard and attendant."

Darian still looked at Sabina in disbelief. "And her oldest son?"

"He is the leader of a village called Asimina, so he lives there. Alcine is probably the best fighter of the realm and needs no protection. Realistically, he is the protection for everyone else."

His voice took on a very careful tone, as if Darian was suddenly walking on a fragile cliff. "Alcine? Is that a common name in this realm?"

"No," Sabina answered, concerned by the stiff way Darian suddenly sat upon his horse. "Alcine is the queen's son through adoption. His mother was Mairi, the woman that mom and I told you about. He came from the other world."

The man swayed on his horse and Rhea reached over to grab him, wrapping a fist in his coat as her mount instinctively moved to press against his horse in support. Faulks fluttered into the air with a squawk of protest at the sudden motion, flapping a few beats before settling on the specially designed perch on the back of Sabina's saddle.

"Darian? Darian, are you alright?" She pulled both horses to a stop and twisted in the saddle to snap her fingers in front of his glazed eyes. "Darian?"

He shuddered before swallowing hard, his eyes unreadable with emotion. "Alcine, son of Mairi, is alive?"

Sabina looked up the trail line, confirming that Henri had turned and was closing in the pair before answering. "Yes, he is alive."

Henri stopped his horse in front them and casually said, "Everything okay back here?"

"We were just talking about Alcine," Sabina said lightly, watching Darian's reaction.

Henri's eyes narrowed, the only part of his face visible behind the scarf and thick hood. "Oh?"

Darian looked between them before shaking himself and releasing the tension. "I was there when Arden was killed, when Mairi and Alcine were declared anathema. The Saverlen still talk of Arden, one of the greatest and most skilled that ever belonged to the order. We thought they all died, had mourned their death for years, and still talk of what could have happened if only Alcine had lived."

118

Sabina and Henri exchanged worried glances as Darian continued, his eyes glazing over in memories. "Arden is, was, considered to be royalty among the Saverlen. Alcine would have been raised to be his heir, our future leader. I was supposed to take care of him and Mairi, but she ran away after Arden's death and I never found her ..." His eyes focused once again and Sabina was troubled by the glint of desperation under the barely-contained control.

"Darian. Mairi and Alcine came here. Mairi killed herself, but Alcine was adopted by Queen Nyssa. All he has ever known himself to be is the oldest son of the queen, and the protector of Asimina."

"He is truly alive?" Darian's voice was rough with emotion as his eyes swung from Sabina to Henri.

"Yes," Henri confirmed, "he is truly alive."

Chapter 17

Kylassame

"They're here, they're here!" The riders heard the cries soaring up from the valley below as they halted their horses on the crest of the rise, letting the mounts catch their breaths.

Sabina looked down at the village of Kylassame with love and excitement. The weather was less biting here, and the houses, nestled in the safety of the valley, were not buried within as much snow as the rest of the realm.

Red-tiled roofs stood out against the soft snow that blanketed the ground around the village. Smoke puffed out of chimneys, gently curling and twisting up from the houses, their fires warming the residents within. White stucco walls blended in with the landscape, while the brightly colored garlands and ribbons that had been hung upon hooks and corners stood out in happy contrast.

Children played in the open areas between the houses, building forts and throwing snowballs at one another, giving happy shrieks as the cold snow dribbled through their layers of clothing. The adults had gathered at the gazebo in the center of the village, drinking hot chocolate dipped from huge vats and waiting anxiously for Rowan to arrive.

He had sent a message several days earlier about the arrival of the children and Darian, as well as several other refugees who they believed would do well in the village of Kylassame. Rooms in the communal apartments had been cleaned and polished, and the dining room had been filled with hot dishes to fill the cold bellies of the new community members.

"Rhea!" Cassie, her mother's best friend, began waving from the front of the gazebo as soon as the party stepped off the winding mountain path. Her daughter, Mya, waved furiously at Sabina. Beside them stood Lily, another close friend of Rhea's, and her daughter, Arielle.

"Cassie! Lily!" Rhea called out, waving back at the group.

Sabina leaned close to Darian, who had suddenly become wary and disquieted. "Those are friends of my mother and father. They have been through a lot together. The girl in the red coat is Cassie's daughter, Mya. She's a little over a year younger than me and one of my friends here. Arielle, in the teal coat, is Lily's daughter and another friend. She's older than me by just a bit."

He simply nodded in acknowledgment, his face betraying none of his emotions.

"Are you all right?" Sabina asked.

"Yes," he responded hoarsely.

Sabina gave him a sharp glance before ordering, "Stay here," and riding to the front of the line to speak with her parents. Moments later she rode back, Henri close behind.

"Come on, Darian. We will have introductions later. Right now I want to look at your wounds. I do not like the shadows under

121

your eyes." She waved back to her friends as they moved along the path toward the house, calling out a promise of a later meeting time.

They pulled their horses to a stop in front of the house and dismounted. Seconds later, Jakob, one of the youths employed by the village livery, arrived to take their horses back to the stables to be fed and cared for after the frigid journey.

Her parents' house was a grand one, and the largest in the village. Originally the design had consisted of three rooms, along with a living room, kitchen, and front porch. That layout had worked fine when Sabina was younger, but after the birth of Aaron it was decided that they needed to expand. Rowan frequently held hushed meetings in their house and would offer a bed for the night, or Rhea would invite a scared child who had just arrived to be protected under their roof. Three bedrooms no longer were enough space for all who sought sanctuary in their care.

Now, the roomy house boasted a master bedroom for her parents, as well as spacious rooms for Sabina, Aaron, and her sister, Katrina. There was an office that was used by Rowan for business negotiations, and a guest bedroom used by many in the village if their meetings with Rowan or Rhea went late into the night. That room was not overly spacious, but had space enough for a large-sized bed, dresser, wardrobe, and mirror.

Her mother's pride and joy was the large bathing chamber that they had created with the help of Jhoni, who worked as a master plumber before coming to the realm. He built the room by adding three walls, created of long planks of cedar wood, onto the back of the house. The floor was covered with smooth river stones that were poured into a binding solution to create a hard floor that had good traction. A water spout on one end of the large room provided a shower area, with a thin, frosted glass wall that provided just the right amount of privacy. The other end of the room boasted a large bathing tub, tall enough for a person to sit with water submerged up to the necks and with enough space to spread out aching limbs.

A large fire pit, similar to those that had been used in the bathing house built in Asimina, claimed the corner of the bathing room. The hot coals heated the space to a comfortable level, and more could be added to create steam used to cleanse the body and mind.

The central living area of the house provided all of the space that the closely knit family needed. Several comfortable chairs and couches were positioned around the large fireplace, while smaller rocking chairs sat against the walls next to small tables. Baskets of yarns and thread sat in specially made drawers under the tables, projects for when the weather turned ill or the house inhabitants needed a moment of solitude.

Henri led the trio up the front steps and onto the porch, which wrapped around two sides of the house and was a beloved area for socialization for the children and their parents. From the porch, a person could see most of the village, easily laugh at the antics of children or watch wildlife frolic in the nearby meadow and fields. Chairs and benches lined the porch and tables were placed at regular intervals to hold refreshments or gaming boards.

Darian's body jerked in pain as he moved from the last step onto the floor boards and he took a long moment before continuing forward through the door. Sabina was uneasy by the stiffness in his gait as he moved toward the bathing room, though that could have been attributed to the long ride.

They shed their outerwear and boots in the small closet just inside the front door, grateful that a member of the village had lit a fire in the large hearth and warmed the house from the outside chill.

Darian winced as he twisted his torso to remove his coat, and Sabina growled as she saw the fresh blood that stained his shirt.

"I knew you should have ridden in the cart! Come on." She led the man to the bathing room, muttering about male stubbornness at his refusal of her assistance.

Once in the room, Henri helped her remove the next layer of clothes from the man. The puncture wound from the arrow seeped clear fluids, aggravated from the constant rub of fabric against the wound. Several of the stitched wounds on his chest and arms had pulled open once again, not enough to require new stitches, but enough to seep blood slowly through the journey.

Sabina sighed and turned the dials that directed warm water to the spout above their heads. "Come stand here and let me help you."

"No," Darian gasped out, wavering on his feet as his body tried to adjust to the temperature change. "No. I will be fine on my own."

"No, you will not be," Sabina snapped in response, tense and tired from the journey.

Henri interceded by gently leading Sabina toward the door, one hand gently but firmly placed on her back. "Let him be, Seb. I'll see that he remains on his feet."

Sabina gave a huff of annoyance as Henri politely but firmly closed the wooden door to the bathhouse just inches from her face. "Stupid, stubborn men."

~ * ~ * ~

She looked up at the bathing room door as it swung open, gently placing the book she had been reading on the table beside the cushioned chair. Henri walked out, his hair wet and wearing one of the thick cotton robes that hung inside the room, away from the water. Darian moved behind him in a matching brown robe, moving slowly and breathing heavily.

Sabina went to stand and help the man cross the room, exasperated that Henri let him walk unassisted when he obviously was in pain.

Henri moved his hand, issuing a subtle command, and Sabina sank back down into the chair. Both men walked into the room designated for guests, where Sabina had built a fire to chase the chills away from the corners and added another blanket to the bed.

A few minutes later Henri walked back out and sank onto a cushioned chair next to Sabina. He still wore the bathrobe but had pulled on a pair of trousers underneath. "Seb," he began.

"He was injured. Why weren't you helping him?" She tried to keep her voice even.

He rested his head against the back of the chair and sighed. "He needs a little space, Seb. I know that the healer in you needs to be around him, to make him better, but he's been through a substantial emotional shock, and needs room to pull himself back together."

She glared at him but refused to answer, unsure now of her next action. Henri was well versed in tending to the wounded from the other world, and rarely made poor judgment calls regarding their health or well-being.

"Sebby, listen. The man is from a warrior caste, plunged into a strange world where nothing is familiar. Judging by the marks on his body, he has probably received worse wounds before, wounds that weren't given nearly as much care as these have received."

Sabina pulled her feet onto the chair, thinking a moment before saying, "Okay, but that still doesn't explain why you threw me out of the room."

This time it was Henri who gave a huff of annoyance. "Because you are a woman, Seb. I know that right now you are thinking as a healer, but look at it from his point of view. He lived as an outcast, and a hero, his entire life. If there were people around, they would have been men, likely of the same age or older. It would have been bad enough for him back at the infirmary, with two pretty women touching his body, but now, without others around as buffers, it would have been even worse. Let him keep his control and sense of pride."

She thought on that for a moment, slowly nodding in acknowledgment. "I guess I can understand that. You are certain his wounds don't need further treatment?"

Henri shook his head, and then turned to face the door as he heard voices approaching. "I gave him the salve to put on them and checked over the stitches. They are a bit irritated but stopped bleeding after the shower. He just needs rest."

They sat in a moment in silence, listening to Sabina's parents approaching the house. Finally Sabina gave a deep sigh of surrender. "All right, I'll leave him be. Can you stay here for a little while in case he wakes up?"

"Of course. Your father offered me Katrina's room while she is at court, so I'm not planning on going outside any time soon. What will you be doing?"

She smiled. "Getting clean while it's still hot in there, which was my original intent before someone kicked me out."

Chapter 18

Asimina

Heavy leather boots crunched in the ankle deep snow as Eric moved over the covered pathways of the village. He had slept late, and the sun was already shining brightly over the horizon as he approached Alcine's house.

The leader of Asimina stood outside in the area designated as his practice yard, the snow underfoot heavily packed with the daily routine of movement.

Eric stood a moment and watched as Alcine finished the routine, steam rising off his bare chest as it hit the frigid air. "Good morning, Alcine. I apologize for my lateness."

Alcine smiled as he turned. "No worries. I will continue on while you warm up, then we can have a practice bout and see if you have improved with the staves."

The moves came fluidly and with ease to Eric now, arms and legs moving independently as he stepped, whirled, struck, and blocked the blows from imaginary opponent. His breath came effortlessly as he moved, lungs contracting and expanding with efficiency in time to the movements, his entire body working as one entity.

He thought of the last week, and the great change that he had experienced after moving in with a member of the village, a young widow named Yasmina. She had been shy when they first met, her eyes downcast as she showed him around the small but well-kept hut that was her home. Her three-year-old daughter, Asli, had clung to her skirts, brown eyes wide at the sight of the strange man in her home.

Yasmina had been married to a man who had emigrated to Asimina from the court when they were both young, and who had become her best friend. Together they built the home where she now lived, and had created a child.

When Asli was just a newborn, he left to go hunting and never returned. The men of Asimina launched search parties but were only able to find his clothing and his weapons, torn and broken. Blood and mountain lion tracks surrounded the area where his items were found, and all had known that the man would not be returning.

She relied on the village for assistance, trading her weavings and cooking skills for food and supplies. The village gave what it could freely, but Yasmina was a proud woman who felt the cut of guilt deeply that she took more than she was able to give back to the village.

Yasmina had been the one to approach Alcine about extending her home to Eric, after watching the man carefully to gauge his personality and determine if her child, her first priority, would be safe. Alcine had seen no reason to fear, and had agreed to the arrangement, provided that Yasmina would approach him if she ever felt doubts or any fear.

Eric had thrown himself into work, and made sure to never give her any doubts or cause to second guess her kind offer. While he could do little about providing food, as his hunting abilities were dismal at best and the fields lay under a blanket of snow, he was able to gather water, firewood, and watch Asli play with the other children while Yasmina worked at preparing dinner.

Cole had proved a steady ally throughout the week, the teenager jumping at the chance to teach someone skills, and before long he had taught Eric the basics of thatching, and helped to do the needed repairs to the hut.

Eric had questioned Cole about those repairs, as it seemed to him that Asimina took care of its own, and Cole just shook his head sadly before replying.

"Her pride is great, and she feels she takes too much already. We have offered but she always refused, saying that it was good enough for them."

Asli had warmed up to him within a day, often clambering onto his lap before dinner for a story. He thought back to the fairy tales and nursery rhymes from his world, and serenaded her with off-key songs and funny voices.

He finished the warm-up and stopped, startled to see Alcine standing at him with a smile on his face. "You have improved greatly since we started working together, Eric."

Alcine tossed him one of the practice staves, a long, stout, and perfectly straight branch of hard oak that was as tall as a man. "How are things going with Yasmina?"

Eric took a moment to think, jumping back as Alcine's stave swung at his stomach. "They are going well, I hope. She is starting to warm up to me and Asli is the most precious thing I've ever seen." He blocked an incoming blow, the movements still feeling clumsy.

"The hut is suitable for you?" Alcine spun his stave deftly in his hands, the motion distracting Eric enough that the stave came down smartly on his hand.

He shook off the sting and took the offensive, jabbing with the stave toward Alcine's abdomen. "Sure. It's much better than the hut I was in before."

Alcine easily parried the jab and flicked his stave toward Eric's shoulder. "And Yasmina? Is she suitable for you?"

Eric felt a flush of anger at the implication and struck at Alcine, then found himself on his back staring at the end of the man's stave.

A quick smile flitted across Alcine's lips as he offered a hand and helped Eric rise. "You must never let anger distract you. You did well before that though. Why were you angry about the question?"

He walked back to Alcine's hut warily, still feeling the sting of accusation from the question. "It's not like that, Alcine, and you know it. Yasmina was kind enough to open her home to a stranger and I am certainly not going to abuse that kindness." He thought of Sabina for the first time in a week and flushed. "Besides, I already have my interest elsewhere."

"Oh, yes, on my cousin?" The warm chuckle was at odds with the fierce look of protectiveness that was on Alcine's face.

"Sabina is an exceptional woman and I owe her my life." Eric rubbed a dry towel that had been heated next to the fire over his body and donned a long-sleeved cotton tunic.

"That she is, but is that enough to risk the anger of her father, and to shoulder the responsibilities that come with desiring a woman of her stature?"

Puzzlement crossed Eric's face. "I don't understand."

Alcine sighed and leaned back on the furs. "Sabina is royalty, no matter how she may present herself while in this village. She is third in line to the throne of the realm of Kaldalangra and one of the most venerated people outside of the court. If you were to further this relationship, would you be comfortable traveling to court, to the refugee villages, or living in Kylassame? Would you be able to remain content under the shadow of her parent's fame and heroics as easily as she seems to do? Would you be able to always be the less powerful partner? Could you share her with the rest of the realm, nearly every day for the rest of your lives?"

No reply came to Eric's lips as the truth of Alcine's words hit his stomach like a stone. "I don't know," he choked out, before walking away.

Chapter 19

Kylassame

"How old did you say he was again?" Mya sat at the kitchen table, munching on a piece of honey-covered pastry while Sabina cleaned the dishes from dinner.

The rest of the family had left the large wooden table that stood in the kitchen and moved to the family room, taking mugs of warm teas and coffees to relax after the large dinner. Darian had joined them just before dinner, dressed in a pair of soft brown slacks and a white shirt that had been borrowed from the village supply store.

"He's actually never said," Sabina realized. "Henri and I are guessing maybe mid to late twenties." She wiped the last of the plates and joined Mya and Arielle at the table. "Why?"

"He's gorgeous, is why. I wanted to know if it was worth flirting or not." Mya fluffed her light brown hair and laughed.

Sabina rolled her eyes good-naturedly. Mya was a notorious flirt and loved to test her skills against the young men of the village. She had reined it in lately though, ever since her mother had told her the story of some woman named Amanda who had once enjoyed the same past-time. Now Mya was more selective, more careful with her attentions and her actions.

"Oh, come on, Mya. Let the poor guy breathe before you go wielding your charms." Arielle flicked her tea at her friend.

"I would say not worth it," Sabina interjected. "Not only is he too old for you, but he's been through a lot. I can't imagine him being the kind of person who would be romantically inclined, or know how to show affection like you would choose."

"That's too bad." She finished the pastry, brushed the crumbs from her fingers, and then gave Arielle a conspiratorial glance before smiling at Sabina. "Anything new with Brendan? You always talk about his attentions like it's a horrible thing."

Sabina let her forehead gently fall to the table in a gesture of futility. "You just don't understand what it's like," she softly moaned, voice muffled by the wood below her mouth. "Brendan is so nice, and so polite, and so horribly correct all the time. All of that means that I have to be nice, and polite, and impeccably correct all the time, and I just can't do it. Plus, I couldn't imagine him actually having fun getting dirty, or being content touring the villages and refugee camps. I don't want to be stuck at court for the rest of my days."

A mischievous expression filled Arielle's eyes. "Speaking of getting dirty, did you see Bryan while you were there?"

"Oh, stop it. I'm never telling you anything ever again." Sabina put her finger in her mug and then flicked the liquid on her friend, who just shook her head and giggled.

Mya snorted and batted her eyelashes. "I want to meet him. A man who is good at coaxing horses to do his whims must be pretty good with his words and hands." Her voice trailed off and her eyes shifted toward the living room once again. "That guy any good with horses?"

"Shut up! Why are you asking about a new guy anyway? What about Philip?"

"Ah, well, I'm not sure quite what to do about Philip." Mya's cheeks turned five shades of red in quick succession, making Sabina suspicious.

"Meaning what?"

Arielle laughed and took a sip of tea. "Wait until you hear this one."

"Well, you see, about two weeks ago we were on my couch when my mom and dad were out, and we were hugging and then we were kissing and one thing led to another ..."

"Mya!" Sabina raised her voice in shock before quickly lowering it and leaning closer across the table. "You did not?"

"Just once!" She smirked. "Well, once that night."

"You are way too young for that, Mya." The words fell from Sabina's lips before she could think.

Mya snorted in response. "Oh, please. I'm not that much younger then you, Seb. You're telling me you haven't had sex yet? Even Arielle has done it."

Arielle flushed and suddenly became extremely interested with the cup in front of her.

Sabina glanced at the living room door to make sure they were still alone. "Keep your voice down, and no, I have not, nor do I have any plans to do so any time soon. You are using drinking the special tea, right? Both of you?"

"Of course!" Arielle looked surprised and hurt at the suspicion. "Anyway, it was only once."

"Yes, Mom," Mya replied. "Come on, you're telling me that you haven't once been caught up in kissing someone and thought about going all the way."

"No," Sabina said, thinking back to her past interactions. Brendan was far too polite and proper to have even suggested the act, and while she and Bryan enjoyed walking the line of propriety, neither was foolish enough to risk such an un-retractable action. She had very little experience with anyone else, always being fully aware and suspicious that any attention was due to her status, and her parents, and little to do with any real affection.

Suddenly the memory of the feel of Eric's strong shoulders beneath her fingers filled her mind, the feel of his hard body pressed against hers in the bath house of Asimina. Sabina felt her face warm at the thought, and the flutter returned to her stomach. She had not thought of Eric since her conversation with her mother, as she had just been solely concentrated on the refugees.

Mya leaned across the table and grinned. "There is someone!"

"Tell us about him." Arielle's eyes twinkled.

"It's nothing." Sabina leaned forward as well and lowered her voice. "When I was at Asimina earlier in the autumn this guy came, from the other world. He was really hurt so I was asked to help heal him. Well, he got better, and then he would do things, like run his fingers through my hair, or put his hand on my back, and they would just send shivers up my spine."

"Well, there you go! So when you go back to Asimina you go find a nice secluded area, rip his clothes off, and-"

"Sabina, may I speak to you a moment?" Her father's amused voice floated through the kitchen, laughter rising as the three girls sat back in their chairs with a loud thunk, each blushing violently.

"Of course, Dad. I'll talk to you later, Mya, Arielle," Sabina answered as the two women scooted into the living room.

Rowan leaned against the door for a moment before coming and sitting on a chair next to his daughter. "Darian was asking if he could meet Alcine. I was wondering how he knew about Alcine, and if you thought an introduction would be a good idea."

She leaned back in the chair, giddy mood instantly sobered and butterflies pinned. "I was telling him about Alcine on the ride here. He said that he was there when Arden died, that they had revered the man as a hero, and mourned the loss of wife and son."

"Do you think Alcine would be in danger?" Rowan watched the thoughts flit across his daughter's face as she carefully considered the scenario.

"No, I don't think so," she replied. "I also don't think he should be moved any time soon though. The journey here was enough to re-open several of his wounds, as well as exhaust him."

Rowan nodded in agreement. "Two weeks' time then, would that be enough?"

Sabina nodded, and then followed her father into the next room to join the family for conversation.

Chapter 20

Kylassame

The sun kissed her skin as Sabina stepped off her front porch and tilted her face to the sky. The snowstorms had finally blown away, and the air felt warm and bright after weeks of blistering cold.

She cocked her head to the side a moment, listening for the male voices that would lead her toward the place where the men had gathered. Rowan had woken up and, after taking note of the break in the weather, had all of the village men gather to inspect the fences, houses, and perimeter of the village.

Rhea had laughingly ordered Sabina out of the house after her tenth visit to the window to gaze at the bright day and let out a sigh. Both women hated being cooped up and Sabina was given leave to saddle the horses while her mother finished cleaning up breakfast.

Sabina had just tightened the cinch on the second horse when her mother walked out with a thick water-skin insulated with layers of leather that was filled with hot mint tea.

"Have you figured out where they are yet?" Rhea smiled at her daughter as the women swung up onto their mounts.

"It almost sounds like they are over at the Jade Stones, but why would they be over there?" Sabina was puzzled, as there were no fences or structures near the Jade Stones.

Rhea's face paled but she put on a brave face for her daughter's sake as they began to move down the path. The Jade Stones were a particular bit of magic that no one understood, and no one went there without a purpose. When Sabina was a newborn she had been kidnapped by a woman of the village and taken to the stones, and when Rhea had Sabina back in her arms they had been pushed through.

It had been beautiful in that space, a beauty that was dangerous with its allure. Newborn Sabina saw the fringes of space, with its myriad of swirling galaxies and shooting stars. She saw images of what could be, and what already had been. People and objects had passed into that strange space as well, some through death and others through circumstance. While her newly born body and mind did not understand or grasp what was occurring, she remembered, and at times the memories came back in her dreams.

Her mother had made the hard choice to step through the veil and back to her life in Kylassame, to the pain of the body that had just given birth, and the uncertainty of life.

Snow fell from the pine branches above with heavy plops; provoking a shriek from Sabina as one of the clumps landed perfectly on her neck and slid under her thick cloak. The geldings snorted, their hooves happily flinging snow in front of them as they pranced through the drifts, happy for a chance to stretch their legs.

They heard the voices of the men float through the woods and slowed their horses to a brisk walk as they approached the group that had gathered at one of the stones.

Rowan looked up and waved at his wife, then turned his attention back to the footprints on the ground.

Rhea dismounted and walked over to stand next to her husband. "Problem?"

"Mm," he answered noncommittally. "Nasta found us over by the horse pasture and brought us here."

Darian looked up from where he had squatted low, inspecting the footprints. "Heavy boots, rubber soles, deep tread so probably fairly new." He squinted as he studied the pattern of prints. "Slightly uneven in length, so the man probably is walking with a limp."

He straightened slowly on legs still stiff from his injuries. "What is in that direction?"

The men from the village followed the path as they considered the trail. They could see where the footprints formed a wavering line along the path before abruptly move into the tree line.

"Away from the village," said Justin, the man who had been governor of Kylassame for a decade before Liam was voted into the position.

Liam nodded his head gravely, small lines forming at the corner of his eyes as he studied the pathway. "Yes, but where are they heading?"

Rowan looked across the circle where Aaron was studying the prints in the snow, brow furrowed with thought. "Aaron? What say you?"

He looked up, and Sabina felt a strong blaze of pride as she watched her fifteen-year-old brother mature and take one step closer to becoming the next protector of the village.

"We have plenty of daylight left, so I think we should send out a small, armed group of men to follow the tracks. Even if we cannot find their end, it would give us a better idea of where to search, or where to avoid until we determine if this person is friendly or dangerous."

His father nodded agreement. "Who should make up the party?"

Aaron thought of the men's different strengths as he looked around the circle. "Nasta should lead the group, as he has a level head and the greatest experience navigating that particular tract of land. Then John, Luke, and Adam." His eyes settled on Darian, the man once again squatting behind the tracks in thought.

Rowan shook his head slightly as a warning and silenced Aaron's words. "That sounds like a solid tracking party. The rest of us will continue the circuit and be back for dinner." He stepped forward to draw Darian's attention. "Darian, would you escort the women home please?"

He nodded and gave a small bow, bending slightly at the waist. "I would be honored, though I believe I could be of better service in the tracking party, sir."

Rowan tilted his head in acknowledgement. "While I have no doubts of your abilities, I would feel more comfortable if you remained with my family until I returned."

Darian gave a second quick bow before stepping away from the group to assist Rhea and Sabina onto their geldings. He then swung onto his mount, wincing slightly at the small tug of his still-healing wounds, and placed his fist on his chest as he told Rowan in Zajedica, "I will guard them well. Happy hunting."

~ * ~ * ~

The trio rode back to the village slowly, both women enjoying the warm sun and Darian relishing the feeling of movement after long weeks of restrictions. He glanced up and gave a small grin as he saw the lean body of Faulks gliding above the leafless tree canopy.

"Your other guard has arrived," he said in passing English, still learning the nuances of the language.

Sabina looked up and smiled. "Oh, yes. He is always close by." She turned to look at the man. "Your English is getting much better, Darian."

He nodded gravely. "I am trying. It is difficult sometimes, sometimes not."

It helped that his fluent tongue, Zajedica, included words in her language. Zajedica become the official language of North America a decade after the breakup of the United States of America, the country where Rhea was born. The land had split into dozens of small countries formed by cultural groups and natural language barriers quickly formed.

In the area of Zajed Seganu, where both Alcine and Darian were born, Zajedica quickly rose in use, a combination of all the major languages spoken on the continent. Within a second decade it became the official language of the continent, though each country still spoke their individual tongue as well.

Rhea glanced at the pair and grinned to herself. She had enjoyed time with the man from the other world, for though he was often grave and somber there was an honesty to his nature that she found refreshing. She was also relieved that she did not have to worry about Sabina when she was in his presence, something she had been doing far too often since men of the realm realized she was of age to marry.

Nineteen and of age to marry. Rhea laughed softly and shook her head. *I have truly become a member of this realm when I think that.*

In Rhea's world, a nineteen-year-old was almost a child, a budding adult. Rarely were they encouraged to marry, have children, or given the great responsibilities that her oldest child had already begun to shoulder.

They arrived back to the village and gave their horses a thorough rub-down before returning them to the warm stable for some water and a meal.

The trio walked up the steps to Rhea's house, Sabina becoming concerned at the careful way Darian moved up the steps. "You should let me take a look at your wounds. I know that Henri has been checking them, but he's not a healer."

Darian gave her a somber look. "With all due respect, Sabina, I am fine. The wounds have healed cleanly; my body has not adjusted yet to the new daily routine."

"All the same," she said as she chewed on her lip, "you should let me make sure they are healing correctly."

Darian gave his head a quick shake of negation. "While I am thankful for the healing you did when I first came here, it is not appropriate for a woman of your age to be alone with a man, especially one that is not fully clothed."

Sabina just narrowed her eyes in disbelief. "You have got to be kidding me."

He shook his head again as he held open the door to the house so the women could enter. "I do not jest. As Saverlen my duty is to protect, not to … to …" he faltered a moment, unclear of how to translate the word.

"You are still doing your job if you let me look at your wounds," Sabina pressed the matter.

"I have already broken one of our oaths by allowing you to help me, and relying on your aid. Please do not ask me to break more." Darian's eyes grew troubled.

She took a deep sigh and, with a stern look from her mother, Sabina backed off the subject. "All right. Can you tell me more then, about the oaths?"

He thought a moment and nodded, sitting lightly on the edge of one chair while Sabina and Rhea settled onto the cushioned recliners.

"The decision to become a member of the Saverlen is not one to choose lightly. Training begins when we are boys and is strict, as well as dangerous. After the death of Sir Arden, we were forbidden to have any ties with women, or any family. We must move through the world as independent beings, brothers only to one another, with all other family forgotten."

"What a hard thing for your mothers," Rhea commented, voice low.

Darian shrugged. "Perhaps. I knew, even before the death of Sir Arden, that I would be leaving my family. My father was a Saverlen, killed with Arden, and my mother could not afford to feed myself and my sisters, especially since she refused to name their father, in fear of the same retribution Mairi received. By joining the order, I was removing the burden of my care from her shoulders, and I watched from a distance as she remarried and my sisters grew into young women."

"Surely the men still give in to mortal desires, though. It would be a lonely life to never know love, or the touch of another person." Sabina listened raptly, chin propped in her palm.

He shook his head again and glanced uncomfortably at her. "In the beginning, before the Oprimata yes, some men did. We soon learned that to give a woman attention, in any form, was to bring a death sentence onto her head. She would be instantly targeted by the Oprimata, tortured for information regarding the man's location, and then killed."

"Oh, that's horrible." Rhea's breathing hitched and Sabina shuddered.

"That is why I keep insisting that it is not safe for me to shelter within your home. I do not want to endanger you."

Sabina leaned back in the chair and drew her knees to her chest. "It's not like that here, though. Yes, people must be careful, but we mingle freely with one another. It's not wrong to be in the presence of the opposite sex, or to touch them." She rolled her eyes at Rhea's speculative look. "I meant innocent touches, Mom, like hugging."

"Different ways," Darian replied as he shrugged.

"Yes, I guess so. Different ways."

Chapter 21

Asimina

"Song! Song!" Asli's small voice rang out.

Eric chuckled and sat down on the fur-covered floor and smiled as the child clambered onto his lap, settling herself in the center of his crossed legs. "What shall we sing?"

She thought a moment, brown eyes serious in contemplation. "Spider song!"

He smiled and moved his hands in front of her little body as he began to sing the story of a spider that went on a long journey, his fingers moving as if they were spider legs.

Peals of innocent, three-year-old laughter filled the hut as she tried to mimic his actions.

They completed the song three times, the third resulting in great squeals as Asli finally was able to coordinate her finger movements.

Eric glanced over at her mother and flushed a brilliant scarlet as he saw Yasmina's shoulders jerking with suppressed laughter. "I think I should go help your mother with dinner now."

"Okay! Can I go play next door?" Asli bounced up, shifting from one foot to the other while awaiting the answer.

"Go ask your mother," he replied.

Yasmina smiled and gave her permission, helping her daughter get warmly dressed before she ran out into the snow. "Thank you for entertaining her."

He gently pulled the chopping knife from the woman's hands and nudged her away from the wooden block. "I'll cut the vegetables for you. Go rest a moment. You've been running all day."

"I am fine." Yasmina reached for the knife, the action stalled by a great yawn.

Eric carefully placed the knife on the block and gently led the woman over to the thick pile of woven mats by the fire, hands on her shoulders. "You need to rest, Yasmina."

"I cannot," she whispered softly, tears welling in her eyes. "There is always so much to do. I cannot rest until everything here is done, and Asli is cared for, and all of the kindness of others has been repaid. And you have already done too much to help me with my duties, how can I let you do more?" She pushed back lightly, trying to move back to the vegetables.

"I know there is much to do, but you need to take a moment for yourself," Eric said softly as he looked into her tear-bright eyes. He could feel the tension in her shoulders as she struggled with sheer exhaustion. His strong hands gently ran down her rail-thin arms as they stood there.

"Yasmina, it is not shirking your duties to take a moment and rest. Asli is happy playing outside, the house is clean, and the community does not expect you to repay their kindnesses in one day. Rest." He gently pushed down on her shoulders.

"I do not know how to rest," she whispered as she sank onto a mat.

"That's okay, you will learn." Eric picked up the basket of yarn from its place in the corner and placed it next to the chair. "Here. If you wish, you can work on a new scarf for Asli while you rest. I'll get dinner going and let you know when I need you."

He refused to move away from the chair until she picked up the weaving needles and a skein of yarn. Eric settled in front of the low table Yasmina used for food preparation, evenly chopping the root vegetables from her dwindling winter supply and placing them in the pot of water that would be set upon the fire to boil.

The weeks with Yasmina had taught him much about responsibility, and shouldering a burden. She had a stubborn sense of duty, and an even stronger shadow of guilt. Her daughter received all of the kindnesses that could be given, the bigger portions of meals, the softest of the borrowed blankets, and Yasmina always had time for a hug or a kiss when they were needed.

Yet, she had let her own health and well-being fall by the wayside in her endless effort to provide a good life for her daughter, and to minimize the burden of guilt she felt by accepting help.

After the first week he had approached Alcine about the amount of assistance she received from the village, for in his eyes it was not nearly enough, especially when so many goods and food items were being taken to court. A deep sadness had filled Alcine's eyes as they talked, and he told Eric that almost every offer of kindness was refused. Yasmina took only what was needed for Asli's comfort, and did not want to burden the community with her own. In their eyes, her fine weavings and textiles were sufficient for whatever goods or assistance she received.

The knife moved rhythmically under his hand and Eric glanced at the woman, now curled tightly in the nest of pillows and soundly asleep.

She had filled out slightly since he joined her household; his gentle coaxing to eat more food and take more snatches of sleep giving her body needed fuel. Her long-sleeved, thick cotton dress still hung from her frame, the fabric falling shapelessly from the angles of her shoulders.

Asli had confided in him that she missed when her mom gave "squishy hugs," and wanted them back, missing the comfort found in her mother's once ample buxom and soft lap.

He moved the pot over to the fire, carefully propping it up just above the flames. A skinny hare sat next to the chopping block and he made quick butcher work, shaking his head in awed delight that he could so easily maneuver around the bones and cut the meat of an animal he once would have never eaten.

The meat gave a small sizzle as he carefully lay it on the thick iron skillet that he had placed next to the pot, and he shot a quick glance toward Yasmina to see if she still slept.

Her mouth hung slightly open as she napped, her face peaceful for the first time that he had ever seen. He crept over to her chair and gently placed a threadbare blanket on her lap for extra warmth, then walked to the front doorway of the hut and slid outside.

The air immediately sucked any warmth from his body and Eric shivered violently as he took the two steps from the door to the small storage shed he and Mikel had built a few days prior. A break in the weather had given the men an opportunity to carefully cut the surrounding trees for wood to heat the houses during the predicted storm, and the woven twig roofs kept the wood dry beneath its canopy.

Yasmina was awake when he re-entered the house and gave him a sad smile as he added more wood to the fire. "I am in debt for your kindness. There is time before Asli returns for it to be re-paid."

Eric looked at her a moment in confusion as to how him helping with dinner created a debt to be owed. If anything he had thought to be found in her debt, as it was her house that gave him hospitality and her food supply that he consumed. His gaze fell upon her face, the downcast eyes and her perfect row of upper teeth biting into her lower lip.

"Yasmina," he began.

"It will be easier if we do not speak," she interrupted, a slight shudder passing through her body.

Eric felt his brow furrow in confusion. "I don't understand." He watched for a moment, uncomprehending, as her thin fingers moved to untie the thick laces that secured her dress.

He stepped forward quickly then, placing his hands on her shoulders and holding the thick cotton material to her skeletal frame. "Yasmina, I do not want this." His fingers gently re-fastened the dress.

Three tears fell as her eyes refused to meet his. "It is all I have left to offer."

"No," he said softly as he gently cupped her cheek and gently forced her gaze, so full of hurt and despair, to meet his. "You owe me nothing."

150

She stared at him, eyes bleak, before glancing over at the woodpile, and gesturing to the food that was cooking. "You give me wood, you fixed my hut, you help care for my child, and you make me dinner. What have I ever given you in return? What else do I have to offer that you could want?" Her breath caught in her throat.

"Let go of the guilt, Yasmina." Eric gently tucked a loose strand of hair behind her ear. "Pick yourself back up, let go of the guilt, and the feeling of despair. See the incredible woman who is inside of you, and let her rise. That is all I want from you in return."

Chapter 22

Kylassame

Sabina shivered as she looked out the glass window on the way to her front door. The noon sky was a steely gray color and a cold wind whipped through the bare tree branches around the village.

The prints found the other day had resulted in a dead end; the scouting party losing the trail at the edge of a cliff-face of the mountains surrounding Kylassame. They had returned later that day, discouraged but convinced that the person would cause no harm to the community if they had gone out that far and were heading into the mountains.

Darian stepped beside her, his thick coat already buttoned, and Sabina's coat draped over his arm. "Are you ready to go?"

She pulled her coat on and nodded. "The hall itself will be warm, but it's going to be horrible getting there. Let's get it over with."

They stepped through the door and pushed through the first blast of wind that threatened to knock Sabina's agile frame right off the steps. The Town Hall was a mere fifty yards away, yet by the time they entered the protection of the building's walled-in porch, their cheeks were chapped and their lungs felt frozen.

"Sabina!" Henri strode over and helped her out of her coat, the fur stiff with frozen snow that had drifted from rooftops. "Happy birthday!"

The hall had been decorated from floor to ceiling with paper streamers and decorative lanterns. Colored ribbons hung from the rafters and swayed as guests danced around the hall. As new guests arrived, the cold breeze sent the ribbons twirling into the air, filling the ceiling with color and gaiety.

She murmured, "Thank you," and then took in the sight. The hall had been decorated for this day, her twentieth birthday. The members of Kylassame always made a big deal for, what they considered to be, the big birthdays. The first birthday of course, then the fifth, tenth, and so on.

Sabina had missed her fifteenth birthday party due to a storm keeping her at court, and she smiled ruefully as she remembered that day.

Her aunt, Queen Nyssa, had done her best to give her niece a spectacular party and Sabina had showered her with gratitude and thanks when it over. The main dining hall of the castle had been decorated with winter greenery and bright winter berries, and the kitchen staff had created a vast spread of delicacies for the occasion.

Sabina had tried to enjoy herself, but felt the responsibility of her place in court the entire time. Old friends began to drift away that day as Sabina was another year closer to the throne, though, they assumed, Alcine stood to inherit first. New people began to flock to her side, honeyed words intending to draw favor falling deaf on her wise ears.

Her true joy came later that day when her friend Bryan had quietly pulled her into the stable and showed her the tiny colt that would grow into her beloved gelding. Her heart had filled with such joy that someone finally understood her, that she had kissed him impulsively, and thus began their long and carefree relationship.

Aaron bounced over, followed by Katrina, who had made the trip solely for this party, and wrapped his older sister in a bear hug. "You're so old now!" he proclaimed, giving her a kiss on the cheek.

"I'm not that old," she said dryly. "Soon you will be just as old as me."

"Will not!" he badgered, defiant out of habit. Aaron looked around the room for an ally, his eyes falling on Darian as he approached with a plate of food for Sabina.

Aaron gestured toward Darian and grinned. "At least you aren't as old as Darian or Nasta!"

Sabina gave a choking cough after simultaneously sipping her champagne and gasping at her brother's rudeness. She waved off Darian's immediate look of concern and took a deep breath, tears stinging her eyes as the champagne burned in her sinuses. "Aaron, that is not polite. Apologize. Immediately."

Stung from his sister's tone, Aaron stared at Darian's boots contritely. "I apologize, Darian. I did not intend to give offense. Besides, twenty-eight isn't that old." He looked up cautiously, relieved to see a small smile, a rare thing, on Darian's lips.

Aaron had immediately formed a strong respect and admiration for the man upon their arrival to Kylassame. He shadowed Darian without shame until Rowan, exasperated on the other man's behalf, told him to let Darian have some peace.

Darian never complained though, and even now he had a touch of humor in his voice as he winked at Aaron. "Apology accepted, young man. It was a false statement anyway. I am closer to Miss Sabina's age than I am to Nastasio's."

Sabina inhaled another sip of champagne, glaring at Henri who solidly thumped her back in a misguided effort to help. "What do you mean; you are closer to my age?"

One eyebrow raised slightly as Darian looked around the astonished group. "How old do you think I am?"

Henri crossed his arms. "I put you at around twenty-eight, twenty-six at the youngest."

Darian shook his head and his lips twitched, though none around him could tell if that was due to mirth or anger. "I am twenty-two, but thank you for the added years." He handed Sabina her plate. "If you will excuse me, I need to go speak with your father regarding our guard detail for the trip to Asimina."

Sabina winced and closed her eyes as he walked away. "Well, that was not well done. Twenty-two? Only two years older than me?"

Katrina hooked one arm around her sister's waist and grinned. "He really is practically your age. He is going to be in trouble when Mya finds out that he is not too old for her, as she thought before."

"Oh, no." Sabina quickly scanned the room for Mya, relieved that she was standing next to Philip, arm companionably linked around his waist.

Katrina looked at her curiously. "Would that be such a negative thing?"

"He's been through a lot, Kat." Sabina answered. "I don't know if he will ever be able to handle the casual dalliance that Mya thrives upon."

"Well that is … unfortunate." Katrina's eyes took on a bored look and Sabina gave her a small shove toward a group of peers.

"Go have fun, Kat. We old people will keep our ancient musings over here."

~ * ~ * ~

Sabina laughed at the raunchy joke that had escaped Henri's lips, one glass of wine on the wrong side of sober, and swayed slightly as she stood.

The party had dwindled down into the late hours of night, with many of the older generation offering congratulations for another year and then braving the cold walk home. Katrina and her few Kylassame friends had left, for soon the festivities had become boring and they preferred to gossip and relax in the comfort of one of their homes.

Henri had dragged out a crate filled with a fruity white wine that he had found in the drop-zone and had been saving for after the older adults had left. All of the younger generation had heard stories about the evils of alcohol, and the events that had preceded the burning of Liam's house twenty years prior, and drank responsibility. However, they did imbibe on more regular occasions than they let on, especially secretive when in the presence of Rowan, their protector and unspoken leader.

Nastasio came over, eyes bright and a smile on his face. "Stellar party, Seb, just wonderful. Happy birthday!"

She giggled as he kissed her cheek. "Thanks, Nasta. It was a good night, wasn't it?"

Henri raised his glass. "To Sabina, the eldest of the de Nespa clan, who still doesn't have to worry about being an heir to anything!"

Sabina snorted. "Oh please. Not officially maybe, but you wouldn't find me acting this way in court. There it is all, 'Lady Sabina this' and 'Lady Sabina that.'"

Darian stood next to her, a solid form offering quiet support for the moments when the wine made the room spin. He looked at her full glass, and, shaking his head, plucked it deftly from her fingers.

"Hey! I wasn't done with that." Sabina looked up at him, at the violet eyes that were a rare and beautiful color.

They are like the color of the sunset, rich and beautiful, she mused as her body leaned forward slightly, wanting to see if there were swirls of other colors in their depths.

"I think you were, Miss Sabina," he replied, voice lowered so that none else heard the gentle rebuke.

Mya approached, still on Philips arm. "Sabina! Lovely, wonderful, Sabina! You need to turn twenty more often. This was awesome."

"Say that again in the morning and I'll think about," Sabina joked, taking in the way that both Mya and Philip gently swayed on their feet with glassy eyes.

Mya blew a raspberry at her friend, and then turned her soft blue eyes on Darian. "Hello, again. Philip, this is Darian, the man I was telling you about with the really cool swirly tattoos."

Philip gave a smile that did not quite reach his eyes. "It is nice to meet you, Darian. Welcome to Kylassame."

Darian gave a curt nod and replied, "Thank you," eyes narrowing as he stared a moment too long at the man.

Philip gave a wary glance at Sabina. "Well, we should be going. Seb, would you like us to escort you home? It's on the way."

"No, thank you. Darian will see me home safely."

Philip's brown eyes darkened slightly and he reached forward to lightly place his hand on Sabina's elbow, the sleeve of his coat exposing his wrist. "I think it would be better if you came with us, Seb."

Darian stiffened as his arm shot out, fingers wrapping in a vice grip around Philip's covered arm. He yanked up on the coat-arm, exposing dark black markings. A series of jagged sunbursts surrounded by Xs extended from his wrist upward, disappearing into the sleeves of his coat. "You!"

Philip jumped back, wrenching his arm from Darian's grip and shoving Mya behind his back. His voice was firm despite his intoxicated state, and he spoke in Zajedica. "I do not want to fight you. I have denounced The Way. I now live by the rules of this village and not the others."

"No one is safe with you here, Oprimata," Darian growled, stepping in front of Sabina who stood in silent shock as her mind tried to sort through the rapid change in language.

"There is no Oprimata here. I am Philip and no one else. There is no Way. There is no conquest or manifest." He held out his hands in a gesture of surrender.

"Where are the others?"

Philip gave an imploring look to Sabina before taking a step toward Henri. Unbalanced, his feet caught on a loose plank and he swayed toward Sabina instead.

Darian's fist shot forward, knuckles connecting with the cheekbone of Philip's face. A punch to the gut had the intoxicated man on his knees and Darian darted behind him, wrapping his strong arms around Philip's neck. Philip grunted as he was forced to his knees, his fingers grabbing at Darian's elbow as it applied pressure to his throat.

"Darian! No!" Sabina yelled, pulled back from the men by Nastasio as Henri moved forward.

"Darian! Darian, release him." Henri stood in front of the men for a quick moment, gauging the time and action needed to end the fight.

Violet eyes burned with rage as Darian tightened his grip and pulled Philip backward several feet. "You do not know what he did, how many he has killed. No one is safe when he is here. Give him time, and he will kill you all."

Mya moved then, surprising them all by grabbing a half-full wine bottle from the table beside her and swinging it at Darian, the bottle connecting solidly with the side of his head.

He flinched for a second before his eyes rolled back and his body slumped heavily to the ground. Sabina gave a sharp cry and fell to her knees beside his chest, relieved at the steady breath and strong pulse she felt.

Philip took a gasping breath and remained on all fours as he sucked in air. "I forgot how fast he moves. I should not have forgotten that. He was always faster than we were."

The group stood around the unconscious man, grateful that none of the village elders were in the hall to witness the confrontation. Finally, Henri gave a huge sigh of resignation.

"Come on, then. Let's get him to a safe room and decide what to do there."

Nastasio gave Philip a hand to help him on his feet. "You alright?"

He nodded. "Yep, nothing too bad. Want some help moving him?"

The group looked at him uncertainly and Philip gave a laugh of disbelief. "I am not going to hurt him. He is right, and I deserved his anger, but I do not return it." He looked at the group and ran his fingers through his hair.

"It's like this," he continued, "back where I come from, where he comes from, it is a different world. There was a different sense of wrong and right, and of how things should be. The group that I was born into, the Oprimata, we believed that our way was the right way, the way ordained by our God, the way that all of man needed to live by to be considered civilized."

He took a shaky breath, bruises already forming on his throat. "And we were so damned sure that we were right that we thought the end justified the means. I think that, originally, we just wanted to help bring advancements to areas that did not have them, to genuinely help the people, but then ..."

Philip sighed. "I know it now, now that I can see a different way. We thought the Saverlen were terrorists, rebels, rogues. They were people who fought against the way of order, against the way that things should be. We declared them outcast, rebels, and any person harboring one of them was to be tried and most often killed. We couldn't understand why the people supported them, when all we were doing was trying to save their souls."

Mya gave a small gasp of alarm and Philip looked at her sadly. "I saw it all when I came here, realized how much we had destroyed in the name of what is right, and decided I would never do that again. We destroyed entire villages, entire cultures, all in the name of our God, all in the name of improving their lives. I saw then that *we* were the terrorists, the occupiers, and not the saviors that we had envisioned ourselves to be, not when it meant massacre and genocide. That man, Darian, and I came through together, and it was my arrow that pierced his chest just as he tackled me and we both fell into a deep, abandoned well."

Sabina quietly spoke. "Time works in funny ways when people cross over. He couldn't know that you had been here for three years already. He would have thought you had been here the same amount a time, a matter of just over a month."

Philip rubbed his tender cheek. "I could understand that, just as I understand his rage for what he has known of my character."

Sabina pressed the heels of her palm to her eyes, forcing herself into a more sober state on sheer will alone. "We were going to leave for Asimina in a few days. Dad will never allow that if he hears about this episode. He won't trust him anywhere near me, or Alcine."

Henri shook his head slowly in agreement and glanced at Nastasio. "Seb, your dad is going to have a fit if he realizes what happened tonight. You know he won't tolerate it, and would send Darian back to the refugee camps."

"I know, I know!" Sabina closed her eyes. "He can't go back there, and he needs to see Alcine. Alcine needs to know about his father and his heritage. What do we do?"

"Leave before your father finds out about it," Nastasio said quietly. "Once Darian wakes up, just the two of you. We know about his code of honor and you know how to take care of yourself. Once you are away, we will tell your dad about the situation, have Philip tell his side as well."

Philip's breathing hitched and his voice trembled. "Will Rowan let me stay once he knows about *my* past?"

Sabina gave the man a small smile. "Dad's good about judging a man by his current actions and not his past. You've been here for three years. You may see a temporary decrease in guard detail, or maybe some speculative glances, but I don't think he will kick you out. The people here consider this village to be a second chance, redemption from any ills done in the other world."

Henri shrugged into his coat. "Let's get your things ready, then."

Chapter 23

Kaldalangran Mountains

Darian snarled as they rode away from the mountains that guarded Kylassame. Clouds filtered the sun's morning rays as they moved through the forest of leafless trees and the crisp air turned their cheeks bright pink. "You should have that man killed. It is not safe. We should go back."

Sabina pushed her gelding into a careful jog on the snowy path, certain the man would push his mount to match her pace. "You can't have someone killed for their past, Darian. He has been in Kylassame for three years. During that time he has been an active and positive member of our community. He has helped build houses, harvested crops, and protected us."

She sighed and pulled her scarf higher on her face. "Look at it this way. How many men did you kill before you came here?"

Darian fell silent a moment before responding. "That is an unfair question. It is an entirely different scenario and cause." His eyes glinted with contained anger and he fell silent once more.

For hours the only sound that could be heard was the muffled swishing of snow beneath their horse's hooves and the occasional call of Faulks above. The wind picked up, blowing up the loose powder to swirl around their faces and sting their eyes.

Finally Darian broke the silence. "Perhaps, too many. Though at the time, it was not enough."

"What?" Sabina shifted slightly in the saddle to glance back at the man.

He sat easily on his horse, back straight and hips moving fluidly with the gait of the animal. His horse snorted happily as they moved, pleased with the man's light touch on the reins. "You asked how many men I had killed. How did you know I had killed any?"

"The child at the camp said that the markings on your body indicate the amount. He also said that you were one of the best of the Saverlen." Sabina stared at the horizon, gauging their need to reach the first camp before the sun began to set by watching the swirling, darkening clouds.

"It was never a matter of being the best." Darian's voice was guarded as he spoke. "I killed only to protect the innocent, only when necessary. If my skills allowed for me to do so more efficiently and without harming myself, then it was for the better." He paused and urged his horse faster until he rode beside Sabina.

"Sabina, you knew my past and yet you brought me into your home. That was reckless." His tone was quizzical and uncertain.

She shrugged and shivered as a cold gust sent airborne snowflakes into her hood. "You needed help and I was that help. I've also been trained in defense by my uncles, who are probably the best fighters in the realm. I was willing to take my chances, especially in my world, where you were at a disadvantage due to unknown weapons, allies, and terrain."

"Plus," she continued, "You could barely hold your head up, much less attack me. By the time that your body had a fledgling amount of strength I felt I had a good measure of your character."

A small smile tugged at his lips. "Still … it was a foolish risk."

Sabina pulled her mount to a halt and gave him a sharp stare. "Look, do you wish I had just let you die?"

Darian thought for a moment before responding. "I do not know how to answer that. I am grateful for your help, but part of me does wish I received an honorable death." His breath puffed out as he gave a sharp sigh, moisture trailing into the sky. "I do not know where my place is here. My entire life was spent training to protect the innocent and dispatch the enemy. I do not know how to do other things. Here, there is no enemy. I have no purpose."

"I see," Sabina responded slowly, mind racing. "It is good that we go to Asimina then. My cousin Alcine may be able to help you find a new role in life."

They passed several more hours in contemplative silence before Sabina judged the position of sun was low enough on the horizon to warrant making camp. They arrived to the safety of the cave just as dusk began to settle.

Sabina moved into the protection of the cave as Darian led the horses to a second protective cave just a few feet away. Slowly, her muscles aching and stiff from cold, she shrugged out of her outermost layer of clothes, sighing in relief at the absence of wind and blowing snow. She quickly gathered wood from the niche cut out in the back of the cave and went to build a strong fire to give warmth and light in the darkness.

Her fingers brushed the old ashes as she lay down the wood, brows furrowing as warmth touched her skin. A heavy sense of dread settled in her abdomen as she inspected the cave closer, noticing a large bloodstain near the back of the cave, and a leather pack pushed against the wall.

A sharp whistle drew her attention and Sabina moved to the edge of the cave. "Darian? Need help with the horses? Do you see anyone out there? I think someone else may have found decided to shelter here as well."

His body was cloaked in shadow as he moved away from the cave and the horses.

Sabina sighed and moved forward, wrapping her arms around her body. "Darian, come on. You aren't breaking any Saverlen oaths of propriety by sharing a cave with me during a snowy night. Nothing is going to happen, okay? Besides - "

He turned and Sabina drew in a quick breath of alarm as she realized the man in front of her was not Darian. He was slightly taller, and the hulk of his mass indicated a much heavier build. His face was crisscrossed with series of old, white scars and narrowed eyes, the lids half shut with blood that had frozen over.

The wind swirled and Sabina's hair whipped around her head as she quickly glanced around the tiny clearing in the woods. They were surrounded by trees, in a small clearing two man's lengths in diameter. While the cave was only a short distance away, the snow came up to her ankles, eliminating any chances of fleeing quickly. Her body had already begun shivering from the lack of her thick coat, though fear pumped hot blood through her veins.

A slow grin spread on the man's thin, cracked lips, revealing several missing teeth. His accent was heavy, the Zajedica he spoke thick and guttural. "My ill luck has turned."

Sabina began to slowly back away. "I am not alone out here. I am not your enemy. I can get help for you."

His eyes were as frigid as the snow surrounding her. "You are not of my family, just called out to a Saverlen, and you are a woman. You are the enemy and I will take all that I need from you, whether you like it or not."

He darted forward, lightning fast for his size, and wrapped his half-frozen fingers into Sabina's blowing hair, jerking her sideways. Sabina landed hard on her side in the snow, scrambling to get her footing. Just as she stood, a sharp, heavy boot slammed into the back of her knee and sent her back to the ground with a shriek. Cold snow filled her mouth and she moved again, darting forward and rolling into a squatting position.

The grin widened as the man watched her stand, and then drew a knife from his belt. "You make this more fun. We play then."

He slashed the knife at her face, the frozen steel glinting in the retreating sun as Sabina jerked back, the blade missing her cheek by a hair. Her ankle wrenched in the snow and twisted painfully as she moved backward and she instinctively glanced down. The knife moved swiftly, its large blade slicing downward through the thin leather jacket and opening a deep gash in the thin muscles on the side of Sabina's ribcage. The upswing caught her opposite thigh and she fell backward into the snow as sharp pain flooded her senses.

Her hand fell on a thick branch and she swung, all survival skills emptied from her mind by the pain and sheer terror. During her life she had learned over one hundred ways to disable a man, with fifty resulting in his death. As she stared at the leering man in front of her, she could not remember a single one.

Wet wood smacked as the branch hit the man's shoulder with a loud thud, resulting in laughter ringing harshly in the air as the impact was absorbed by his layers of clothing.

The knife was shoved back into his belt as he towered above Sabina in the snow, grin growing wider. "Enough of that game. Now we play new game, eh? Be good girl and I give you fast kill after."

Sabina pushed through the pain and flipped over onto her hands and knees, knowing that she needed to escape. The wind howled louder, pressure building against her ears until she could hear nothing but her heart pounding and the ragged breath coming from her chest. Somewhere a hawk screamed, angry and distant, and a horse squealed in answer. She scurried forward, gaining several fast yards before her lacerated leg muscle seized and her body froze from the intensity of the pain.

Suddenly his weight was on top of her, knocking the breath from her lungs. The knife tip bit her skin as it traced her spine, opening her shirt as it easily sliced through the fabric, her back muscles seizing as the cold air sank deeply into her flesh. Sharp pain exploded through her head as the steel-point burned into the flesh at the base of her spine before cutting through her waist band. A heavy hand pushed down on the back of her head, shoving her face in the snow so that she could not breathe just as she felt her pants being cut and tugged from her hips.

Her fingers moved across the snow, desperate to find something, anything that could be used a weapon. Her hot breath melted the snow directly under her mouth and nose, the resulting liquid causing her to cough and gasp for breath. She had known caution and anxiety when training in defense, but never this fear, so bright that it caused stars to swim in her vision as her body prepared to shut down from the overwhelming emotion.

Sabina felt the weight of him jerk strangely to the side just before a hot liquid snaked down her bare back, smelling of a copper and metal. Suddenly his full weight was upon her, pushing her entire body into the snow, heavy and suffocating yet unmoving. Two heartbeats later and the weight disappeared. Gloved hands lifted her face and she gasped in a breath of cold air before she turned onto her side, too cold and in too much pain to do more.

He lay beside her in the snow, eyes staring straight into hers as the snow beneath his head began to melt away with the heat of the blood flowing from the deep slash across his neck. Six parallel lines pumped blood from his face and neck, the result of vicious talons that had evolved to snatch prey and tear flesh.

Sabina fought the urge to vomit, acutely aware of her own blood spilling onto the snow and forming a crimson outline of ice around her body. She let herself roll onto her bare back, eyes focusing on the snowflakes that fell onto her body, large, puffy crystals of snow.

It's so beautiful, she thought absurdly as she watched them drift down to gently fall onto her hair, frozen ringlets forming as the snow melted from her body heat, then froze again.

A series of high, statico chirps encouraged her to turn her head to the side and Sabina gave a small smile. Faulks, his beautiful white chest feathers splashed with red, hopped forward across the snow. His beak tenderly nuzzled her cheek and she felt a tear freeze on her lashes as she realized she could not move her leg, and that her body was becoming stiff with cold.

"Sabina? Stay with me. You are safe now. I have you." The male voice was filled with concern and husky with fear.

Sabina shifted her focus toward the man standing above her, his features blurring through the snowfall and then doubling as her concentration failed from the blood loss. She stared at Darian a moment, and felt herself falling into those rare, violet eyes that matched the sunset before the storm. A weak smile fell upon her lips as her mind vaguely recalled their earlier conversation.

"Looks like you found your purpose," she whispered hoarsely.

He bent down and carefully scooped her up, his body wonderfully, blessedly warm. Cocooned into his cradle of warmth, Sabina let herself drift into the darkness.

Chapter 24

Kaldalangran Mountains

Another round of violent tremors wracked Sabina's body as she lay in her torn clothing in front of the fire. "Need warmth," she whimpered, holding on to her role as a healer to keep the fear at bay.

"I know. It is coming," Darian replied as he moved several logs onto the fire and blew, hastening the bark to catch flame.

"Looks like my self-defense sucks," Sabina said, sucking in a sharp breath at the pain that encompassed her body.

He glanced at her sharply before replying. "You lasted longer than most of the trained men I fought with. You did well, Sabina. You could not have beaten that man without assistance, no one could. Jugar was an Oprimata, one of their best fighters, and known for his ruthlessness. You are alive, that is all that matters."

Sabina simply nodded, too weak from the fight and too cold to continue talking. Darian, content with the increase in heat from the fire, moved quickly to her side.

"I need to treat those wounds, Sabina. We also need to get you out of the wet clothes before your body temperature drops too dangerously." Darian squatted beside her, placing a tentative hand on her shoulder, aware of the necessary breach in propriety.

"I promise I won't try to seduce you." She gave him a tiny smile of encouragement as he gently began cutting her shirt into strips; the only way remove the frozen garment without causing unnecessary pain.

He gave a small snort of surprise and shook his head in disbelief. "Even now you joke. Save your breath." His hands carefully pulled away the shredded leather jacket and inner shirt, then gently draped a fire-warmed cotton blanket over her chest.

Sabina turned her head away as his fingers, surprisingly gentle, began to clean the gash on her ribs with water warmed by the fire. She could make out the entrance to the cave, although they were far enough in to avoid the worst of the wind and cold. Two large shapes loomed in the entrance, shifting as if they intended to move toward her.

"The horses," Darian said as he felt her body tense and followed her eyes. "I thought the cold was too biting and we would have enough room. I had just brought them in when I heard Faulks scream and followed your prints."

A sound of tacit agreement fell from her mouth before Sabina shuddered, flares of pain momentarily overtaking her senses as he began to sew the wound closed with the small needle and thin sinew she kept in her healer's pack.

"I am sorry," he said, voice rough with concentration. "I am used to having different supplies."

She gritted her teeth against the pain, taking in gulping breaths until he finished. He gently wiped away the last of the blood and covered her torso with the blanket.

"I need to do the leg next, okay?" Darian waited for her nod of confirmation before methodically shredding her pants and removing the torn undergarment. His eyes averted, he carefully placed the blanket to cover her hips and uninjured thigh, only exposing the injury to the air.

Tears escaped her tightly closed eyes as Darian gently poured water over her leg to wash away the worst of the blood. Her leg and ankle were an increasing flood of misery, alternating between throbbing agony and the feeling of being stuck with millions of tiny pins as her flesh began to warm.

She looked to the cave entrance once more, alarmed by the wall of snow that had built just inside the opening. "Darian," she began, and then swallowed hard as another spasm of pain overwhelmed her.

He glanced at the opening and took a deep breath. "Nothing to be done about that. We will have to wait for the storm to abate before we can continue to Asimina." He gently cut off the end of the sinew and sat back on his heels. "I need to move you to a dry blanket. Is that permissible?"

Sabina gave a small nod, her body screaming with pain as he slid his arms underneath her shoulders and knees and carefully transferred her to the opposite side of the fire. A soft nest had been created from their pile of soft furs, and she sank down into the cushioned surface with a grateful sigh.

Darian placed a hand on her forehead, frowning before wrapping her nearly naked body tighter in the warmed cotton blanket. "I am going to go and check on the horses. Try to sleep."

~ * ~ * ~

Her skin felt on fire, lungs heavy and rasping, and her fingers clawed ineffectually at the pressure surrounding her body, slowly smothering her. Sabina's sleeping mind caused her to gasp for air as it remembered the attack, the feeling of the man's heavy weight bearing down on her wounded body. Sharp, burbled cries of distress poured from her lips, causing her to jolt into awareness.

Sabina panicked, still feeling the heavy weight bearing down on her body and acutely aware of the lack of clothes upon her skin. Her arms were trapped to her side, unmovable and useless in this cocoon of weight and pressure, her fingers scratching and shoulders straining at the confinement.

"Sabina? Sabina! Calm down. You are safe. It is just the blankets." Several pairs of alarmed violet eyes stared down at her as she felt some of the weight being lifted and her arms freed.

The blurred eyes slowly came together to show her one face, and after a moment of searching her memory she gave a breath of relief. "Darian. Darian," she repeated, reassuring herself.

His hand felt cool on her brow and he gently slid another layer from the heap of blankets covering her body. "You are burning up. Drink this." He held a small wooden cup to her lips and she gratefully sucked in the moisture.

"My valiant protector," Sabina sighed as pain flooded her body and she drifted into unconsciousness once more.

~ * ~ * ~

The shivering began the next night, violent tremors that threatened to pull apart the delicate stitches holding her together. Sabina was pulled into awareness by the pain and carefully curled her body into a tight ball under her nest of blankets.

Her body hurt, the gashes pulsing with every beat of her heart, and her lungs felt full and heavy. Cold tears began to fall from her eyes as she took in a gasping breath, unable to generate the warmth her body needed. She closed her eyes tightly against the misery, seeing stars dance in the darkness behind her eyelids.

"Sabina?" The rich voice was there again and she felt a gentle weight cover her body as Darian draped another blanket over her.

She shivered again and forced her eyes open, smiling slightly as the fire in front of her suddenly rose, the warmth seeping through the blankets. "So cold. Can't warm up."

Darian put his hand on her neck, alarmed by the chill that had settled over her skin. "Sabina, you are losing too much body heat. We need your body to warm up faster than the blankets and fire will allow."

Sabina moved her head slightly to view his face. He looked different in her pain and fever-induced state, surprisingly vulnerable and human. His eyes were worried, brows drawn together and lips taut as he gently inspected her wounds. She could see shadows on his face, indicators that he had not slept in the days since the attack, and there were small lines of apprehension at their corners.

"How?" she whispered, feeling her strength ebbing quickly and not caring about his reply.

Unexpectedly, he blushed and moved away, returning with another blanket, which he lightly drooped over her body. "Flesh heats flesh faster than other means. I swear to you that I will not abuse the situation and only do what is necessary."

The disquiet in his voice brought a light smile to her lips. "Come on then," she said, averting her eyes as he shed his layers of clothes, leaving only the thin cotton shorts worn in Kylassame as undergarments.

She chuckled at his sharp intake of breath when his chest pressing against her frigid back. His legs curled against hers, his entire body was perfectly sized to cocoon her in warmth from the back while the heat of the fire seeped into her from the front.

Sabina felt his arms cautiously wrap around her waist, for lack of a better position, and let her body wiggle itself more snuggly against his heat. "Don't try to seduce me, okay?" she teased as she let the blessed warmth take her back into slumber.

~ * ~ * ~

"Ow, ow, ow!" Sabina winced as she sat up on her pile of furs, carefully holding the thin cotton blanket to her chest. "I feel like someone beat the crap out of me."

"Half right," Darian replied in a wry voice. "I take it you are feeling better?"

"Thirsty, and hungry." She looked over to where he was tending the fire, dressed only in cotton trousers. "Why are you half naked?"

His lips tightened slightly and he quickly moved over to his pack, pulling a linen shirt over his tattooed chest before returning to
176

the fire. "Ah, well. Your body kept shifting from burning to freezing, so it was easier to just leave my shirt off in between the freezing spells. I tried to warm you up while wearing a shirt, but you kept grumbling to me that the fabric was cold."

Sabina felt her face flush as she remembered the feeling of his firm chest against her back, warmth seeping through her muscles as they lay there, his arm a comfortably heavy weight on her hip. "Oh, um, right. Thanks for that by the way."

She shifted the blanket to the side carefully, sucking in a breath as she looked at her wounds. "That's a fun one."

Darian crouched by the fire, eyes wary as he stirred a pot filled with slivered beef and root vegetables that had been boiled in broth. "I am sorry. It will likely leave a scar. I am not as skilled with a needle and thread as you or your friend."

"I am grateful to be alive enough to worry about a scar. You did well, Darian, and I'm really lucky you happened to be here."

He shrugged, pensive and silent once more, and Sabina took an experimental breath, wincing slightly as the stitches pulled.

"How long has it been?" she asked.

His eyes glanced at hers before they went back to studying the pot. "Four days." His gaze shifted to the entranceway. "It still has not let up out there, so we may be stuck for some time more. Did you pack any clothes in the saddle bags? I can get it for you."

"Um, in a way." Sabina suddenly averted her eyes as Darian reached into her saddlebag and she remembered the one outfit she had brought from Kylassame to Asimina. She had expected to be riding in the same garb for the three-day journey, and had a full trunk of clothes in her family's house at Asimina, so she packed lightly.

177

"Is it ceremonial?" Darian asked as he pulled the silk fabric from the pouch and looked at it curiously. It was a small robe made of silk that wrapped around her body, the hem falling to just below her hips. He looked over at Sabina who had begun squirming uncomfortably under the blanket.

"Not exactly." She drew in a breath, wincing slightly at the soreness of her ribs, before giving a resigned sigh. "It will have to do though. I can hardly move with the blanket wrapped around me and," her voice paused as she realized the implications of the robe being her only option of clothing. "Oh, hell. I can't ride into Asimina wearing that!"

Darian's lips drew into a brief grin as he handed her the robe, and then turned to face the wall so that she could wrap it around her body in as much privacy as he could give.

"Okay, I'm … decent now," she said, her voice strangled with embarrassment.

He turned and gave her outfit a quick, restrained glance. The top of the robe formed a deep V above her breasts, the fabric clinging to her body as it slightly flared out at the tops of her thighs. The silk fabric had been woven with swirling designs in a myriad of colors, and edged with golden threads.

Sabina sat on the pile of blankets, uncomfortably aware of the amount of skin not covered by silk fabric. "I suppose I shouldn't be embarrassed, if I've spent the last four days naked under a blanket."

"There is nothing to be embarrassed about. This covers what needs to be covered and is the best we have for right now." Darian's tone of confidence and lack of desire gave Sabina an unexpected pang of relief. "What if," he continued, "we were to cut the thinner blanket and then sew it into a crude dress? Would that make an outfit sufficient for travel, at least underneath my travel garments?"

"I can't take your clothes!" Sabina protested, though she did not relish the prospect of riding another two days in the cold with no outerwear.

"Of course you can, and will," he replied curtly. "I am used to such hardships, and we can use the largest of the blankets to cover us both."

"Wait, what?" Sabina asked.

This time Darian looked uncomfortable before answering the question. "Sabina, your wounds are deep, and, stubborn though you are, your body will not be able to support you for the two-day ride. My gelding is strong enough for us both and this way you can use my body for support."

"How about we decide that in a few days and see how I feel?" Sabina offered.

He nodded in reply and crouched next to the fire, ladling the soup into the bowls they had brought for travel. "While we wait for the storm to cease, would you mind telling me about Asimina?"

She accepted the bowl of soup and felt part of her stress ease as she took her first spoonful. "Sure." She took another spoonful and thought about where to begin.

"Asimina is a village that has seen great, drastic changes throughout its existence. We actually don't know much about it before my uncle's lifetime, for he actually belongs to the oldest generation of the village.

"When my uncle was a young boy, King Verikhan, my grandfather, began his annihilation of the outlying villages that surround the court of Kaldalangra. Sebast, my uncle, remembers his childhood being wary but unafraid prior to the attacks, and the village had no need of defenses. Its people preferred to live in peace with nature, erecting houses of wood and thatch, with cloth-woven doorways and communal fires."

She smiled and slowly stretched her injured leg in front of her, encouraged by the ache of the muscle that had become a manageable pain.

"In that way, it is much the same village as it was, oh, at least forty years ago," she continued. "It is a beautiful village now, but it was basically destroyed by the king; only the strongest of my uncle's generation surviving the reign of terror to push on."

"My aunt discovered the village when she was just a young girl, and then she met my uncle, Sebast. They worked together for over a decade trying to protect the people from the attacks led by the king, and later by his heir, the High Prince Mateo. They would give warning to the village before the attack, giving Sebast time to hide as many inhabitants as possible, and then sneak into the village after the damage had been wrought and help the people to rebuild."

Darian gave a grunt of approval. "The life your aunt and uncle live sounds like they would make good members of the Saverlen."

Sabina gave a wry smile at the thought of her aunt as a Saverlen. "Yes and no. They do work very, very hard to make sure that all people in the realm receive justice, and that none are persecuted. But most of the time, at least now that she is Queen, my aunt and uncle reside in the court and do their good works through politics and regulations."

"You mentioned that before, but I don't understand, if you aunt is the queen," Darian's brows furrowed in confusion, "then why are you tending to the injured at refugee camps instead of living in finery and luxury?"

"Oh yes, that. Well," Sabina said thoughtfully, "in truth, I hate that life. Technically the lineage descends by order of birth with no regard to the sex of the heir. My father is older than my aunt by two years, but they both decided that the court would have an easier transition with her in place as the ruling monarch. But since I am the oldest of the children born to the co-reagents, my aunt and my father, I am technically the first heir to throne."

"And yet you are out here?" Darian's voice was filled with confusion and rebuke.

Sabina shrugged, wincing as the motion pulled on her stitches. "My parents decided early on that they wished me to have a life unfettered by the court, or at least the ability to make my own decisions. I very much dislike the court life, and felt I can do greater good to the realm by helping its people in the flesh, rather than sitting upon the throne."

"Yet the life you choose is a harder one," Darian replied.

"In some ways, I suppose. In others, it is far preferable." Sabina took a deep breath. "If we are going anywhere soon, I will need to get my legs back in working order. Help me walk around a bit?"

He walked over behind her before carefully easing her onto her feet, hands held firm beneath her elbows for support. "Are you sure it is not too soon? Those are not small wounds, Sabina."

"Oh, I'm sure it is." She took a few shaky gulps of breath as her injured leg trembled beneath her supported weight. "But," she continued, "I'm equally sure that we are going to run out food before I will be healed, and we need to be able to move as soon as this storm blows over."

"You are stubborn."

She gave a breathless laugh before replying. "I can't argue with that statement." She took one shaky step across the floor, then a second. Her leg buckled on the third step and only the solid support of Darian behind her kept Sabina from crashing to the stone floor.

"I hate being this weak," she grumbled as she gathered her legs for a second try.

"You will be ready by the time you need to be. Do not needlessly push yourself too far. Trust yourself that when the time comes, you will be ready."

Chapter 25

Asimina

Children scampered around in the snow between the houses of Asimina, shrieks of joy filling the air. The storm had lasted a full week, a never-ending fall of dense snow that trapped people into their houses and had the community calling through the open smoke holes in their roofs to make sure neighbors were still alive.

Eric and Yasmina had been kept busy diverting Asli's attention from the terrifying storm that had turned them all into captives within their own home, and which had greatly alarmed the small child. Together they had created dozens of new songs, dances, and games.

True to her promise, Yasmina had begun to eat and rest more, a soft fullness rising in her face and easing away the lines of stress that had cut so deeply. She had begun to laugh and smile more as well, and the look of desperation had all but disappeared from her eyes.

She carefully moved up the snow staircase that had been created outside the door, her hands warmed by two ceramic mugs filled with a hot tea made of dried rosebuds, and stopped at Eric's side.

He accepted the cup with a nod of thanks and used the vessel to warm his fingers, cold even through the thick gloves that Yasmina had created for him from the fur of a rabbit he had shot just before the storm hit. He looked around the village and felt a sense of pride in the work that he, and the other men, had done to free the people.

The snow fall had truly buried the homes of the villagers, only their tall domes peaking above the snow, and the smoke from their fires looked as if it were spiraling from the earth itself. The villagers would have suffered greatly had it not been for Cole, who had been in the village on a visit and devised a plan of insulating the roofs of the huts with thick bundles of wool, creating a thick barrier to keep the deadly low temperature outside of the walls.

When it was over, Eric had been the first to dig through the snow, carefully bringing the white matter into the house bucket by bucket and melting it into drinking water as the tunnel slowly connected their doorway to the surface.

Once on the surface, he was able to create an exit for Alcine. Together, they were able to dig out the doors of all the houses, molding the snow into a firm staircase that could be walked upon by the healthy and the frail alike.

Alcine shuffled over and stood beside Eric, quiet and subdued. After watching the children play for several minutes he spoke, his voice guarded of emotion. "I received a confirmation from Rowan from a messenger hawk. Seb left Kylassame two weeks ago. It should have taken her three days to get here, four at the most with that storm. Where is she? I've been worried sick about her but unable to search due to this damned storm."

Eric's breath caught in his throat. He had not thought of Sabina since moving in with Yasmina and felt a pang of guilt. "I hope she's okay."

184

"I'm giving her one more day and then going to search. Will you come with me?"

"Of course," Eric agreed. A shudder coursed through his body as he thought of Sabina missing. His thoughts filled with the feel of her body in his arms before she left, but it was not as sharp, did not grip him as tightly as it had in the past.

He did not see the look of resigned sadness in Yasmina's eyes, or the way she set her jaw with a silent decision as the men talked about organizing the search.

Asli bounded over then and, after hearing the conversation, hugged her mother's legs tight. "Will Miss Sabina be alright?"

Yasmina put up a front of assurance for the child. "Of course she will, dear one. Sabina is far tougher than any snow storm." Her breathing hitched a moment before she continued. "Besides, she knows that she needs to return to the people who love her. That will drive her home."

Eric looked over at her questioningly. "Are you alright? You should go back in and rest."

"I am fine," she replied quietly, eyes downcast. "I will go inside and leave you to your planning."

He reached out to give her shoulder a squeeze of encouragement, surprised at the way she twitched away from him before quickly descending the stairs into the hut. Asli followed her mother, sliding down the steps on her thickly padded winter pants.

Alcine was the first to break the tense silence that followed. "When she does return, will you be moving in with Seb, or remaining with Yasmina?"

His heart lurched as Eric answered with a soft, "I don't know," and once again looked down the staircase. A small glass lamp acquired from the court had been lit in the dark interior, the door weaving closed against the frigid air outside, and he could see the shadows of Asli and Yasmina moving in the small hut.

Eric swallowed a sip of the tea and sighed. "It would be cruel for me to stay with Yasmina while courting Seb. I guess I will have to hope that she will invite me into her home, or find other arrangements."

The other man gave a non-committal grunt in reply. His eyebrow raised in disbelief as he saw the way Eric looked toward the place he had called home for the past few weeks.

A sudden cry of surprise rang through the village, sounded by a young boy who had been playing on the edge nearest to the woods. More voices rose, this time in alarm, and the two men exchanged worried glances as they made their way through the snow, following the relay of calls that sounded through the crisp, otherwise-silent winter air.

They had crossed to the edge of the village when the two horses walked out of the woods, and Alcine swore sharply as he recognized Sabina's riderless gelding. The second horse was carrying an unrecognizable rider thickly wrapped in blankets and furs, and Alcine slowly drew his curved hunting knife from its scabbard in the event the rider was hostile.

The horses drew closer, and Eric gave a shocked murmur as he saw Sabina's face, pale and frighteningly gaunt, looking out from a fur-lined hood folded within the blanket. "Sabina!"

Alcine tensed beside him as the second figure could be made out, a stranger who was similarly concealed within blankets. Alcine studied the gloved hands that held the reins and felt anger begin to smolder as he realized the man's arms were firmly wrapped around his cousin's waist.

He strode across the snow to close the gap, and held his knife loosely at his side. He took a small satisfaction in the way the stranger tensed. *Good,* he thought. *Let him know that he has cause to be concerned, wrapped as he is around my cousin.* While being mounted gave the illusion of added height, the man seemed tall, and his eyes easily met the hostile looks of the village men as they gathered.

Eric moved beside him, weaponless but feeling the rush of adrenaline at the obvious threat. "You take out the stranger and don't worry about Seb. I'll get her out of danger if necessary."

A quick nod was the only indication Alcine had heard Eric's words, his mind already preparing his body for the possibility of a fight. His mind became clear of all concerns, becoming analytical, cold, and mechanical. White clouds billowed from his parted lips as his lungs prepared for the quick burst needed to surprise the stranger, while his body flooded with energy needed for a long bout.

He was unable to get an idea of the man's physique under all of the heavy layers, but, judging from his head in relation to Sabina's, he seemed to be of the same height as Alcine. It was never to his advantage to go into an altercation with no knowledge of the opponent, but he had not spent his entire life training in combat to worry about the unknown.

"Where have you been? What are you doing with my cousin?" he barked out, ignoring the pit of fear that had begun to settle as he realized the implications of Sabina being alone with this man during the time she had been missing.

The stranger's featured hardened and he pulled the horse to a stop. They were far enough away from Alcine as to have the opportunity to turn and flee, and Alcine quickened his stride. He watched carefully as Sabina turned her head slightly, dropping the hood to speak in quiet tones to the man.

~ * ~ * ~

Her cheek brushed against his lips as she turned, quietly murmuring, "Be still, that is my cousin," before turning back. She forced a smile to her lips, the effort exhausting after two days of painful travel.

"Calm down, Alcine. This is a friend and we have been stuck in the storm. It is a long story that I would prefer to not tell from horseback. All I want is a bath, and some food, and then a long nap under thick blankets."

Her cousin narrowed his eyes in suspicion as he gestured to her riderless gelding. "Why are you not riding your horse? Do you know how long it has been since you left Kylassame? We have been worried sick about you! Why would you run off with some stranger?"

Tears pricked her eyes at the accusation and Sabina felt a rush of indignant anger course through her, causing her head to pound painfully. "I didn't run off with him, you jerk. We got caught in the storm and I was," she paused, considering her cousin's anger. "I was sick," she finished weakly.

"Come on," Alcine replied brusquely. "Let's get you inside and warmed up." He pointed at Darian with the long hunting knife. "He goes to solitary," he snarled.

Another wave of anger pulsed through Sabina at the insult to Darian, the emotion leaving her dizzy and gasping for breath. Darian dropped the reins and gathered her in his arms, one around her shoulder and the other at her hips, as he felt her body sway in the saddle.

"Sabina," he murmured reassuringly into her ear. "Calm down. It is fine." He kept both of the men in his vision as they moved rapidly toward the horse, her cousin wielding a vicious hunting knife.

"No!" She struggled lightly against his grip as she tried to turn in the saddle. "It's not right for him to insult you by sending you to solitary, not after what you have done for me."

The two men leapt forward, misinterpreting her struggles as an attempt for freedom. Darian quickly threw off the blankets that had cocooned Sabina and him together as they approached and raised one hand in a gesture of surrender.

"Take your hands off of her." Eric approached him from the left side, unarmed but eyes darkened with wrath.

Darian shook his head slightly in refusal. "She is injured and will fall. I cannot."

"Let me help her down, then." Blue eyes shifted to wary concern as the man laid a gloved hand on Sabina's thigh.

An involuntary cry of pain lifted from Sabina's lips as Eric's glove fell on the wound and suddenly she felt as if the world was tunneling in upon itself. Her body toppled to the side and she felt herself sliding from the horse, a hard body keeping her upright as her feet sank into the thick snow.

The world before her eyes swam and spun, and her stomach lurched at the sudden vertigo. She swallowed back her twisting stomach and forced her eyes open, sluggishly taking in the actions around her, acutely aware of Eric's arms wrapped around her shoulders.

Alcine had pulled Darian from the horse, the gelding bolting toward the pasture in alarm as his rider was knocked from his back. The hunting knife was held loosely in Alcine's hand, that lethal blade pointed at Darian as he quickly recovered from the fall.

"Surrender yourself and I will not kill you." Alcine's voice was as cold as the ice surrounding them, his concern over Sabina's injuries overriding her insistent pleas on Darian's behalf.

Darian glanced at Sabina and gave a quick nod, sinking to one knee in the snow. "I mean no harm to Miss Sabina or to the people of this village. I surrender myself to your goodwill, provided Sabina is given the safety and care she needs."

His eyes flashed up, taking in the face of the angry man staring down at him. "Alcine, son of Arden. You look like your father. I am forever in your service."

Chapter 26

Asimina

"What were you thinking, Seb? You could have died out there!" Alcine had carried Sabina back to his own hut as Eric, Cole, and Rafael moved the stranger to the solitary hut with little gentleness.

Rafael had arrived to the village minutes before the encounter and had run hard when he heard the shouting. As the bastard son of Agrafina, the two men considered themselves near cousins, for their mothers had been close as sisters throughout their lives.

They also shared the knowledge of the stigma of not being blood related to their lineage, though Rafael held more anger in his heart at the circumstances surrounding his birth.

"I almost did die out there," Sabina gasped as she sank onto the pallet bed, soft furs cushioning her aching muscles. "The only reason I am still here is because Darian was there to keep me alive."

"You mean your father let you ride out, into an impending snow storm, with a man that just came to our realm. Alone and unguarded." Alcine crossed his arms in front of his chest, the fear of her unaccounted absence and frustration at his own anger still needing an outlet.

Sabina winced as she shrugged out of Darian's thick coat, and then lifted her shirt, crudely sewn from the cotton blanket, to inspect the stitches on her side. "Not exactly," she murmured. "He didn't exactly know we left until after the fact, and we would have made it here before the snow storm if not for this lovely addition to my physique."

The newly healed wounds had not re-opened, much as she had hoped, but the skin around the scar was inflamed and red from the journey. She dropped the shirt back down and looked up at Alcine, surprised to find his eyes bright with restrained tears.

"What, Alcine?" She raised her eyebrow at him and then added, "If you think this is bad, you should see my leg," in an attempt to lighten the mood. Sabina hated to quarrel with Alcine, though their combined stubbornness had them squabbling more often than either preferred.

"Gods, Seb. What happened?" Alcine gingerly sat on the bed beside her and helped her out of the thick traveling pants so that she could inspect the leg wound. It was also inflamed but the wounds held up as well as could be expected for the physical exertion of the trip.

She closed her eyes as exhaustion set over her body and rested her head on her cousin's firm shoulder. "We had just stopped at the midway cave when I heard a noise. I went to investigate, thinking it was Darian with the horses, and instead was attacked. That man did this to me, and would have done worse, but Faulks distracted him long enough for Darian to kill him."

"Seb," Alcine interrupted.

"And then," Sabina gasped in a moment of pain as she pushed on, the hurt and fear causing her words to fall faster as she sank into the safety of her cousins presence. "And then, I came down with a fever, and the storm hit, and we were stuck in the cave until we could dig out and ride back here."

"Seb," Alcine once again interjected.

"He's a good man, Alcine." Sabina forced her eyes open, their usual bright green muddy with fatigue. "Darian, I mean. He didn't fit into Kylassame, but I think his soul is a good match for Asimina. He is strong, and brave, and believes in justice above all things."

She gave a nervous chuckle before continuing. "Honor, too. He's big on honor. I was pretty much naked in front of him for almost a week and he never once made me feel uncomfortable, or vulnerable. What are the odds of that?"

Alcine sputtered incoherently at the thought of her naked in front of any man.

"Can I sleep here tonight? I don't know if I can make it to my house." Sabina felt as if the weight of the world had settled upon her body and sighed gratefully as Alcine helped her curl onto her side on his bed.

"Of course you can. Get some rest, now. I'm going to go talk to your honorable stranger." He gently stroked her hair and covered her with a thick blanket as she sank into a deep sleep.

~ * ~ * ~

Alcine paused in the doorway of the solitary hut to allow his eyes time to adjust to the drastic plunge into darkness. The stranger sat on his knees in the back of the hut, arms tied behind his back and head bowed in contemplation. Red and orange waves danced across his face, reflections from the hot fire that Cole had flared in the pit of the house.

Eric guarded the door, arms crossed and feet wide for easy movement. "How is she?"

"Sleeping. Exhausted, but surly as ever." Alcine studied the man across the hut for a long moment. "Did he give you trouble?" he asked, motioning to the bonds.

Cole cleared his throat. "Ah, no. We just thought it might be a good idea, at least until you talked to Sabina. He has actually been quite a polite prisoner."

The leader of Asimina stepped beside the fire. "Darian," he said, his voice harsher than intended from the emotions swirling within.

Darian raised his eyes but did not otherwise move, remaining passively on his knees. "Will Sabina be okay? Is she finally resting? She refused to rest until we arrived here."

Alcine cocked his head to the side, interested and somewhat amused that a man who was bound in a strange land would first ask about the health of a woman he barely knew. "Yes. She is sleeping and I thought I would take the opportunity to come decide if I should allow you to have further contact with her. You do realize that she is a princess of the realm, do you not?"

"Yes." A smile fell upon his lips briefly before his features shifted back to neutrality. "Miss Sabina had mentioned it."

A sigh escaped from Alcine as he found himself already tired of the charade. "Alright, look," he said, squatting down in front of Darian. "Sabina is my cousin, and I love her dearly. You, however, are a complete stranger, who happened to be in a cave with my naked cousin who is horribly injured and vulnerable. Give me a reason why I should not just haul you out to the snow covered woods and send you on your way?"

Darian glanced warily toward Eric, who had released a garbled sound of anger at the information. "I shall give you two. Firstly, because I was in a cave with Sabina, who was naked and vulnerable and hurting, and yet did not touch her beyond what was necessary for her healing. I think few men can say they would do the same in my position, so you have a good idea of my character, especially in relation to your cousin."

His violet eyes gazed defiantly into Alcine's for a moment before they softened. "And second, because if you turn me out into the snow, I will never be able to tell you about your parents and close the circle of honor and debt."

Chapter 27

Asimina

The snow has begun to recede before Sabina was able to move through the village on her own, her wounded thigh finally strong enough to support her weight for short lengths of time.

Rafael wrapped his arm snugly around her waist as they stepped onto a slippery patch of ice and gave her a jaunty grin. "You created quite a stir leaving court as you did. Now Asimina is all a-flutter with your stranger. What else will you do to surprise us, Seb?"

Her free hand lightly thumped his stomach. "What was I expected to do? Just accept the crown and change everything?"

"That is what many of the Patrons would have preferred. It was difficult for them. Not only did they have the proverbial carpet ripped out from under them by learning that Alcine was not of a pure bloodline, but then to have the actual eldest heir blatantly refuse the crown and pass it to one who is just barely touching adulthood?"

Sabina gave a despondent shrug. "I never wanted it, you know. That life is not for me."

"Oh, I can clearly see that." His blue eyes sparkled and he gave her an affectionate but gentle squeeze. "You would not have nearly as much opportunity for rescuing handsome strangers while seated in the throne room."

"Yeah, okay." Sabina rolled her eyes at the insinuation. "I wasn't going out to rescue handsome strangers. He's not even interested in women so that doesn't matter."

Blue eyes twinkled and pink lips curved into a smile as Rafael purposefully misinterpreted the phrase as a way to badger the woman he considered a cousin.

Sabina looked up at his expression and flushed violently. "Not like that! He's not interested in anyone, Raf. His entire life has been devoted to justice and vanquishing evil. There isn't any room left for romance or domesticity."

"Unlike Brendan?" Rafael questioned.

Brendan had been one of the first of their peers to befriend Rafael, and became his most loyal friend. Life at the court was not easy for Rafael and he often spent his time traveling through various encampments, returning only for brief, scheduled visits to remind the court of his existence and confirm his loyalty to the crown.

None of Sabina's generation knew the actual story of Rafael's conception, only that even the mention of the event would cause terror to surface in his mother's eyes. Brokkan, one of the elite guards in Nyssa's order, had formally adopted the boy when he was three, after several years of courting his mother, Agrafina.

Brokkan had never cared about Rafael's questionable parentage, and was the first to forcefully silence those who wished to parade it for ill intent. Sabina had once heard the man speaking to her father and heard him say that protecting Agrafina and her child was the least he could do, as so many events may have been avoided if only he were braver in the past.

The two paused at the edge of Alcine's hut, unwilling to disturb the masculine peace that descended over the area when the three men went through their daily exercise.

It had taken only two days before Darian had joined Eric and Alcine with their routine, the three moving through the graceful movements of strikes and blocks in stunning synchronicity. He had picked up the routine quickly, and the other two began to ask for instruction on new moves, new sequences which he used to dispatch them with ease while sparring.

The three men had become inseparable, something that sat quietly at odds with Sabina's heart. Eric and Darian had moved into Alcine's roomy house while they waited for the spring thaw that would enable a house to be built for the two to share.

Sabina had offered to allow Darian to live in her house, for it was built to accommodate a family of five and roomier than Alcine's, but Darian had refused. The identical offer to Eric had perched on her lips but never happened, something that surprised even her. Instead, Rafael would be staying with her to help with any movements that were still restricted by her injuries and acting as her temporary personal guard.

Not that Darian had relinquished his self-assigned duty to oversee her safety. He and Rafael sparred wildly as the latter proved his abilities to defend Sabina in the event of an attack. She had thought the entire thing an overreaction until Darian reminded her that of the three Oprimata who came to this world, they had already encountered two. It brought chills to her spine to think there could be another waiting in the snow to strike.

"I'm safe here," she whispered.

"What's that, Seb?" Rafael asked.

She shook her head to clear the worry. "Nothing, Raf. Just thinking." Sabina heard the crunch of boots on snow and turned her head. "Hi, Gia."

"Hey, Seb," the newcomer grinned. "I'm sorry I missed you last time you came through the village. I was spending some time at court with my dad and we must have just missed each other on the road."

Gia was one of the many children who resulted from a union between a woman of Asimina and a man from the court. Her mother, Alissandra, had survived the cruelties of King Verikhan's reign and offered fledgling trust to Mikel, a lower-caste man from the court. They had built a life in Asimina and resided there most of the year, but Mikel insisted that Gia accompany him to the court on occasional trips to know the other part of her heritage.

"How was court?" Sabina asked.

"The same," Gia replied. "The older Patrons hate that they have to acknowledge me since Nyssa is fond of me, and the younger ones all want to get in my good graces so they can improve their standing in the eyes of the royal family."

Sabina chuckled, the motion pulling slightly on her scars. "It's probably a good thing that Henri is still in Kylassame then."

Gia rolled her eyes as her lips turned upward. She and Henri had become a couple years earlier, after many refusals on her part. The life of the roamer was never one for her, and Gia was hesitant to constantly wait at home for Henri's return.

Then she realized that she would rather wait for his return, than never see him again, and finally said yes to his courting request. Ever since then, the two developed a relationship that suited them both. Henri spent less time traveling, and Gia timed her visits to the court or nearby friends with his time away from the village.

Sometimes Henri accompanied her to court, interested in that part of her life. He quickly found himself to be embroiled in the court politics, and untrusting of the intents of many Patrons. While he trusted in Gia's loyalty, he never passed up the chance to remind the people of the court that she was not interested in pursuing other suitors.

"So who is the new addition to our village?" She tipped her chin toward Darian.

"His name is Darian. He's from the other world and a great guy." Sabina cut her usual introduction to the man short, having said it at least fifty times in the last two days.

"Well, that's certainly good then. A new fling to get your mind off of Eric?" Gia glanced over at Sabina and raised an eyebrow at the confusion on her friend's face.

"Why would I need to get my mind off Eric?" Sabina asked, watching as the men finished a routine and began to stretch their bodies.

Gia and Rafael stared at their feet and, for a long moment, the only movement was the white puffs of air from their breath. Finally Gia bit her bottom lip and spoke. "Oh boy. Um, well. It might be nothing, after all. It's only, after you left, he agreed to temporarily move in with Yas to help her out. I'm not sure what his plans are now that you are back, but she hasn't spoken to anyone in two days, ever since he moved in with Darian and Alcine."

Sabina felt her breath hitch, the sharp intake uncomfortable on her ribs. "Well, it's not like we are married or anything. He's free to choose someone new." She was surprised by the lump that formed in her throat, but wondered that the rejection did not sink all the way into her heart.

"Maybe there is nothing between them other than feelings of friendship and mutual respect," Gia offered in consolation.

"Maybe," Sabina agreed doubtfully.

"Or maybe they've spent the last two months getting to know each other under thick blankets," Rafael chimed in tactlessly. His face took on sheepish look as both women turned and glared. "Or maybe not."

Sabina looked toward the three men thoughtfully. "I'm actually surprised that Yas agreed to have a stranger in her house. She has been so destructively self-reliant and closed off over the past year."

"She didn't have much of a choice." Gia watched as the men finished their routine and began to towel off their bare chests. "She had run out of fire wood and her hut was in desperate need of repair. Alcine told her she had to take in Eric as a way to help her get those things fixed without feeling further obligation to the community."

"He didn't!" Sabina felt her brow furrowing in indignation on Yasmina's behalf. "They both know that Asimina protects her own, through good times and bad."

Rafael rubbed the back of his neck uncomfortably. "Well, yes, but she wouldn't accept help otherwise, and her situation was getting dire. It was a brilliant ploy to get her to accept help, along with giving Eric a place to stay while you were otherwise occupied."

"I was coming back, you know." The cold air burned in her lungs as Sabina took a steadying breath. Waves of heat rose from the men as they moved into Alcine's hut to clean up. *Why would Alcine push him into the house of another woman when he knew I would be returning in just a little time?*

She shook her head to clean her thoughts and gave Rafael a forced smile of encouragement. "Anyone else hungry?"

Chapter 28

Asimina

The thin layer of frost-covered snow crunched under her feet as Sabina made the chilly walk to the bath house. The white blanket dumped by the storm had almost fully melted back into the earth with the warm, sunny weather of the past week and water steadily dripped from the trees and thatched roofs.

For the people of Asimina, the break in the weather was perfectly timed. Tempers had been sharpened by the close confinement within homes and emotions were running high. They rejoiced in the warm sunshine on their face and the tiny winter crocuses that had begun to pop through the remaining layer of snow, purple buds bringing color to the otherwise monotone landscape.

For Sabina, the warm weather was even more of a relief. Darian had not given her more than polite interactions in the past week, refusing to enter her home and citing impropriety. Eric had come to visit her but had been sullen, the air between them charged with an awkwardness brought on by the events during their time apart. While she thoroughly enjoyed spending time with Rafael, his dry humor was beginning to wear thin on her strained nerves and she craved additional company.

She tipped her head up to let the sun's rays fall onto her face and smiled. At least now she was able to take slow walks around the village, slowly strengthening her body after the attack. Her scars had faded from being puffy and red to smooth white markings over her pale skin, with just a tinge of pink surrounding the slightly raised skin.

The changing room was chilly and Sabina shivered as she slid out of her wool-lined, long-sleeved tunic and thick cotton pants. Both items had been borrowed from Alcine, for her own clothing rubbed against scars as they healed, causing her constant irritation that threatened to drive her emotions beyond reason. His clothes were larger and she was able to secure the pants with a woven strip of cotton, causing the hem to fall low on her hips instead of her waist. She knew the overall image was less than flattering, but had ceased caring.

The blue bikini she wore into the bath house left her feeling exposed, but it was necessary. She did have a more modest suit given to her by Mya during her last visit to Kylassame, but the tightly-fitting material scraped against the wounds on her ribcage. Sabina briefly entertained the idea of simply covering her upper body with a cotton T-shirt she had brought back from Kylassame, but decided that the community would see her body eventually, so it might as well be now.

Embarrassment crept to the front of her mind as she looked down at the jagged pink and white lines that could easily be seen on her torso and leg. She pushed aside the feeling and gave herself a mental shake before stepping into the bathing house.

"Hi, Seb!" Gia called out from her position in the center of the largest pool.

Sabina walked across the packed dirt floor to the steps of the pool. Her chin lifted in a gesture of false confidence as she looked around the room and realized that all of the current bathers had shifted their gaze to her body.

There's nothing I can do to change what happened, she told herself sternly. *I can't take back the past and I can't magically heal my body, so I just need to accept it. At least the court will never need to see the scars.*

The water rippled around her as she slowly descended the built-in stone steps and submerged her entire body below the water. After nearly three weeks of limited bathing opportunities due to the healing wounds and frigid temperatures, the feeling of cleanliness washed over her like a caress. Sabina rose and shook water out of her eyes, her long hair lightly draping over her shoulders and raining water from the tips.

A group had gathered at the corner of the pool, an area where the water came neck-high on Sabina's body. Gia spoke quietly to the group and they moved toward the center of the pool, a shallower area. Here, Sabina's body would still be concealed by the dark water, but the women's head and shoulders would be above the waves and ripples caused by exuberant bathers.

The men - Darian, Eric, Rafael, and several men of the village - stood with their chests exposed to the fire-warmed air of the chamber. Three women who had been sitting on the edge of the pool nearest to the group stood up gracefully, repositioning themselves at the nearest point once again.

Sabina fought the urge to roll her eyes and sigh in annoyance at the presence of the three women. Her opinion of Keri and her friends was well-known among the village ever since the woman had pursued Alcine. The moment he turned eighteen and was named Protector of Asimina, the woman was suddenly proclaiming that she was in love, and they were meant to be together. Alcine had been too polite back then, too concerned with giving the impression of a friendly and approachable ruler, to give Keri the firm refusal that was necessary to end the one-sided affair.

Sabina had taken matters into her own hands, less caring of the impending whispers and speculations than her cousin. While her voice was never raised and her manner never became threatening, it was made perfectly clear to Keri that she was to keep her intended affections far from Alcine. Since then, she had toned down her affections, but still acted as if every new man to enter the village was a potential love-match, like a bored cat deciding which mouse to pounce upon and play with before spitting out.

Why wouldn't she think that Darian is attractive? She tried to reason with herself. *He is attractive. They have no way of knowing about his past, or about the ghosts that lurk in his mind. Those women just see the outside and want to touch those beautiful muscles. They would run screaming if they knew how many people he had killed, or how he had grown up. They wouldn't know how deeply his oaths of fidelity and honesty run. To them, he is just a handsome man to be conquered and paraded on their arm.*

Rafael's eyebrow lifted in curiosity at her expression. "Hey, Seb. We were just talking about your next visit to court. Mother said Nyssa wanted you back for the Heart's Festival."

"Wonderful," she muttered in response. Sabina had planned carefully to miss the Heart's Festival that was celebrated by the court. While she understood the history of the day, a chance to send anonymous tokens of affection in a time when love was punished, it had since deteriorated. Now, the day served as a chance for the unwed men of the court to pen verses, often vulgar, and inundate unwed females with their unwanted affections. As a child of the royal family and second-in-line to the throne, Sabina had her fill of false affections daily, and did not see the need for any additional excuses for it to be thrust upon her without recourse.

Keri leaned back on her arms to elongate her flat stomach and purred. "I don't see why you have to be negative. It sounds like a wonderful tradition. Perhaps we should start it here? I can already think of someone who would get my token of affection." She blinked coquettishly at Darian as her full lips pulled into a sexy-shy smile.

This time, Sabina could not help but roll her eyes, resulting in an ill-concealed snort from Rafael. Darian simply raised his eyebrow their direction, but smiled politely back at Keri before turning back to Alcine.

"Alcine, can you explain to me again about the caste system of court?" Darian glanced at Sabina briefly before fixing his attention onto her cousin.

"Of course," Alcine answered.

Gia sighed in tedium at the turn in conversation and motioned for Sabina to follow her to the deeper end of the pool, far enough away from the group to have a private conversation.

"Seb, you know I love you like a sister, right?"

Sabina lightly ran her hands through the water, making small waves around her body. "Uh-oh, what is it?"

Gia took a quick breath. "The thing is, I don't want you to get hurt." She paused and shook her head. "Okay, you know I'm bad at subtlety and nuances. Seb, in less than a week you and your male escorts will be going to court for an undetermined amount of time."

"My escorts?" she questioned.

"Yes." Gia ticked off a finger as she said each name. "Alcine, because he has to be there, Raf, because he is a sadist who enjoys watching the drama, and Darian as an extra guard. Alcine and Raf told him about how," she paused, searching for the correct word and coming up blank, "hectic the Heart's Day can become and they all agreed you might need someone to watch over you."

She sensed where this was going and glanced at the group. "But Eric will be staying."

"Yeah, Eric will be staying. He hasn't said why, but he was adamant about not going to the court. Almost to the point where we thought he would bolt. I'm just," she halted again.

Sabina gave her a tentative smile. "I know. Eric and I will talk before I leave and figure out what is going on. Both Yas and I are the kind to find a person to love and not share, and I do not want to lose her friendship over this. There is too much potential for hurt on both sides if we don't draw the line."

They drifted back to the group and Sabina was aware that Darian's stoic face had turned to watch their progress. His dark hair had begun to grow during his time in the realm and was several inches long. As if he read her thoughts, his hand ran through the hair, ruffling the thick mass of waves.

Darian glanced at Alcine. "Remind me to use your shears before we leave for the court. It would be unseemly for me to appear before your mother, the queen, in this state."

Keri smiled and spoke sweetly. "I could do that for you, Darian. Just stop by my house later and I will give you what you need."

His voice was polite yet firm and he gave a slight nod at Alcine's telling look. "Thank you for the offer, Miss Keri. I have already asked Sabina to see to it, as she is fine attuned to the presentational standards in the court, but I appreciate the offer."

Sabina pasted on a smile to hide her surprise as the group turned toward her. "Oh, right. We will be sure to do that tonight."

Darian moved closer to her body, the motion sending small waves to lap against Sabina's shoulders. "If you do not object, I would like to get a closer look at your scars now that they have been cleaned and make sure that you have healed sufficiently for the journey."

Her eyes looked into his violet ones dubiously before she reluctantly nodded. She gritted her teeth when, as she stepped forward into the shallower water, the entire group also shifted. It appeared her friends were also going to observe the inspection. While she understood his refusal to do this in her home, a piece of her burned in embarrassment at the public inspection.

His touch on her ribcage was professional as he gently examined the pink flesh surrounding the stark white scar, then murmured approval at the healing. "I apologize, again, for not being able to give you a cleaner stitch. May I see your leg?"

Sabina awkwardly shifted her body so that the scar on her thigh could be seen over the water. "You did what was necessary and saved my life. There is nothing to apologize for."

"Yes, but if I did it better, you may not have had these scars at all." Darian's eyes looked troubled.

Rafael's sardonic voice floated over the pool. "I seem to recall a certain female standing next to me saying that scars are an attractive trait on a person."

Gia groaned. "Oh, please. Scars are attractive on *men* because they show their physical prowess, their ability to defend themselves and handle pain. On women," she shrugged, "they just suck."

"I respectfully disagree," Darian countered. "I think on women the scars would show the same prowess, the ability to withstand attack and persevere. They should be considered a badge of honor and heighten beauty, rather than a disadvantage."

A shrewd smile played across Gia's lips. "Really? So you would rather have a woman who is scarred, than a woman like that?" Her head gave a small nod in Keri's direction.

All three men shifted their eyes to the woman who was now moving toward them on the packed dirt floor surrounding the pool. She had a lean, supple body that swayed seductively as she moved, and her thick, long hair brushed against the waistline of her string bikini. A perfectly symmetrical face and a clear complexion caught men's attention instantly, their fascination enhanced by the unscarred, unblemished, perfectly proportioned body.

Sabina had never felt more self-conscious as she did that moment. While she always thought herself attractive, she had ample hips and was more muscular than lean. Her days were spent working hard and her skin bore the marks of that life, small scars or bruises on her arms and legs, her movements purposeful, instead of seductive.

The combined stare of three male eyes swung back to her body and she had to forcibly resist cringing under the scrutiny. Alcine looked amused, Rafael's lips kept twitching, and Darian's face held no expression at all.

Finally, Darian broke the thread of tension pulling between them. "My original statement stands. Sabina, please let me know when it would be convenient for you to assist me in becoming presentable for the court."

She nodded mutely as he walked out of the pool.

"He's a unique one," Gia kept her eyes on Darian until the curtain closed to the changing room closed behind him.

"That he is, Gia. That he is."

Chapter 29

Asimina

"Eric, may I speak with you?" Sabina quietly approached Alcine's hut, where Eric stood leaning against a support post and staring into space.

Eric gave her a tentative smile and moved away from the pole, taking one step toward her. "Sure, what's up?"

She forced herself to stare into his striking blue eyes and not hesitate, not give herself time to cave and walk away. "We need to talk about us. Do you still have the feelings for me that you confessed before I left?"

His smile faltered and he softly put his hand on her back as he led her away from the hut. He knew that Darian and Alcine were inside preparing for the upcoming trip back to the court and did not want them to emerge and interfere with the conversation he had been dreading ever since Alcine reminded him of Sabina's return.

"Sabina, I do. I missed you so much while you were gone. For weeks I dreamed about the feel of your body pressed against mine that day in the pool." He flushed as he remembered that moment. "My heart still beats wildly when you are close, and part of me wonders what a future with you would be like."

212

"But," she prompted, as she saw the way he averted his eyes from her gaze.

"I do feel these things for you, but I don't know if I can be what you need. I can't go to the court, and I dislike frequent travel. You are so beautiful, and strong, and courageous, and need someone who can match you, step for step, in those traits."

Her fingers quivered as she rested her hand on his shoulders, tracing his scars as if she could see them through the thick shirt covering his skin. "You are all of those traits, as well. To survive what you did, you must have been extremely strong and courageous."

"No, another person was the courageous one. I was just a stubborn coward who should have died." His skin crawled under her touch, a faint memory floating to the surface of a cat-like creature sitting on his shoulder, razor-sharp claws shredding his flesh.

Sabina began to respond, but saw Eric's eyes light up as they shifted to the side, filling with deep wanting and affection. She followed his gaze, unsurprised to see Yasmina walking up the path from the river, water jug balanced carefully upon her head. Yasmina gave one longing glance at the couple before quickly diverting her eyes and hurrying forward.

"Now I see." Sabina kept her voice understanding, though her mouth had gone dry and her stomach tightened.

Still, he flinched and ran his hand through his hair nervously. "Seb, when I moved into her house it was truly with the only intent of helping her through a tough time. But then," his voice trailed off as Sabina held up her hand.

"Stop. I understand and it's okay. It happens. We'll still be friends." Sabina gave him a quick embrace as she blinked back a tear of rejection, trying to find the strength to not let her emotions run away with her words. "Be good to her, okay? She's one in a million and deserves the best."

She ran after Yasmina on the path, leg only aching slightly with the movement, nothing more than a nuisance. After just a few seconds she caught up to Yasmina, placed a gentle hand on her shoulder, and turned her back toward Eric.

~ * ~ * ~

Yasmina approached him hesitantly, clutching the water jug to her chest to hide her quaking body. "Sabina said you needed to speak with me?"

Eric felt his mouth go dry and swallowed hard. "Yas, I'm sorry. I made a horrible mistake when I moved out of your home. Somehow I didn't realize ..."

"It was to be expected. Everyone was aware the arrangement was for convenience only. I should not have forgotten that you were already spoken for and it was just a matter of time until the arrangement would change. It was my fault entirely, I apologize for being presumptuous." Her voice was steady, though her body continued to quiver and her eyes were bright with unspoken emotion.

"It's true that I did have feelings for Sabina," he admitted, his eyes steady upon Yasmina's face, his heart heavy at the doubt and sadness she reflected. "Then, I met you. Together we worked to build a good home, a solid home, for Asli and we developed a shared trust. I don't want to walk away from you two. I can't walk away now."

Yasmina set down the jug with a heavy thud and filled her lungs with the chill air. "I will speak frankly, Eric. I am not a woman to wait around for a man to decide what he wants. If you want to pursue a relationship with Sabina, I will not stand in your way. If you want to move back in with me," her voice wavered before growing firm once again. "If you want to move back in with me, I need ... for you ..." She dropped her gaze as her voice cracked, unable to continue without bursting into sobs.

He reached out his hand and lightly caressed her cheek, encouraging her to meet his gaze. "Yasmina, I chose you. Sometime over the past few months I have fallen in love with you. I want to be there to help you through all things, if you will forgive me for this small confusion."

She nodded curtly, and he swept her into his arms as tears of relief and joy trailed down her cheeks. Yasmina sniffed and shyly wrapped her arms around his waist.

"I have not been held like this since my husband."

Eric kissed her forehead. "I know, sweetheart. I will never seek to replace Asli's father, but only wish to offer you, and her, a chance to be loved once again. I choose you, always and forevermore."

Chapter 30

Asimina

"You should not be out here by yourself. It is not safe."

Sabina turned her head slightly in the darkness as she felt, rather than saw, Darian sit down on the log beside her.

"I couldn't sleep and didn't want to wake up Raf."

It was the dead of night, and the moon had just crossed its halfway point in the journey across the heavens. Sabina had used its light bouncing off the dusting of snow to guide her way to the edge of the water. The river surface was still and quiet, its movement slowed by the thin layer of ice that remained across the wide expanse of water. Several smoothed logs had been dragged over by enterprising children at the beginning of the winter to provide a seating area for adults to watch them while they slid and ran across the ice.

Darian shifted, the movement causing his knee to rest against Sabina's leg. "I saw that Eric moved into Yasmina's dwelling. I was told he moved out after we arrived, and I was under the impression it was because he was courting you. "

Sabina blinked back a tear. "So was I," she murmured quietly. "But it was a good decision for him to move in with Yasmina to help her in my absence."

"Is it customary for an unwed man to move in with an unwed woman here?" Darian's voice was carefully guarded, unsure if the question would cause offense.

A white puffy cloud rose in the air as Sabina let out breathy laugh. "Customary? No, but it does happen. Mostly the women object to the arrangement, unless they have a great need for the help or are attracted to the man enough to want him around all the time. Our houses are our sanctuaries and our places of safety. Most women do need a man to help provide food, safety, or manual labor, but the house is still considered ours."

Darian's eyes twinkled and he cleared his throat before softly asking, "When you offered for me to stay in your hut, was it out of need or attraction?"

Sabina felt a warm flush rise on her face and stood up rapidly, too full of contradictory emotions to remain calm or stationary. "I was just trying to be nice, okay? I didn't want you to feel like I abandoned you after you had done so much for me, and thought since you had been so content to be in my presence in Kylassame you wouldn't mind. Just forget I ever said that, okay? It was nothing."

He rapidly stood and gently grabbed her shoulders, halting her retreat. "Sabina, I am sorry. That was intended as a joke. I am afraid I am not very good at making them."

A low sigh sounded in the still night as Sabina rubbed her forehead. "No, I am sorry. I am not in the best of moods at the moment." She allowed Darian to sit her back on the log and leaned against his solid shoulder. While her wounds had healed and the time

217

of food and rest had greatly improved her condition, she still tired easily and had difficulty sleeping at night. Added to the emotional pulls she felt over the last day, and the anxiety of returning to court, Sabina felt as if she had no energy left to give.

Darian held himself very still as she closed her eyes. "Eric confided in me that you two had a past. I am surprised he would cause you this much dishonor by moving in with another woman after asking me to limit my contact with you. I had thought him better than that. He did not seem like a man who would intentional cause emotional distress to people he supposedly cared about."

Sabina frowned as she thought about the myriad implications of that statement. "Yes and no. I mean, we kissed once or twice, and I did have feelings for him, but I barely had time to get to know him before we left for court, and later for Kylassame."

She sniffed and hastily wiped at the tears that had begun to silently fall from her eyes. "It's kind of funny, really. My whole life I've been so careful to keep my feelings and my actions in check. I'm a princess of the realm, and had only ever been kissed once before Eric came to our world."

A sharp laugh rang through the night as she continued. "Then here comes this total stranger, babbling about how he needs to find a woman, his long-time love, who wasn't me by the way, and I just fall into his arms like a love-starved puppy."

They sat for some time in silence as Sabina mulled over her feelings. "The strangest part though," she finally said, "is that I'm not as upset as I feel I should be. I feel sad for a future that may never be, but not for any actual, immediate events. It's mostly just stung pride mixed with a bit of self-pity, but not heartache. I would have thought it should hurt more to lose at love."

"Perhaps, you have already matured beyond the woman who kissed him." Sabina rolled her eyes and started to stand as Darian continued. "No, hear me out." He gently placed a hand on her arm. "Sabina, when I first met you, you were a formidable woman who had seen much of people's suffering, but was still relatively naïve when it came to personal matters. I suspect that have always held yourself apart from altercations, or fully investing yourself into another person's emotions and life. That is not intended to be negative, for you are a princess, and must hold yourself apart from the emotions of all who rely on you if you ever wish to stay sane. Then, you heard about the atrocities committed to those children at the camp, the horror of what man can do to the innocent and defenseless. You saw the worse part of my nature come out in Kylassame when I attacked the," he stopped and bit back the words. "When I attacked Philip," he amended.

His bare fingers gently touched where he knew the scar was forever imprinted on her thigh. "And, you realized just how vulnerable you are, and how frightening life can truly be. You have grown. It is hard for a couple to grow equally under conditions like that, perhaps impossible. Add to it that Eric found another who truly needed his help, and was able to fully receive his aid, and you have the perfect opportunity for two hearts to move away from one another."

"I never thought of it that way." Sabina wiped the last tear and gave a small smile. "It makes me sound much less pathetic when you put it like that."

"Oh, Seb," he said, voice filled with absolute sincerity. "There are many things a person could say to describe your character, but pathetic would never be one."

That brought out a small, hiccupping chuckle and Sabina stood up gingerly, legs stiffened by the cold night air. "Why don't you tell me some as we walk back?"

Darian held out an arm for support as they walked together on the pathway. "Well, there is kind, generous, courageous and perceptive." He glanced at her and gave a conspiratorial wink. "And stubborn, definitely stubborn."

She rolled her eyes but could not help the smile from forming on her lips. "Flatterer."

Chapter 31

Asimina

It was just past noon when the party from Kylassame arrived in Asimina. Rowan, Rhea and Henri dismounted stiffly and took a moment to stretch their legs. The journey from Kylassame had not been overly difficult in the cold yet sunny day, but Rowan and Rhea were no longer in their youths and their bodies were impacted by traveling very differently than their younger companions. Furthering the issue were Henri's pleas for a faster pace the entire trip, as the man was eager to return to Asimina, and Gia.

"Mother!" Sabina ran to her Rhea and embraced her tightly. When she pulled back it was to see tears in Rhea's eyes.

"I was so worried," Rhea said. "Alcine sent a message that you had been trapped in that storm and had arrived injured." She pulled her daughter into a tight embrace again out a need to reassure herself that Sabina was alright.

"I know, Mom. But I'm okay," Sabina began to defend herself.

"And your father was furious with you for leaving with the stranger. Sweetheart, we all liked Darian, but you hardly knew the man and then you were attacked and had no one to protect you because you left without any warning."

"I know, Mom, and I'm sorry. The situation warranted that we left abruptly and without telling Dad. I will explain everything and you will understand. I'm sorry that it caused you pain. I was lucky I had Darian with me though, he is the one who saved me from the Oprimata who tried to kill me."

Her mother wiped away tears with the back of her hand and smiled. "Enough grim news. Tell me about this man, the one who gives you butterflies. Can I officially meet him, now that he is healed and no longer in shock?"

Sabina fingered the hem of her shirt and cleared her throat. "Um, well, actually no. We have gone our separate ways but I'm okay. It was for the best." She nodded vehemently to reassure herself.

Rowan approached then, his green eyes concerned. "That is troubling. While I did not approve of the man's affections for you, I had hoped that he would be willing to ride with us as an extra layer of defense for a brief time before returning to Asimina."

She looked up at him in surprise. "Do I need that much protection? It's just court."

Steady eyes looked down at her. "Darling, the court was rocked with your rescinding of the throne last time we were there. I do not fear for your safety, but rather your sanity. People will be trying even harder to vie for your attention now. There will likely also be a concentrated effort to see if a wedge can be driven between our families now that there is a potential division."

"Begging your pardon, but I caught the tail end of the conversation." Alcine's voice was a welcome addition and brought a rush of relief to Sabina. He stopped and clasped Rowan's hand respectfully. "Darian and I agree that, while introduced as a peer to the realm-born Patrons, his main responsibility will be to deflect unwanted attention from Sabina. He has the attitude and the physical ability to keep her from harm, as well as not having the concern of being drawn into any court disputes."

"Absolutely not." Rowan's voice was like ice. "Perhaps you do not know the manner in which this man left Kylassame, but I forbid him to be alone with my daughter."

Alcine straightened his shoulders, muscles tense as he became alert and wary of his uncle. Rowan rarely showed his temper but when he did, it was unwise to be on the opposite end of the dispute. "I am well aware of the details, Uncle. Sabina and Darian both gave me an independent accounting of their departure and the events leading up to their arrival in Asimina. They also gave me great detail about their time in the mountains, after Darian saved Sabina's life. After that, I fully trust him to behave accordingly in Sabina's presence."

He continued with a sideways glance of apology to Sabina. "When they first arrived, my mindset was that of your own, sir. To that effect I made sure that Rafael was assigned to protect and aid Sabina as she healed and kept Darian close to myself. During that time I was able to get an unemotional appraisal of his character and found it admirable. His conduct has been nothing but respectful and he holds his commitment to honor above all personal wanting."

Sabina puffed out a breath as she bit down the temper that rose from knowing Alcine had questioned Darian to such a degree. Aware that her father was carefully watching her reaction, she forced a smile upon her face. "See? So now are we good to go?"

Rowan nodded reluctantly and moved his attention back to Alcine. "When will you be ready to leave for the court?"

"As soon as we saddle the horses, sir. We are already fully packed and it will only take a moment."

~ * ~ * ~

Darian rode adjacent to Sabina on the path, his horse instinctively timing its steps in sync with Sabina's gelding. She had been sullen and silent since they left Asimina, in sharp contrast to Rhea and Rafael chattering away down the line of riders. The entire group moved at an easy trot, their horses at ease on the road between Asimina and the court, and the weather perfect for late-winter travel.

"Sabina, did I do something to upset you?" Darian asked quietly.

"No," she replied curtly, her mount skittering on the path as it channeled her tension.

"Are you sure? You have not said five words since we left Asimina, which is rare for you. I would like to fix the problem, if I am the cause." He risked a glance in her direction, surprised at the anger clouding her face.

Sabina bit her lip sharply before turning and looking at him. "Were you aware that Alcine was purposefully keeping you away from me?" Her hazel eyes flashed in resentment and her fingers flexed on the reins, needing an outlet for her energy.

"Yes. I was aware of that," he replied.

"And it didn't offend you?" Her voice was husky with shock and exasperation. Rafael coughed from his position behind the couple and she fixed him with a glare until he shrugged and continued gossiping with her mother.

Darian rested a hand on his thigh and picked his words carefully, aware that her temper danced on a knife's edge. "Sabina, I am a stranger here. You are a princess of the realm and beloved by very many people. You had been attacked, injured, and missing, and I am the one constant variable to all of those events. It was only in your best interest that I was kept away from you until Alcine could get a measure of my character."

"And you were okay with this?" She forced her fingers to loosen from their fisted grip in her horse's mane and focused on not grinding her teeth together.

"No," he replied frankly, violet eyes becoming shadowed. "It alarmed me to be away from you, especially when you required assistance, but there was the most prudent option and I do not regret my compliance. Once you were well, I stayed away at Eric's request." Darian looked at her and his eyes softened. "That action, I do regret, given how it ended. I cannot help but to wonder if I could have spared you some of the pain had I not allowed his actions to confuse your emotions."

"He is better off with Yasmina, anyway." Sabina stroked her gelding's neck with one hand while holding the reins in her other. "He was right. It is nearly impossible for a relationship to survive when one member is constantly bouncing around a realm. That's no life for anyone, and why I'm better off alone."

"Perhaps. That is certainly one way to view the situation."

Sabina glanced over at the odd tone to his voice, as if he were on the verge of disagreeing with her statement. "Is Alcine what you expected?" she asked, purposefully changing the subject.

A reserved grin brightened Darian's somber features at the question. "Yes and no. I look at him and I can very much see his father, even though he was raised by another. He shares his father's dying conviction for truth, justice, and working toward the common good. He is a formidable man who would have easily earned his markings, had he grown up in Zajed Seganu."

She looked forward on the path and stared a moment at her cousin's back. Alcine had chosen to ride at the head of the party, eager to utilize the hours of travel by discussing strategy and politics with her father. Sabina also firmly suspected he was still arguing for Darian to be allowed to remain at her side, as the pair kept turning in their saddles to watch her and Darian's progress along the path.

"He would have died there, though." The sobering thought popped into her head. "Did you know his father well?"

"Oh, yes," answered Darian. "He was the mentor of my mentor, and one of the greatest Saverlen that lived. I was sixteen when he was executed, and had spent many years in the same camp, learning under his guidance."

His features darkened momentarily at the memories. "I think he knew that something was going to happen when we returned home that last time. A few days prior, he ordered all of us who were not yet adult men, at least in years, to remain in the woods while they entered the village. We were under strict orders not to enter the village for any reason, but instead to flee if anything abnormal happened."

A quick glance from Sabina confirmed that the stoic, unshakable man was fighting tears. His jawbone clenched and unclenched and he swallowed several times before continuing. "We had argued with him when he told us to remain behind. We were young and brave and sure of our fighting prowess. I had approached

226

him that night, asked him why we were to stay behind. I argued that it was dishonorable, cowardly even, for us to not enter the village with the others. I told him, if something dire was to occur, he would need us even more. If we were to die, then we would die, but we would do it with honor instead of living in shame."

Their horses slowed their pace slightly, giving Darian time to wrestle his memories as the outer villas around the castle came into view. Sabina noticed that his words took on an accent when he became upset and spoke quietly, aware of the tension. "But you stayed away?"

"Yes. He told us we would be needed to guide people along the path to justice and peace. Sir Arden said that if all those who could protect the innocent were killed, there would be nothing but corruption to fill our steps. It was better for us to survive, even if it meant assimilating into their culture and following their rules."

Sabina felt her eyebrows furrow. "At some point you would have to take off your shirt though. Wouldn't that ruin the entire plan?"

"Yes," Darian replied as his shoulders stiffened and his purple eyes looked far beyond the horizon. "Those of our number who had not yet earned the markings melted back into the village the night before the senior Saverlen were captured. They were brave, and allowed themselves to be stripped and branded with the mark of the Oprimata. It was difficult for them to swear allegiance and obedience to the enemy, but we all knew that was the only way for our kind to survive."

"The rest of us disappeared into the woods. It was only a short time before the Oprimata went hunting. For years I slept in the trees, or under brush, as I dodged their footsteps and aided their victims. One day, three cornered me in the forest and in my flight, I arrived

227

here. I do not know what happened to the other Saverlen who stayed behind."

Sabina let the clip-clop sound from the horse's hooves fill the moment of silence after his story abruptly finished. The castle walls rose on the horizon as they crested a rolling hill and drew closer to their destination. She tipped her head to feel the warm sunlight on her face, then sighed and pulled the purple veil up to cover her head.

"It is still customary for women to cover the head while in court," she explained as Darian gave her a quizzical look. Sabina thought another moment, and then glanced at the man who rode beside her. "I think you should spend some time with my aunt."

"The queen?" he confirmed.

"Yes, the queen." Sabina thought about her aunt's life before she became queen. "When her father was the king of the realm, he did some truly horrible things. She had to go along with it, had to live with the actions, because if she didn't, there would be no one to change things for the future. If anyone here could understand you, and offer a way to let you forgive yourself, it would be her."

Darian gave her a tentative, quick smile. "I think your aunt and I may be able to understand one another then. Yes, if you would request the audience, I would be honored to speak with the queen."

Chapter 32

The Court

The sky was settling into a blanket of stars by the time Sabina was able to slip out of the castle proper and enter the stables. Nyssa had become fond of Darian immediately, and requested his presence after dinner so that she could hear more about Alcine's birth father and heritage. The queen had met Alcine's mother, Mairi, during her brief stay in the realm and confessed that hearing more about Alcine's parents brought up bitter sweet emotions, but she felt she owed it to Mairi to know about Alcine's heritage.

Their return to the court had been as difficult as Sabina had anticipated, and, though they had only been in the castle long enough to attend dinner, she already felt emotionally drained. Her relinquishing the crown to Josef had caused a large ripple in the small pond of the Patron's lives, and they felt the need to thrash amid the waves rather than let them become still waters.

Half of the people were requesting private meetings with Sabina so that they could sway her mind, and return her as the immediate heir to the throne. While the older population still held deep discriminations against her father and were elated that his daughter would not inherit the throne, the younger population railed against the decision. Those of an age with Sabina had spent their entire lives carefully conducting their interactions with Sabina to curry her favor since Alcine was impenetrable.

Now, they were faced with the choice that would determine their future. Some had immediately moved their attentions to Josef, attempting to convince the teenager that their affections were genuine and not superficial. Most still remained with Sabina, certain that she would come to her senses and reclaim the crown as the rightful heir.

A small sect declared that the entire debacle was proof that the lineage was fabricated by Nyssa and Rowan to remove power from select patrons. Sabina and Alcine had been astonished to hear, upon arrival, that this group was pushing for Rafael to be acknowledged as the legitimate heir to the throne.

"Why Raf?" Sabina wondered aloud as she slowly moved through the center aisle of the stable. Covered glass lanterns were secured at regular intervals along the wall to provide light in the dim building, and she smiled as one lantern illuminated the lanky figure of Bryan, leaning against the wall.

"Why Raf?" he repeated as he pushed off from the wall and moved toward Sabina.

She immediately let herself be folded into his arms and took a deep breath, the comforting scent of horses and hay releasing some of the tension in her shoulders. "Yes. I was just informed that there was a group who want Rafael to be declared heir to the throne. I cannot understand where that claim would have even originated. If Alcine, as the adopted son of the queen herself, has no claim to the throne, then Rafael would not even be at the end of the line. His mother may be as close to the queen as a sister, but has no blood relation to royalty."

Bryan pulled back and looked into Sabina's face uncomfortably. "How much do you know about Lord Rafael's heritage?"

"Not much, I will admit. We only know that for the last twenty or so years he has been mocked for his heritage and for not knowing the identity of his sire. Why would it be brought up as a good thing now?"

"Well," he said hesitantly. "It would seem that some information has surfaced about Rafael's father. It has been told that his sire was the High Prince Mateo, who was the true heir to the throne."

Sabina stumbled backward out of shock. "The High Prince? He was stripped from his title though, accused of deception, and the man disappeared shortly before the king's death. Even if he did sire any children, he was not the biological son of Sula and Verikhan, and therefore his claim void. His title was only in name, and …"

"Yes, it was stripped from him, and he did disappear," Bryan admitted quietly, his eyes growing dark and his voice taking on a distant quality. "But no one truly knows what happened. How did it so conveniently happen that the man who was hand-selected by the king to be raised as the High Prince and be his heir suddenly disappeared from existence days before the throne became available? Added to that, the only people who know what truly did happen are members of the current ruling family, who, for obvious reasons, would not say if there was a conspiracy to place their own upon the throne."

A wave of anger rolled over Sabina and she took another step back. "Bryan, tell me that you are simply repeating what you heard and do not believe that." Her eyes filled with angry, astonished tears as he stared back at her wordlessly. "Bryan, that is *my family* you are

231

accusing of treason. They love this realm and would never do such a thing."

"I do not know, Seb." Bryan took a step toward her and reached for her hand, startled and disoriented when Sabina snatched it from his grasp. "I do not know what to believe anymore. We had all assumed that Alcine would inherit, or you, and then to hear that Josef was the heir," he paused and shook his head, his eyes growing warm again and his features puzzled. "Sabina, it makes us question what the truth really is about the past, and about the lineages. What did happen to the High Prince? Where does he fit in all of this? No one remembers where he came from, just that he was always the heir. What if he finds his way back one day? What then?"

A tear spilled from her hazel eyes as Sabina asked, "Then what becomes of us? You are my best friend, how could you betray me this way?"

He looked genuinely baffled and gathered Sabina into his arms once again, surprised that her body stiffened in rejection. "What does this have to do with us? You already abdicated the throne. Why would it matter who claims it in your stead? Josef or Rafael or even Katrina, what does it matter?"

She looked up at him with blazing eyes and fire in her tone. "It matters because it is my family you are speaking about, my family you are accusing of violently removing an heir to the throne without just reason."

"But … " His eyes clouded and he shook his head as if unable to finish the thought.

Realization dawned in Sabina's mind and she gently placed a hand against Bryan's stubble-covered cheek. "Who told you this, Bryan? I can tell you that I know, with absolute truth, that Rafael has no intention of ever sitting upon the throne. I can tell you that I know, with absolute truth, that Josef is what the realm needs to continue in the direction of peace and love."

His face was as still as carved stone, but a single tear dropped from his eye. His eyes twitched to stare down into her hazel ones, and she saw the answer to her question in their fear.

She wiped the tear away, and then leaned forward to whisper into his ear. "It was Cademar, was it not, who planted these ideas in your head?"

Bryan jerked his head into a nod. When he spoke, his voice was hoarse with shame. "Seb, I am so sorry. Why did I not realize that Lord Cademar would have his own intentions by convincing people of his suspicions? How could I have even thought of believing him?"

Sabina took a deep breath and rested her forehead on his shoulder, disturbed by the ease at which her friend turned, but relieved that he did not have these intentions in his heart. "Because he is a member of the elite class who has spent a lifetime learning how to convince other people to do his bidding. He is a pretty talker who has a way with words, and knows just enough of the realm's dark history to bring people to his cause. His family has also lost just enough status and power to be willing to do anything to have it restores, especially if it hurts my family in the process."

"Sabina, I'm sorry," he choked out as his arms wrapped tighter around her waist.

The sound of the stable door sliding open had them springing apart, and Bryan quickly took a protective step in front of Sabina. She hastily wiped the tears from her eyes as the tall silhouette of a man strode down the aisle. Her breath released in a long sigh of relief as she recognized Darian's figure.

"Lady Sabina? Is everything all right?" Darian stopped a few feet away from where the pair stood, Sabina's tear-streaked face shining in the torchlight.

She was taken back a moment by his appearance. He was cleanly shaven for the first time since she met him, and his face seemed sharper, more refined. His hair had been carefully combed back and he wore a fitted dark-gray doublet and well-tailored black trousers. Had she seen him this way from the start, she would have never suspected his fighting ability and suspected him as nothing more than a peer of the realm. The man would fit in perfectly with the other men his age, provided he could hide his accent.

"Yes, everything is fine now. Darian, this is Bryan, one of the lead stable hands. Bryan, this is Darian, a man from Zajed Seganu who is staying with my family." Sabina slid from her place beside Bryan to stand between the two men. She was uneasy with the way they both held their bodies, as if ready to spring at any moment's notice. Bryan was no fighter, but if he felt she were threatened he would not hesitate to try to eliminate the enemy with no regard to his own physical well-being.

Darian was the first to speak, his eyes never moving from the man in front of him, and behind Sabina. "Lady Sabina, your aunt asked me to come find you and escort you to the family room. There are some disturbing rumors that appear to be circulating through the court. She wishes to address them with all members present."

"So it would seem," Sabina murmured. "Give us a moment and I will meet you at the door."

His eyebrow raised in wordless question as his eyes shifted from Sabina to Bryan, and then Darian gave a quick nod. "I will be just outside."

Sabina felt afraid to breathe until the stable door slid shut behind him, and then whirled around to place her hand on Bryan's shoulder. "Listen to me. Something is happening, and you are going to be forced to choose a side." Her heart felt heavy as she drew the line, unsure if their easy relationship would survive. "Either you give me and my family your support, or we will be nothing more than a princess and a stable hand the next time we meet. I do not want to lose your love and friendship, Bryan, for I treasure you more than any man I have known, but my family and my duty to the realm comes first."

He leaned down and gently kissed her cheek. "I am forever loyal to you, Sabina. Whichever direction your loyalty lies is the path I will take. I shall not doubt it again."

"Good. If anyone asks, you will tell them that you were aware of this plot but considered it political gossip and desired to wait to reserve judgment. I know the way this will end, and do not want to see you hurt."

She took several deep breaths of as she walked down the aisle, grounding her spirit with the earthy smell of hay and leather, then slid open the stable door.

Chapter 33

The Court

Sabina found herself once again in the solitary, sound-proof room where the DamaTalous shared their deepest secrets and fears. She had taken her usual seat on the couch, her legs curled beneath the long skirt and knee slightly touching Katrina's hip.

The entire family was there. Nyssa and Sebast sitting on the plush couch, with Josef and Alcine perched on the cushioned arms. Rhea sat on one of the elegantly carved wooden chairs, while Rowan stood protectively at her shoulder. Sabina's brother Aaron leaned against the wall beside their father, looking more serious than he ever had prior. Katrina was curled on the couch with Sabina, surprised and frightened by her inclusion in this meeting.

Katrina was often left out of family meetings such as this one, for she had less of an understanding of propriety and covertness than her older sister. While she was never ill-intended, Katrina had a difficult time sorting out which family meetings were allowed to be discussed among her peers and which were to be held in confidence. As fifth in line for the throne, behind her father, sister, brother, and cousin, her presence was not usually required in matters of politics.

Four members of the court who were not blood members of the DamaTalous also stood in the room, quiet and shadowed. Agrafina stood with her back as straight as a rod and blue eyes swirling in silent outrage and confusion. Brokkan stood next to her, a protective arm wrapped around his wife's waist and eyes dark in silent challenge. He was a large man with black hair and brown eyes, with enough muscle to be imposing figure. Brokkan had been one of her father's best friends since they were young children, and only his respect for Rowan and Rhea kept his anger chained now.

Darian stood with his side to the door, muscular arms crossed at the waist and attention focused on the moving shapes in the hallway, hazy images of court Patrons walking by the translucent walls of clouded glass blocks. The blocks were designed to prevent any sound from carrying to the hallways beyond, but still allowed visuals of outer movement, thus creating an ideal, safe, meeting location for the royal family.

Sabina was surprised to see him there, but silently agreed that it was best to have a person not directly involved with the emotions present in the room both as a guard and potential mediator.

Rafael stood with his parents, leaning against the wall. When he caught Sabina's gaze upon his face, he winked, then sauntered across the small room to lean against her chair. "So it would seem I have my eyes upon the throne," he said nonchalantly, unaware of the explosive reaction he was prompting.

Sabina shook her head at him as she felt the tension swell in the room. "Raf, this is serious. The Patrons are saying that you have the legitimate claim for the throne, even over me, and that you are prepared to claim offense against the royal family in order to restore that status to yourself and to your mother."

Darian's voice quietly added, "And that you are prepared to remove the DamaTalous through violence, if necessary, to restore that lost status."

Rafael bowed his head to the room. "I apologize. I did not realize that these protests to raise my position to heir were being taken seriously by anyone other than the voices saying them. I am well aware of my place within the machinations of the court, and would never dream of putting myself into that position. If nothing else, it would mean spending more time within these stone walls, which is not something I ever plan on purposefully implementing."

Agrafina's face visibly relaxed at the words of her son, and the mood of the room lightened as everyone took a cleansing breath. "I have been an honorary member of this family for my entire adult life, for better and for worse. I hope you all realize that I would never, ever, work to overthrow the throne or cause strife in this court."

Nyssa looked at her lifelong friend in astonishment. "Of course, we know that, 'Fina. We only called this meeting so that all of the family members would know that the rumors were out there, and develop a unified response. We never believed you or your family had a position behind the words. You have always been like a sister to me, and I would never accuse you of such things without first asking you if such rumors were true."

Brokkan's shoulders dropped from their defensive position. "Then, I apologize for doubting this meeting's intent. We did not realize the rumors had already been dismissed and thought we would be accused of treason against our dearest friends. Are we aware of who started them and what is the course of action we shall take? Why would they even think Rafael had a claim to the throne? 'Fina may be a friend of the DamaTalous, but that hardly gives her son a claim."

"Who do you think started them?" Sabina answered without thinking.

All eyes swung to where she sat on the couch and Sabina straightened instinctively under the scrutiny. "I will not reveal my source, but one person heard the rumor that Rafael is the son of the High Prince Mateo, and rightful heir to the throne, from Cademar and his peers."

Alcine's eyes gleamed dangerously. "Does that man have nothing better to do with his time than start trouble for our family?"

Sebast's voice held no amusement as he answered his son. "It would appear not." He glanced toward Rowan. "What course of action do you suggest?"

Rowan stared at the wall as he tapped his fingers against his thigh. "How many people saw Darian arrive with our party?"

"Not many," Alcine replied.

"Darian, do you think you would be able to meld into Cademar's group for the next few days and get them to speak more of this plan?"

Darian's features gave no indication of his emotions as he nodded, though his eyes flickered momentarily to Sabina's position on the couch. "If that is what is required, it shall be done."

"I should introduce him," Rafael shifted his hip on the chair, uncomfortable with the sudden attention from the room. "That is to say, obviously I had heard these rumors, and would seek to put myself into a better place to gain the throne, if they were true. Would it not make sense for me to want more support at my back? It would be a double blow to the DamaTalous as well, a peer they recently brought to court taking the side of the opposition."

Sebast inclined his head thoughtfully and straightened his legs as he carefully though over the ploy. "Yes, I think that would work. How will Darian relay the information back to our ears without causing suspicion?"

Josef cleared his throat. "He should meet with Sabina, at night." His face momentarily flushed before he took another step toward becoming a king and swallowed his discomfort. "It would add another layer of thorns onto the betrayal. Darian meets Sabina at night in order to exchange information. If caught, and maybe they should allow themselves to be caught once for added effect, he would tell Cademar that it was exciting to be seducing a princess of the realm while working to overthrow her family."

Nyssa shook her head in disbelief as a smile grew. "My son, I do not know if I should be very proud of you right now, or very frightened by your plans for your cousin."

"When shall I begin?" Darian's voice was rough, mentally preparing to step over to the opposing faction.

"In the morning," Rhea answered in a soft voice. "Let us remain friends one last night before the world is tipped upside down."

"Where should we meet?" Sabina shifted in her seat uncomfortably.

"The arena," Agrafina's voice was harsh as her mind filled with ghosts. "You should meet in the arena. No one but Cademar and his allies would go there after dark, so it would be a likely location for you to be caught."

Darian and Sabina dipped their heads in deference, both mentally preparing for what must be done and dreading what will happen with the sunrise.

Chapter 34

The Court

The grand ballroom had been lavishly decorated by the house servants under the direction of Dezba, the ancient but expert gala planner for the court. The marble floors had been cleaned and scrubbed until they gleamed, and the multi-colored windows polished so that they sparkled. Colored candles and glittering lanterns filled the stone room with light, and beautifully carved chairs and side tables provided a place for the party-goers to rest and socialize.

Endless lengths of rich silk streamers draped from the ceilings, filling the room with the gently fluttering colors of purples and blues. They spanned the length of the room, creating a roof of billowing colored silks, and then cascaded from the rafters to form long curtains that kissed the marble below.

Sabina gasped in alarm as a hand snaked out from an invisible break in the fabric and pulled her through the curtain. Visions of her previous attack flashed through her head, and her hands balled into fists as she spun toward shadowed figure. Her eyes fluttered shut in relief as she saw Darian standing before her in the darkness, a look of concern upon his face. Sabina's hand pressed over her wildly beating heart as she slowly felt the panic fade from her blood.

"You scared me."

"I apologize. I need to speak with you and it is best not for us to be seen." He gave a curt bow, his eyes trained on the curtain behind Sabina, wary of the shadowed figures as they glided through the ballroom. Darian was dressed in finery that had been borrowed from Alcine, and the formal clothing fit well on his impressive body, drawing stares the moment he walked into the room. An ink-black vest studded with tiny blue crystals rested over a deep blue shirt, the overall effect causing him to meld into the shadows created behind the curtain. Black velvet pants had been artfully tucked into knee high leather boots, polished to a gleam and freed of any dust. His entire being reminded Sabina of the night sky, endless, dark, yet with glimmers of light from the stars above.

Sabina took another deep breath, the tight fastenings of her gown squeezing against her ribs as she drew in air. Corsets had come into fashion in the last few years and she detested the tightness around her chest and torso, though she appreciated the overall hourglass effect. Her gown was a deep, forest green, with golden geometric lines embroidered around the hem. It brushed the floor in the front, with a slight train that flowed across the floor behind her when she moved. Long sleeves made of a green lace covered her from shoulder to fingertip, and the fabric of the bodice rested so low on her chest that she found herself seeking the shadows whenever eyes drifted her way.

"You look beautiful tonight." Darian's lips twitched into a brief smile before his countenance once again became serious. "Sabina, this could be worse than we thought. Cademar was extremely happy to meet me and bend my ear to his plans, and I believe I have already convinced him of my duplicity to the throne."

She took a step closer to him, afraid of sharp ears on the other side of the thick curtain of fabric. "What do you mean? How could it be worse?"

"They do not seek to put Rafael on the throne. He is the figure which they will use to overthrow the current rule; however, Cademar seeks the throne for his own purposes. Rafael will be disposed of as soon as the DamaTalous, and their supporters, are removed from power."

There was a noise on the other side of the curtain and Sabina saw a hand slide along the fabric. Her fingers subtly waved toward the threat and her hazel eyes flashed fear as she slightly raised her voice. "This is too dangerous; you should not have taken a risk in seeing me. You know that father would never approve."

Darian's eyes darkened and his lips grew taut as he realized the threat. He moved closer and took her hands gently in his, using the contact to tug her closer to his body in case the person on the other side was watching as well as listening. "Your father does not frighten me. Soon, he will not have the power to keep us apart. It will be a brighter day for everyone."

"When?" she whispered audibly, hoping the quiver of fear in her voice sounded convincing to the eavesdropper.

"Soon enough, all it will take is the right moment and your father will never be a problem again." He gave a harsh laugh, only his eyes revealing to Sabina how the words disgusted his sense of duty.

A plan quickly formed in her head, and Sabina looked around furtively, acting as if she did not see the shadow against the curtain. "I must return." She raised her voice slightly again, giving just enough volume to allow the eavesdropper to hear her clearly. "I must see you again."

"Tomorrow night. Slip out after dinner and I will meet you in the arena." Darian gave a slight nod to indicate that he understood her plan.

"Be careful." Sabina did not have to fake the concern that twisted around her heart as she slipped out from behind the curtain and moved back toward her family.

Alcine gave her a wry smile as she moved toward him. If Darian was a figure dressed for the night shadows, Alcine was one for the light. A snow-white shirt lay under a cream-colored jacket with gold embroidery around the collar. Alabaster pants had been perfectly tailored for his physique, and his dark hair had been tamed with a bright gold ribbon.

"You were aware that another was listening to your conversation, correct?" His eyes continued looking over the crowd as Sabina stood beside him, their bodies slightly touching.

"Yes. They will be eagerly awaiting our next meeting. Tomorrow night, in the arena." She kept her face passive, giving small smiles to those who passed by without revealing the nature of the discussion.

"Be careful, Seb. Both of you." Alcine's face faltered as Irena walked toward him. "Oh, spirits help me."

Irena flounced up to the couple, her corset pulled so tightly that her chest was in danger of falling out, and her voice slightly shrill with too much wine. "Sabina, my best of friends, you must introduce me to that deliciously dark stranger you brought into our midst!"

Sabina kept the genuine surprise from her features and smiled at Irena. "Why, I have no idea of whom you speak."

The sickly sweet perfume Irena wore almost overpowered Sabina as the woman pushed between her and Alcine. "That one," she clarified, pointing to where Darian stood. "I have never seen a man so handsome, so mysterious, so intriguing."

Behind her view, Alcine rolled his eyes. "Ah, yes. He is quite the object of discussion. A man from the other world, and one who has already been granted into elite society, he is attracting quite the crowd."

The truth of that statement unsettled Sabina as she silently observed Darian. He was across the room from her, and in the center of a small group of Patrons. Cademar was there, with his current romantic interest on his arm. Caela stood next to Darian, laughing in response to his words and wrapping her thin arms around his forearm. Rafael stood on the outskirts of the group, quietly conferring with one of Cademar's friends.

"Oh, pooh!" Irena pouted. "While I was coming over here to get a proper introduction, Caela just swooped in! Perhaps Rafael would like some company."

Sabina fought to keep the smile on her face, especially when Darian's eyes glanced up from Cademar to meet hers across the room. Caela had moved closer to Darian, her bare shoulders brushing against his chest. She laughed again, lifted a hand, and suggestively caressed the blond curls on her shoulder before brushing her fingers against his chest.

Heat coursed through her body at the sight and Sabina felt her muscles tense and chest constrict. Heart pounding and head buzzing, she flexed her fingers and moved to step toward the group.

"Steady, Seb. It is just a game." Alcine nodded politely as Cademar's eyes swung to where he and Sabina stood. Irena had left them to make her slightly unsteady way toward Caela and Darian, intending to introduce herself to the new man.

Flushed and confused at the strong reaction, Sabina gave Alcine a small smile before excusing herself. "I am going to get some air. I will be back for the dancing. Watch your back while I am gone."

She moved toward one of the small, open balconies at a smooth but rapid pace, needing to clear her head. Her lungs gulped in the cold air and her skin rose to form tiny goose bumps along her exposed flesh.

"I thought I saw you come out here." A hand touched her back as the male voice sounded behind her.

Sabina's body recoiled instinctively from the touch and she pushed against the balcony banister, whirling around in a fluid motion with her fingers flexed. "Brendan," she gasped. "Do not sneak up on me like that."

Brendan took two rapid steps backward and held his hands up in surrender. His hands slowly lowered and he held one out to her, his fingers lightly enfolding hers into a firm grip. "I apologize, Sabina. You are not usually so easy to startle. I had thought you heard me crossing the balcony."

"Yes, well. Almost getting killed tends to make you less trusting of the shadows."

"Almost getting killed?"

A curse silently went through Sabina's mind and she pasted on a smile. "It is nothing. An exaggeration only. How have you been?"

Brendan's smile did not extend to his eyes. "It has been an interesting time since you went away. Sabina, I do not wish to be the bearer of bad news or ominous tidings, but I think it is only fair that you should know." His free hand moved to her back and gently pulled her closer. "Sabina, there are events coming that put you in grave danger. If you would finally acquiesce to my request at marriage, it would keep you safe. We could move out to a village in the countryside, have a family, and live a life of leisure and peace. You would never have to worry about politics again."

Rafael's voice boomed through the night, sparing Sabina the necessary refusal. "I have found you at last!" He swaggered over to the balcony and wrapped an arm around Sabina, displacing Brendan as Sabina fought for balance. "I have been looking all over for you!" His voice was slurred and his arm gestured wildly, smacking Brendan unceremoniously in the face.

"I will speak with you later, Sabina. Please, think about the offer, and your future." Brendan gave a small bow to both Sabina and Rafael before stalking back into the room.

"You are not really this drunk, are you?" Sabina asked, then fell forward, off-balanced, as Rafael quickly straightened his posture.

"Of course not. It just seemed like the easiest way to remove his hands from your obviously unwilling body." Rafael laughed and leaned his elbows against the railing, eyes pointed toward the inner ballroom. "Seb, this is bad."

"I know, I know." Sabina pushed the heels of her hands against her eyes in an effort to release some tension. "Darian is going to meet me tomorrow and tell me more. They have no intention of placing you on the throne, you know."

247

"Oh, I am well aware," he said sardonically. "I have no intention of letting them remove the current heirs to the throne so that my neck is the next to get slit. We are going to have to move faster than originally planned though."

Rafael cursed quietly as Cademar's voice preceded his arrival. "Rafael! I see you have found Dauphine Sabina. I have a friend I would love to present to her."

Sabina felt her cheeks ache with the effort of keeping the smile on her face. "Oh? Well, then, lead on." Her skin crawled as she linked an arm through Cademar's and allowed him to escort her into the midst of his friends.

The friend was tall, over six feet in height, and had a deceptively lean build. Sabina could see the arm muscles flexing under his tightly fitting long-sleeved shirt as he gave a short bow to kiss her hand.

"I rejoice in the great honor of meeting the beautiful Dauphine. Lord Cademar has told me much about you, and I see that, at least, the reputation of your beauty is truly spoken." The man smiled at her, his grin too friendly to be genuine.

She curtsied in reply and gave a polite reply as she worked to place his strange accent.

Cademar slung an arm over the man's shoulder. "Lasarre here just came to the realm. We found him out back, wandering all alone and in need, and now he has promised his undying loyalty for rescuing him. It is a powerful thing, loyalty, don't you think?"

"Well, Lasarre," Sabina said pleasantly, ignoring the barbed question, "welcome to the court of Kaldalangra. I hope that you enjoy it here."

"I am sure that I will." His eyes were an odd color of gray, the color of dull slate. "Would it be permissible for me to call upon you tomorrow? I wish to tour the castle and Cademar informs me that you would be the best of guides."

Sabina's heart was in her throat, but she managed a quick, "Of course," before removing herself from the group.

Chapter 35

The Court

"Take Rafael."

Sabina brushed her hair with such ferocity that it fairly crackled with tension and glared at Alcine. "What good will it do to take Rafael?"

"A good amount, seeing as he can protect you." Alcine paced around her chamber as Sabina lightly fastened a long veil to her hair with small, gem studded pins.

"What exactly do you think this man is going to do?" She glanced at the mirror again, and then turned around when she saw the fear in Alcine's reflection.

"I do not know, Sabina. Who is he? Why is he here? Why is Cademar pushing him to meet you when he knows that Darian is seducing you? It just does not make sense and it scares me." He plopped down on her bed and stared at her unnervingly.

A knock at the door startled them both, a feeling that was getting to be too familiar for Sabina's emotional well-being. Her honorary-uncle, Savin, was standing in the hallway when she opened the door. Her father had requested his presence in the court after seeing the tension and hearing the plans of rebellion.

"Hello, Lady Sabina. I found this poor soul looking for you and decided to serve as an escort for you both." Savin dwarfed Lasarre in both height and build, and the man looked deeply unhappy by the older man's presence.

"Hello, Uncle. Hello, Lasarre. Where would you like to start the tour?" Sabina quickly closed the door behind her, hoping that Lasarre had not seen Alcine sitting on her bed.

Lasarre grinned, his even, white teeth gleaming. "Cademar has told me much about your sporting arena."

Sabina nodded and accepted his arm as escort. "Well, then we shall start there. It is a short walk, at least."

They moved through the castle, footsteps ominously echoing through the stony structure. Lasarre asked many questions, though Sabina gave as brief of an answer as would be polite. He was particularly interested in the history of the realm, and the reign of King Verikhan, her grandfather.

Finally, they reached the arena and Savin pushed open the thick, wooden doors.

Under the rule of King Verikhan the arena was once the scene for bloodshed and murder. The old and sickly would be abducted from Asimina and brought here to fight to the death, all for the entertainment of the patrons. Back when her mother first entered the realm, the sand of the arena would be covered in red blood.

Now, the walls were a bright white, with clean, fine sand creating a thick layer of padding below their feet. The arena was now a place for controlled contests such as horse competitions, wrestling matches, and sporting events. Tiered benches rose around the arena floor, seats for the spectators who thronged to the events. A thick canvas roof covered the benches, but did not extend completely over the center, leaving the arena floor open to the elements.

Lasarre pointed to the bench where the royal family sat for events. "That was where he sat? The King and High Prince?"

"I suppose so." Sabina shrugged, forever disquieted when speaking of her tyrannical grandfather and his false heir. "It is where the DamaTalous sit currently, so I would imagine it would have been the same back then."

He looked around curiously. "And what is that door?" He pointed at a large wooden door on the far side of the arena.

Savin answered. "That door leads to an inner chamber. It is where the contestants prepare for their events."

Lasarre looked at the door thoughtfully. "It is a great arena. Hopefully there will be an event that I can witness during my stay here. We had similar things in my old world."

"Oh?" Sabina looked up at his face in unfeigned interest, though a hard knot settled in her throat.

"Contests of strength and fighting skill, though not often in such a formal setting," he confirmed. "I may not be the biggest of the participants, but I have never lost a match." Lasarre rolled up his shirt-sleeves and pointed at a series of spirals tattooed into his arm. "The winners are marked thusly. Each spiral for a match won."

Sabina stared at his arm in sick fascination. His entire right arm was covered in the tiny, intertwined spirals, each the size of a coin. Then she fought the jolt of panic as she saw the sunbeam design on his inner wrist.

"You must have great skill." Savin's respect was clearly heard in his voice. "Perhaps you will agree to a bout one of these days?"

She felt a moment of relief as the two men began to talk about fighting moves, relief only because it distracted them sufficiently that they did not notice how pale her face had become.

Chapter 36

The Court

Silver moonlight filled the arena, casting an eerie glow over the white, sandy surface. Sabina remained motionless on the bench above the arena floor, her breathing shallow in fear that the white vapor might reveal her position. She was dressed for the darkness in a cotton dress of deep indigo, with an opaque black head-scarf dulling the moon's glow on her shining hair and pale face.

A slight wind sailed through the area and rustled the canvas above, causing silver streaks of light to dance across the arena and surrounding benches. For a moment, there was a man beside her, so close that she could see his white-blonde hair and shining eyes. His face was cleanly shaven, and the features were familiar, though she was certain she had never seen the man before. A transparent gold crown sat upon his head and he looked down at the arena floor and smiled at events only he could see. His lips alone were colored, a bloody red that stood out in stark contrast to the ethereal white of his body.

Sabina felt herself frozen in place as she realized she could see through the man, certain she was seeing the ghost of her grandfather and terrified he had come to take his final revenge upon the family. Then swishing footsteps could be heard in the arena below, and he abruptly vanished. All light was extinguished as a dark cloud passed over the moon, and Sabina felt the violent thudding of her heart as a man-shaped shadow across the arena floor, heading directly toward her.

The form stopped in the center of the arena, turning slowly as if searching. "Sabina," he called out quietly, and she relaxed slightly at Darian's voice.

"Here," she softly called back as she cautiously stood and made her way down the steps toward the arena floor.

Darian moved across the sand, his boots whispering over the surface, the quiet sound magnified by the stillness of the night. He reached the edge of the high arena wall and looked up, his naturally tanned skin blending into the darkness.

Sabina pulled her skirt close to her body and carefully sat down onto the high wall surrounding the competition area. Steady hands grasped her hips as Darian guided her careful drop from the wall and light landing on the sand below.

"You have to leave, now," she started.

"It is too dangerous for you here," he finished.

Sabina stared into his eyes a moment before glancing around furtively. "Darian, the man named Lasarre; he has the starburst marking on his wrist, the same one as Philip and the man on the mountain. I think he is the final Oprimata that you spoke about earlier. You must leave before he finds out who you are and comes after you."

A creak from the large, wooden arena doors being opened carried through the night, and Darian shifted his body to hide Sabina from view. "Sabina, they are planning on putting Rafael's position forward in just a few days. You need to get out of here, now. I dislike the way people of this court listen to Cademar's fervent, insistent stories of your family's betrayal of the High Prince and the former king."

A shadow man moved through the door and melted against the wall, only the shine of eyes under the moonlight revealing the figure as more than a trick of the light. A second shadow slid through, creeping along the wall in the other direction, every inch of the arena fully in view to the newcomers.

"Hold me," she whispered as she wrapped her arms around Darian's firm waist. "We have company, and cannot afford to end this conversation yet."

His body jerked at the sudden contact. "I do not know how to be affectionate with a woman, not enough to be convincing." Darian moved his hands awkwardly to rest on Sabina's hips, aware that they were being watched and needed to portray the image of a night-time tryst.

Subtly guiding him, Sabina moved until his arms were around her waist and his body was pressed closely to hers. As she softly spoke, she kept the shadows in her peripheral vision, careful to make sure her words did not meet their ears.

"Cademar thinks that he will rise to be king, and put Lasarre as his second-in-command." Sabina stood on her toes and tilted her head up, her lips brushing against Darian's cheek as she whispered, assurance that the words would not carry to the spying figures as they moved closer. "You need to get out of here before then. It is not safe for you, and not right that you should be in danger because of politics not of your doing. Get Alcine out of here, and live your life in Asimina."

The shadow-man moved into a different position, able to clearly see Sabina's position with Darian, unaware that his presence was known. Moonlight lit thin lips that curled into a smile at the compromising position of the Dauphine of the realm.

"I am not going to leave you and your family when I can protect and serve." Darian flexed his hands where they rested upon her hips, frustration and anger building at the danger. "Sabina, we are still being watched."

Sabina's eyes flicked to the sky as the cloud drifted away from the moon and a silver beam bathed them in light. "Gently push me backward so I'm trapped against the wall. It will put us back into shadows, though not enough that they cannot see us completely"

He did, his hand instinctively cupping the back of her head as the stucco wall pressed against her dress. "Seb, how do we ..." he trailed off, his eyes filled with uncertainty.

Impulsively she leaned forward, sliding her fingers into his thick, short hair and pulling his head toward her own. Their lips met, and Sabina gasped as a spark coursed through her body and caused the tiny hairs on her neck to stand. His hand moved to caress her hip, and she melted into their ploy of a covert affair.

Pulse racing within her chest, she could feel his heart pounding in tandem, strong and steady beneath his light jacket. His hand slid to the small of her back, involuntarily pressing his body closer to hers. Sabina murmured uncomprehending words in between kisses, her fingers flexing against his shoulder as if her body could not stand to be parted from his for one second.

Finally, they separated, their breath rasping through the night as they fought for some control, each afraid at the depth of feelings in a kiss which had started as an act. The watchers slid out of the door, the slight creak betraying the departure.

Darian tilted his head toward the sound, then looked down to where Sabina's forehead rested against his chest. He reluctantly removed his hand from her back and stepped to the side, allowing her body freedom from its position between his own and the wall.

"Darian, I'm," she began.

"Sabina, I'm," he interrupted. "You first."

She took a shaky breath, still feeling flushed and anxious over her body's immediate and unexpected reaction to his closeness. "Darian, I'm scared for what's going to happen. It's too much. There is too much at stake now."

His fingers lightly tucked a stray lock of chestnut-colored hair under her black scarf. "I know. It will be fine. Do not worry about me, only take care of yourself. Stay close to Alcine until this is over, okay?"

Sabina nodded, unable to trust her voice to answer. She rose to her tip-toes and kissed him lightly once more before walking across the sands of the arena, tears of fear and desperation raining onto the sand with each step.

Chapter 37

The Court

The low, stony wall that surrounded the roof of the northern tower bit into Sabina's hands as she leaned against the ledge. It had been two days since she last saw Darian, days filled with anxiety, restlessness, and frustration that there was nothing she could do to fix the situation. She was certain that events would be moving along very quickly, as the entire castle and its inhabitants seemed hushed and suspicious as the rumors and plots spread through the court like a plague.

She had climbed the winding staircase that led to this tower for the silence, and a moment of peace. The high ranking peers of the realm scrambled as they sought to ally themselves with the differing factions, betting their lives and reputations on which family would emerge with honor, and their lives. Brendan had become frighteningly aggressive in the pursuit of her hand in marriage, insistent that they remove themselves from court and move into the countryside immediately.

I'd rather grow old alone or die young than be with him, Sabina realized as she cupped her chin in her hand and gazed out over the castle grounds. The wares of the marketplace had been set out in the early morning, and just replenished for the afternoon crowd after

Sabina had climbed atop the tower. Shawls, dresses, veils, and shirts were all freely displayed for purchase in a staggering variety of skill and fabrics. Jewelry created of gold and gems were carefully watched by the Patron who supplied the precious materials to the crafter. Both ordinary and exotic foods were available for purchase and the vendors regularly split a fruit open so a passerby could sample the taste.

A high-pitched laugh carried up through the air, and Sabina shifted her gaze over to the far side of the market where the Patrons loved to gather for gossip. Cademar and Lasarre leaned against the wall, talking in low tones, while Caela and Irena each were standing with their slender arms wrapped around Darian's elbows. Irena had been the one to laugh, and Sabina's stomach twisted in a knot as she watched the other woman slowly slide her hand down Darian's chest as she spoke with him.

Her veil lifted with a sudden breeze, and Sabina turned her head slightly as the large body of Faulks settled beside her on the wall. "Hello, handsome. I have not seen you in a while."

Faulks regarded her gravely with his clear, golden eyes. She reached out and scratched his favorite spot, the small section on his neck where his beak had difficulty reaching. The large raptor leaned into her touch, and his eyes closing in contentment.

The moment of peace was disturbed as a creak signaled the opening of the wooden door at the top of the tower stairs. Sabina turned her head and gave a tense smile as Alcine stepped onto the roof with Josef following behind.

"You can feel it too, can you not?" Josef stood at the space to Sabina's left, while Alcine, who settled at her right, leaned forward against the wall.

She sighed and turned back to view the stables. Her small filly was growing rapidly, and it gave her a brief moment of joy to watch as Pearl galloped around the pasture on twiggy legs, her mother encouraging her along the way.

"I do not know what is worse, knowing something will happen or when it actually does."

Alcine clasped his fingers together and rested his hands on the top of the wall. "It will be over soon enough. Darian told me that Cademar is going to push the issue sometime today, probably when everyone gathers before dinner."

Sabina's breath came out in a painful shudder before she realized she had been holding it inside. "We are going to win, right?" Her voice cracked as her heart dropped with the thought of Cademar emerging victorious.

The usual sarcastic and self-assured grin rose upon Alcine's lips. "Of course, we are going to win. The only real question is what to do with Cademar after he loses."

"He should be exiled or killed for treason to the crown." Josef's voice was hard and unforgiving and Sabina felt dismay rush through her body at his rapid loss of innocence in his new role as heir.

"I agree," Alcine conferred. "Although, my personal choice would be to just take him outside the castle walls and let the cruel world tear him to pieces."

"You said Darian spoke with you?" Sabina kept her voice neutral, even though her fingers were digging painfully into the stone wall. He was still visible in the marketplace, although now he was quietly conferring with Cademar and Lasarre, the women having walked away to continue browsing the goods.

"Yes, earlier this morning." Alcine's cheek twitched. "I am surprised he did not come and see you after your meeting in the arena."

"He told you about that?" Her face began to feel hot as the red flush touched her cheeks.

Josef looked between his brother and cousin in confusion. "Why would that make you blush? It was just part of the strategy."

"No reason," she sputtered, embarrassed at her lack of composure. "I am going back downstairs. Care to join me?"

Alcine winked at Josef. "It would probably be best to move as a pack right now. Come on; let us go see what other plots have thickened."

~ * ~ * ~

The trouble began well before the dinner hour, when the Patrons of the realm gathered in the great hall to socialize and drink prior to the meal. The DamaTalous had gathered behind the long table at the far end of the room, talking in low tones. Their eyes were always watching the crowd, while their bodies conveyed none of their suspicions.

Sebast positioned himself at one end of the table, with Rowan on the opposite, and Alcine and Josef at the center with Nyssa safely tucked between her sons. Katrina and Aaron remained in their rooms, protected by the anticipated events of the evening by several trusted guards. Sabina and her mother stood at the end of the table next to

Rowan, their matching hazel eyes viewing the crowd with misgivings.

"You never told me about your meeting with Darian," Rhea casually mentioned.

"There is nothing to tell. He warned me of potential future events that we all know about and I haven't seen him since." Sabina found her eyes darting through the crowd until they rested upon Darian, where he stood next to Cademar, a clear goblet filled with red wine in his hand.

Her mother followed her eyes and tilted her head in curiosity. "Since when does Darian drink wine?"

Sabina found her heart aching as she answered, "Since he befriended Cademar. I'm starting to grow concerned that he has forgotten he is only playing a role. Mother, what did my grandfather look like?"

Rhea frowned at the sudden change in topic. "His features were like your father, but with all of the kindness and joy stripped from his soul. He had short blonde hair, blue eyes, and a tall build. Why?"

The memory of the ghost fit that description and Sabina nodded to herself in confirmation that the sighting was not just a figment of her imagination. "I saw him, that night at the arena. He looked like he was anticipating something."

Her mother visibly shuddered, then held up a hand to prevent Rowan from joining the conversation. "His ghost would continue to haunt us. He was a cruel man, Seb, who did vile, evil, unspeakable things. If his ghost returns, you run and get me or your father, understand? I do not trust him, even beyond the grave."

Rowan snapped his finger behind his back to get their attention. "Cademar and his allies are looking excited. Be sure to keep your guard up at all times."

As if on cue, Cademar and his group, with the exception of Darian, sauntered to the long table and stopped in front of Alcine. Cademar gave a malevolent grin before turning so that he faced the hallway.

"Good people of Kaldalangra! You have all heard the rumors flowing through the air of this court regarding the lineage of the throne! I am here to clarify some issues for you." He bowed once he had everyone's attention, feeling secure with Darian and Lasarre flanking his position in the room.

"My friends, I would like to introduce you to the son of the High Prince Mateo, and the rightful heir of the realm. Rafael Mateo Verikh de Kalda, come and declare your claim!"

Rafael moved forward from his position at the edge of the crowd, the cold smile on his face growing sharper as he studied the varied reactions of the crowd. "Why, thank you for the introduction, Lord Cademar." He turned to Alcine. "Why is it, Alcine, that you sit at that pretty table while I must beg for scraps? You, the adopted son of Nyssa and Sebast, born to a woman and man not of this world, a Skov in the truest sense of the word." He turned back to the crowd and flung his arms open. "That is true, people of Kaldalangra, he was not even born in this realm, yet you all opened your hearts to him, desired him, and were ready to accept him as your future king!"

Sabina felt her breath burn as it left her lungs, and tears prick her eyes at the words. *It's a game,* she reminded herself, while desperately hoping that it was still a game to those who had been entrenched on the other side for days.

Rafael turned and his finger pointed at Sabina. "And her, the precious Dauphine, princess of the realm. You all lamented and railed when she gave up the crown, but it never should have been hers to begin with. Her father was disowned by King Verikhan, who recognized him for what he truly was, filth. For years he competed with the dogs for scraps of food, until he was finally given a position as a guard to a woman from the other world. His daughter should be the lowest of the low, created by filth and a Skov, and instead, you revere her and grovel for her favor."

The punch of the words stabbed through Sabina's heart and she saw, through tear-blurred vision, her mother tightly grasping her father's hand to keep him from vaulting the table. She was more unsure than ever now if this were still simply a game of politics. Surely Rafael would have warned her father about bringing the past to light, or Sabina into the ploy. Yet, her father's rage was genuine, and there was no remorse in Rafael's black eyes.

She blinked her eyes to clear her vision and glared at the crowd, slightly reassured that most of the anger coming from the crowd was sympathetic for her, if doubtful. They milled about, giving furtive glances between Rafael and the DamaTalous, most refusing to meet the gaze of Rowan or Nyssa, who challenged the crowd with their stares.

Alcine gave a harsh laugh and raised his voice over the rumbling din. "Really, Rafael? You would bend so low as to bring Dauphine Sabina into this ploy for power? You are the bastard son of Lady Agrafina and the gods only know who else, and that is all. This rumor of you being the son of the High Prince is just that, a rumor created by vipers for the sole purpose of stirring up trouble."

"Oh?" Rafael raised his eyebrow and grinned. "Then let us prove, once and for all, who has the rightful claim to the throne. You and me, Alcine, in the arena, tonight. Let the gods of this land determine who has the rightful claim to the throne of Kaldalangra."

A jagged laugh flowed from Alcine once again. "Yes, because that would solve the issue, a duel between the bastard-born son of Lady Agrafina, and the adopted son of Queen Nyssa. Maybe you should do more research, Rafael, because last time I heard, neither one of us had as much as a sliver of claim to the throne."

Rafael gave a small nod to Alcine, invisible to the watching crowd. "If you are afraid to fight me, you can just say it."

A third time, Alcine laughed. "As angry as I may be with you right now, near-cousin, I have no intention to kill you in front of witnesses."

Cademar interjected. "While it pains me to agree with a Skov, he does have a point." His fingers rubbed against his smooth chin as if deep in thought. "Would it not be better to have Rafael duel the intended heir to the throne, Josef?"

"Absolutely not." Queen Nyssa's voice thundered across the hall, shaking the stained-glass windows and causing the chandeliers to shudder and dance on the ceiling. Her blue eyes blazed with anger and the power pouring from her body caused every person's heart to skip a beat. "This charade and false speculation will end. Now."

Cademar bowed his head to Nyssa. "My apologies, my queen, but it cannot. Perhaps I could offer another option? What if we were to have a divine contest, current heir and he who deserves the title, through proxy? After all," his face fell into a charming grin that wooed the crowd, "it would be horrible for the winner to be so badly injured that this entire contest was for naught."

Darian grinned darkly then, and the expression was so natural that Sabina felt a hot tear roll down her cheek. "Allow me to bring justice, Lord Rafael, and serve as your champion."

Rafael gave Darian a cold look. "Yes, that would be acceptable. Josef, name your proxy."

Josef began to speak but was immediately silenced by Alcine's hand upon his shoulder. Alcine gave a dangerous, feral smile as his eyes fell upon Darian, and Sabina was now certain this was no longer going by the plan.

"I shall stand for my brother. Darian, you disappoint me. I had thought a man of your character would not have thrown his dice in with this lot. We healed you, welcome you into our family, and this is how you repay the kindness?"

Darian's eyes were dark as he nodded toward Sabina. "I already received my every desire from the Dauphine in the dark of the night. Now, I throw in my lot with those who can ensure that I can have her at any time I so desire."

Sabina was shocked into silence, the pain lancing through her chest as acute as if she had been cut open and beaten once more. She began to open her mouth to deny Darian's words when Lasarre cleared his throat and drew the attention of the room.

"Lord Rafael, Lord Cademar, might I make a suggestion?"

Both men tipped their heads to Lasarre.

"It would seem to me that Darian's loyalties may be questionable. After all, he did arrive to court in the presence of the royal party, have his way with the Dauphine, and then become sympathetic to our cause." His lips rose into a dangerous smile as he focused on Darian. "It would not be a stretch, then, to assume that at some point this man will once again change allegiance. Who is to say, that he will not do so in a fight with Alcine?"

"You insult me, Lasarre. I thought we were comrades in this endeavor." Darian's voice was smooth and emotionless, though one eyebrow raised in surprise.

"At times, we are. But I am probably also correct about your fickle sense of loyalty. In any case, it is clear that many in this audience would not be pleased if Lord Alcine were killed during this contest, which is a likely possibility against a man of your violent nature."

Cademar again stroked his chin with his thumb and forefinger. "And what would you suggest as an alternative?"

"A simple solution. I shall go against Darian. The winner gets to choose the heir of the realm and walk among its people, free of retribution from those who do not appreciate his choice, for the winner will speak the words directly from the spirits."

"And the loser?" inquired a member of the crowd.

"Oh, them?" Lasarre grinned as he rolled up his shirt-sleeves, displaying his myriad of black spirals and the sunburst of the Oprimata. His shrewd eyes watched for Darian's reaction, of which there was none. "The loser will be very, very dead."

<u>Chapter 38</u>

The Court

The sun had begun to set while Sabina kneeled with her head bowed in the clearing of her mother's garden. She had come here for solace, and to steady her heart before watching two men fight to the death. The air suddenly grew freezing cold, and she began to shiver violently despite the thick wool cloak that was draped over her shoulders.

"You are strong enough to heal from this. You all are. As long as there is love and hope in your heart, the evil will be defeated."

Sabina's head jerked up and she gasped at the spectral image of a woman standing at the edge of the trees. "Who are you?"

The ghost-woman was dazzling, with glittering hazel eyes that seemed to stare through Sabina's body and expose her heart. The figure was not transparent, though her image blurred with every movement and her outline seemed to fade into the air. A thin dress of shimmering blue hung on the woman's curves, with lace and cobwebs that trailed from her sleeves, and formed a beautiful belt upon her hips. Loose curls of golden locks flowed over her shoulder, moving in the still air of the garden as if there were a breeze only felt by the ghost.

"My name is Sula." She glided forward as she spoke, until she stood just in front of Sabina. "I am your grandmother. I have been in this garden a long time, watching over my family as best I could. This has ever been a sanctuary, a garden intended only for those with goodness and love in their hearts. From here, I have seen the results that come from the very bloody actions of my husband, and, the very beautiful from the acts of my children."

Sula's hand lifted to gently wipe away the tears that had begun to fall from Sabina's eyes. "Watching you and your siblings grow has been the most beautiful of all. My son chose well when he let himself love your mother. You hold love in your heart, but it is circled by thorns. Why is that?"

"Because when I thought I found it, it slipped through my fingers and cut my heart into pieces." Sabina's eyes closed against the pain.

"Do you speak of the man who returned to our realm, or the man who speaks words of betrayal?" Her grandmother tilted her head sideways to study Sabina, eyes gentle and understanding.

"I do not know of whom you speak. Who is the man who returned to our realm? I do not know of anyone like that, much less thought to love them. Yes, my heart is hurting right now over Darian's betrayal." Sabina's voice cracked as she spoke his name. "The stupid thing is, I did not even realize how I felt until it was too late."

"That is how it happens, far too often." Sula's voice sank to a whisper as her hazel eyes drifted out of focus. "For you, however, I do not think time has run out just yet. Until his heart turns black and empties of all but despair, there is hope."

Sabina studied the woman, surprised at how fragile she looked. She had heard stories of her grandmother, mostly from her Aunt Agrafina. She had always seemed like such a strong woman, in both heart and body, and yet she was smaller than Sabina. She realized, then, that Queen Sula must have been young when she died, barely more than her own age.

Sula gave a small smile of understanding. "I do not look like a grandmother, do I?" she asked at the expression of confusing upon Sabina's face. "I was seventeen when my parents died and I became queen. I gave birth to your father when I was but your age, and died a few years after having Nyssa."

"Did you come back with Grandfather?"

The former queen tilted her head once again and delicately furrowed her brow. "No. Did you see him recently?"

"In the arena, just a few nights ago."

"Ah." The look of understanding fell upon her features and her lips turned upward. "It would appear there are more forces at work here than we suspected."

Sula's focus was suddenly shifted, and she looked through the dense tree-line a moment before resting her slight hands on Sabina's shoulders. "Have faith in love, and trust your heart. I am so proud of you, my brave granddaughter."

Her image abruptly disappeared as quick footsteps were heard on the path behind Sabina. The air suddenly warmed and Sabina scrambled to her feet, turning to face the path.

Darian stepped out of the tree-line, his movements stiff and unsure. "Seb, I have been searching everywhere for you."

271

"So you can have your way with me? I don't see why you bothered. I want nothing to do with you, Darian, nothing." She strode over to the pathway, intending to stalk by the man who had filled her heart with a sense of security and then ripped it in two.

As she stepped beside him, Darian's arms reached out and encircled her body, pinning her own arms tightly. "Sabina, please tell me that you knew it was part of the game. I would never willingly betray Alcine, or you. Everything changed since last we spoke, with the game, with the plan, with us. It has all gone into chaos and I am doing all I can to put it back into rightful order."

Sabina forced herself to look up into his eyes, surprised to see they were filled with regret and pain. She broke the contact, staring at the ground as she swallowed her anger. "I don't know what to trust anymore. Why would you say those things about me? Why would you offer to kill my cousin? Is the game worth the pain that you inflicted upon me in front of the realm?"

He flinched at her words and loosened his grip, allowing Sabina to take a step back. "I said those things because Cademar was starting to suspect my motives. It devastated me to say all of that, and I deeply regret that I was not able to tell you, or Alcine, the plan. It changed after I spoke with Alcine, and Cademar was suspicious enough to keep me in his sights at all times."

She balled her fist. "Why did you offer to kill Alcine, then?"

His eyes grew wide with shock. "I would never kill Alcine! He is the son of Arden, and I owe him undying loyalty as long as there is breath in my body. I offered to take place in the fight for that exact reason. It was my intent to either let him win, as long as he would not kill me, or to accept his surrender. At that point I would name Josef as the rightful heir and say that your gods spoke through me."

"Why did you seek me out now then and take the chance of being seen? Why not just play out the game that you began?" Sabina's voice fell to a whisper, her mind still jumping from belief to suspicion and her stomach twisting in painful knots.

He gently wrapped his arms around her body and drew her toward him. His head grew heavy as his cheek pressed against her soft hair, and a tear fell onto her shoulder. "Because I have tangled with Lasarre in the past, and I am not certain I will win. Sabina, you know my past, and my inability to allow my heart to be open for love. Yet, it hurt worse than any wound I have taken when I saw your pain in the hall. My heart felt as if it had been crushed to see you holding back tears, and it was as if someone had stabbed me through the gut. I do not know if I can love without caution, or give you all that you need, but I know that I am not the same man who first came into this realm. Because of you, I am more, and I want a chance to see if that more is enough to pursue a lifetime with you. I wanted to make sure that, in the event I lose this fight, you knew the truth of my heart. I did not want to die with you thinking I had betrayed you. I did not want to die without you knowing how I felt about ..."

Sabina tilted her head until her lips found his, silencing him with the action. Their tears fell hot upon their faces as they kissed, hope bursting through her body. "Tell me that again when this is over, because you have changed me as well, and I do not want to know who I will become if you die."

~ * ~ * ~

Deep within the stones of Steinbrekka, the Gormellyn stirred. His beady eyes snapped open and he yawned, his long, black muzzle opening wide and blood-red tongue flicking out to taste the air. His back arched in a feline stretch as he rose on all four limbs, muscles stiffened after the long repose. A purr of contentment turned into a low grown as he lifted his paws to the side of his den and extended his claws, the razor-sharp talons screeching as they scraped thin lines in the hard stone.

The lair was not large, just big enough for a medium-sized dog or large cat. This was the den where the Gormellyn slept in eternal peace, only awoken during times of great need. The last time his long slumber had been disturbed was when the foolish High Prince Mateo had answered the summoning of Steinbrekka, the call to power that was released for Lord Rowan to claim twenty-three long years ago.

Foolish, High Prince. Foolish, King Verikhan. The creature stretched once again, ancient bones cracking and shifting until he was able to move in a sinewy, snake-like smoothness once again. He could still taste the blood of the High Prince on his tongue, and the fear and rebellion of Verikhan lingered in his finely tuned nostrils. For this immortal being, the events of the past decades were as clear as if they had just occurred, and he momentarily lost himself in the deep betrayal of the past king.

Then, his head turned from side to side as his tongue once again darted into the air, seeking that which pulled him from his two-decade-long slumber. His eyes narrowed down to nearly invisible slits and he hissed, steam rising into the frigid air of the cave.

Foolish, foolish, two-faced human. You should have never come to this realm. Now you shall suffer.

Chapter 39

The Court

She should have felt safe, surrounded by her family, with her father before her and her mother to her right. Yet Sabina felt her very soul shaking in fear as she took her accustomed seat in the section of the arena reserved for the DamaTalous. Her breath refused to come easily, and she felt light-headed and clammy, afraid that her entire life would unravel over the course of the next few minutes.

Queen Nyssa was there as well, seated one bench to the side with her husband and children. Rowan had sent Aaron away during the dead of night and the teenager should have arrived safely in Asimina long ago. Aaron had orders to keep riding to Kylassame, and stay there until he received word of the day's events. None of the court would even notice his absence, as he routinely stayed away throughout the year.

Katrina sat next to their father, her face even paler than usual and eyes red from terror-induced tears. Her friends had been forbidden to speak with her until this drama played out, and for Katrina the feel of being a pariah had been nigh unbearable.

Sabina placed a hand on her sister's shoulder and leaned forward to whisper, "We are strong. We will rise. We are the rightful children of this realm and we will not lose our place to lies and manipulations."

"Pretty speech." The unfamiliar male voice whispered from the empty seat to her left.

She looked over quickly and jumped in her seat, grateful that her family's attention had been transferred to the arena as Lasarre and Darian walked through the wide doors.

A man sat beside her, a figure in full color, but Sabina could see the outline of the wooden bench upon which he sat. There was no crown upon his head today, but his self-assurance, even in death, gave no doubt as to the identity of the man sitting beside her.

Blue eyes looked down at her and a chilling smile played across his crimson lips. "Blood will flow today. I can smell it. It has been a long time since a fight to the death occurred in this arena. Too long since the sand was heavy with its weight, the air filled with its metallic balm."

A soft, mournful feminine voice spoke from beside him. "It should never have flowed in the first place, my love."

Both Sabina and her grandfather turned to see her grandmother, Sula, sitting regally beside Nyssa. They looked like mirror images, though her father had been the child to inherit his mother's green eyes. She felt the ghost-man beside her grow rigid with shock. Terror and panic pulsed from his image in waves, the air shimmering in its wake.

"Sula," he whispered. "My love."

Sabina looked at the arena as the former king moved to kneel before his wife in the space between the benches. Lasarre and Darian had shed most of their clothing, each electing to fight in the cold twilight air clad only in trousers and thick boots. The markings across Darian's torso and shoulder glistened and snaked around his body in the light of the setting sun, enhanced by the hundreds of torches that had been hastily hung on the walls of the arena.

He had a viciously-sharp, curved knife in his right hand and a thick, sturdy pole in his left. Two smaller knives rested in sheaths on his leather boots. As he twisted his torso to loosen up, Sabina stared at the jagged black marking on his ribs, given when he proved his loyalty to the Saverlen, before lightly touching her own scar through her cotton dress. The image was nearly the same, though his was created with delicate care and hers through the quick slash of a knife.

Her attention shifted back to the ghosts beside her. She barely recognized the man now, his body racked with sobs and on his knees. This was the tyrant king who had terrorized the realm for nearly two decades, who had nearly killed both her mother and her father, along with every adult she loved. Now, his cheek rested on Sula's lap, her long, delicate fingers stroking the short blonde hair above his temple as tears fell from his blue eyes, evaporating once they fell from his chin.

Rhea leaned over and touched Sabina's leg softly, causing her to jump in surprise. "I am sorry, Seb." Her hazel eyes grew concerned as Sabina took a shuddering breath. "What are you looking at?"

Sabina glanced at the ghosts again, surprised to see Sula place a finger in front of her lips and give a small shake of her head. "Nothing. Just, thinking, and trying not to think too much."

Her mother took her hand and squeezed it. "I had hoped that you would never have to live through terror, like today. I know what it feels like, to sit and watch and pray that those you love come out of evil's grip and walk through to the other side."

"You mean, Father?" Sabina was surprised to see large tears roll down her mother's cheeks.

"Yes, and also my best friend. We never talk about it, but my best friend from my old world was the one who had been transformed into the High Prince Mateo. When he tried to claim himself as heir to the throne, a creature from another world interfered. I watched as the creature shredded his skin as if it were fine silk, and knew for certain that he was going to die."

"Shredded his skin?" Sabina felt the prickling of unease begin at her neck and slivered down to her toes.

Rhea nodded absently, her eyes snapping toward the arena floor as the first clash of weapons rang across the arena. "From shoulder to mid-torso, the claws of the Gormellyn shredded his skin and muscles, as if they were streamers. It was one of the most terrifying things I have ever lived through."

Then Lasarre's knife hacked a notch in Darian's pole, and Sabina's attention was reserved for the fight in front of her. The crowd roared with glee at every move, every strike, caring not which opponent was attacking or defending. The older generation, accustomed to seeing fights to the death, screamed for their chosen victor, cheered on every injury, every near-fatal strike. Sabina's generation watched in dumb horror, and she could hear Katrina rapidly praying to every deity her sister had ever heard of for the entire thing to be a nightmare, a figment of her vivid imagination.

Darian darted forward then, his knife jerking out rapidly as he spun around Lasarre. Lasarre caught the blow on his own blade, wincing as the blades crossed and slid to his hand, his blood spilling onto the sand. Lasarre countered, the small wooden buckler in his left hand catching Darian on the elbow, causing his defensive stick to drop and his arm to hang stunned and useless at his side.

Together, they danced a waltz of death. Each making progress and then giving ground back. Both men darted, spun, and jumped; narrowly missing the blade of the knife. Their weapons locked, and Lasarre slammed his knee into Darian, the man dodging so the blow landed on his thigh, instead of the intended target. Darian cursed as pain shot through his leg and shot his elbow upward, cracking Lasarre on the jaw, and then darting away.

"They are evenly matched." The former king had moved so that he was standing behind his beloved wife.

"Do you know who will win?" Sabina asked her grandfather in a barely audible whisper, unsure if ghosts had that power.

Sula shook her head sadly. "We cannot see into the future, my child. I do hope it is the man with the brilliant markings across his torso, for the loyalty and love in his heart glows as brightly as the sun."

Sabina noticed the air shimmering around the two ghosts. "Will I see you again?"

Both ghosts looked at one another before Sula answered. "I do not think so, sweetheart. It is long past our time, and you will do fine without our presence. Hold onto your strength, and hold on to your convictions in the goodness of people." Her lips curved sweetly and she gently placed her hand within her husbands. "Always remember, our actions in life live on after death, and one must act to cause joy, and never pain. All men can be made monsters, or heroes. It all depends on what happens when they reach their darkest moment."

A scream of victorious anger sounded from the ring then, and Sabina's head swiveled with such speed that her neck muscles cramped painfully. Lasarre had knocked away Darian's knife after scoring a hit, blood running from a long slice in Darian's back.

Darian edged back, dropping into a crouch to avoid a sweeping blow aimed for his neck, and returned upright with two small boot knives, one in each hand. Lasarre struck at Darian's ribs, landing a blow with his wooden buckler just as Darian's small knife scored a line across Lasarre's chest. He swung wildly in anger, luck causing his blade to sink into the soft flesh beside Darian's left shoulder and lodging there.

The Saverlen simply grunted at the pain, swinging his right arm and slashing it toward Lasarre's eyes to drive the man back. Darian reached over and yanked the knife from his shoulder, flicking the cold metal once to rid the blade from his blood.

Now Lasarre retreated, his only offensive weapon in the enemy's hand. He thrust outward with the buckler, using his last remaining resource as he began to panic. A sharp cry rang from the bleachers, then an arrow whistled through the air, flying from an archer positioned above, sliding into Darian's flesh with a sickening wet thud. Lasarre grinned as he once again advanced; reassured the battle was now over.

The shrill scream of Faulks reverberated around the arena, causing the people who watched the grim dance to hold their ears in pain. The huge talons reached down and snatched the buckler from Lasarre's grip, carrying it high above the man. All human movement ceased as the fighters and viewers watched, entranced, as the hawk gracefully circled inside the arena, finally landing on the open bench next to a very-stunned Sabina.

"I am done with you now, Oprimata. The gods of this place have spoken." Darian gave a low growl as Lasarre tripped in the sand directly in front of the royal family. The back of his fist slammed into Lasarre's temple, and he fell onto the sandy floor, stunned.

280

Darian knelt with Lasarre's own blade across the man's neck. His burning, feral, purple eyes looked up to see Alcine standing just a few feet away. "What would you have me do, my Lord Alcine?"

Alcine looked down at the man on the sand. Lasarre was already beginning to stir, and lay passively, aware that he was caught between two people, either of whom could end his life.

"Lasarre, do you swear to leave this place and never again plot ill against those who dwell within the realm?" Alcine's honor still overruled his better judgment as he gave the man a second chance to live.

"I do so swear it," Lasarre rasped out.

Darian made a sound of disgust as he stood back to allow Lasarre to rise. As soon as he regained his balance on the sand, Lasarre attacked, grabbing the knife from Darian's hand and lunging toward Alcine.

Sabina stood in terror and felt a scream lodge deep in her throat as she saw Lasarre launch his body at her cousin. Alcine turned to parry, but he was weaponless and surprised by the immediate breach in honor. Lasarre raised the knife, aiming for Alcine's heart, and Sabina closed her eyes. A spray of warm blood fell upon her exposed neck, and her eyes snapped open to see the Oprimata crumpling to the ground, a gaping wound across his neck.

Her legs gave way and she sat down abruptly, staring at the arena where her cousin stood, his eyes on Darian. Darian held his two little knives, the blade of each dripping with Lasarre's blood. She had moved forward involuntarily when Lasarre lunged and found herself at the edge of the arena, standing by the low wall. Blood had spattered across the front of her chest and dress, but had missed the rest of the royal family. They sat in stunned silence, momentarily shaken by sudden, bloody end of the match.

Darian moved forward and dropped to his knees in front of Alcine. His voice was so low that only those in the immediate area could hear. "You are my Lord and my oath-sworn ward; I shall do whatever it is you require in making amends for my previous actions. I will support any person you deem worthy of the throne. I place my life in your hands and my future upon your judgment."

Alcine turned to where Cademar and his supporters stood in amazement, paralyzed and disbelieving that their chosen fighter had lost. "I want those traitors locked up. I leave their fate to the justice of Queen Nyssa, and the heir to the throne, Josef de DamaTalous." He looked down at Darian. "You saved my life, and that requires me to absolve you from your words of treason." Alcine glanced up at Sabina, who stood at the edge of the arena with a knuckle-white grip on the low wall and tears raining from her eyes. "We will speak later. I have yet to determine if I can trust you around my cousin, or my family, ever again."

Darian's voice was rough with emotion as he quietly acquiesced, "Yes, my Lord."

Chapter 40

The Court

The thick, stone walls that lined the hallway seemed to grow ever-closer as Sabina walked down the narrow passageway. She wrapped her wool-lined shawl closer to her body and continued to descend a flight of steps, for this lower and private wing of the castle had been created below ground level, causing the chill of the castle to deepen into a stronger cold.

She stopped at the thick door and closed her eyes. *Can I trust him? Do I dare?* Eyes opening, she reached out to gently push the door open, and then stepped into the bleak room. Her mind was reeling from the events of the past week, and she was still raw from the loss of Eric's affections, the deep feeling of betrayal, and the confusion of emotions she felt when her mind dwelled overlong on Darian.

Is what I feel for Darian true, or just a reaction to Eric's rejection? She asked herself as she walked into the empty first chamber. The room was a small receiving room, an open chamber which served as a waiting area for those who came into the realm from the other world. Several doors led off from the room, two currently opened and one closed.

The first led to the room that housed those who arrived near death. The only furniture in that room was a low, canvas cot to recline the body of the dying inhabitant, and a low table to place any needed implements or anesthetic brews. Sabina let out a sigh of relief that the door was closed, signaling that Darian was in one of the other rooms and was not determined to die.

She poked her head in the second room, the recovery chamber. The room was empty of people, and she could tell by the crisp, untouched linens on the bed that he had not yet been brought to this space. A low mattress stuffed with soft, fragrant grasses rested on a short, wooden bed frame. A small side table stood on either side of the mattress, pushed against the wall. On the tables stood a small glass filled with water, a pitcher, several clean cotton bandages, and a pouch filled with pain-relieving herbs.

Voices trailed through the door to the third room, so Sabina crossed the stone floor and gently knocked on the half-closed wooden door.

"You may enter," answered the voice of her aunt, Lianna. The sound was muffled by the thick door and Sabina was unable to determine the tone.

Darian was seated in the deep soaking tub, his naked body concealed from the waist down by thickly leafed aquatic plants that floated across the surface of the dark water. Lianna had discovered that these plants, gathered from the outskirts of a village named Albadarl, had potent abilities to fight off infection and inflammation when added to hot water. The bath had been filled with the plants, giving Darian a measure of privacy while Lianna tended to his upper wounds.

His back was toward the door, and he twisted stiffly to see who had entered. "Hello, Sabina. I did not lose, as you asked." Filled

284

with equal measures of fear and hope, his body was stiff and his voice hoarse.

Tears instantly flooded her eyes as she took in the sight of his wounded body. The long slash across his back had opened slightly when he turned, the stitches pulling with movement, and blood beaded along the wound. The arrow was still lodged in his flesh, and she watched as Lianna jerked it from his body in a swift, clean motion. Blood trailed from the wound to mingle with the bath water as Lianna covered his skin with salve and tightly bandaged the puncture.

Darian gave a small smile of reassurance. "Do not cry over me. I have had worse injuries than these and will heal in no time."

Sabina sniffed and tried to smile in return. "I'm just so sick of seeing you with an arrow sticking out of your body."

That brought an unexpected chuckle to Darian, although he winced at the pain of the movement. "I will be more than happy to end that tradition, if it would please you."

Lianna gave a delicate snort and tied the final knot in the bandage. "I am going to go grab some garments from your room for after the bath. Sabina, can you help him out of the tub when he is finished? The effects of the healing plants will begin to diminish in about five minutes."

"Of course," Sabina murmured as Lianna left the room, tactfully closing the door behind her.

The water sloshed in the tub as Darian adjusted his aching body, never dropping his gaze from Sabina as she moved to the side of the tub. "Rafael?" he asked.

"He is fine. After you left, Queen Nyssa addressed the crowd, and Rafael told the entire court the true events and treasonous plots that had occurred over the last week. They know full well that he has no eyes on the throne, nor cares who sired him, for Brokkan will always be his true father. They also know that you and I never ..." Her face flushed red and hot as she dropped the end of the sentence. "He also spoke with me just before I came down here and told me about everything that happened while you two were within Cademar's social circle."

Plants sloshed to the side of the tub as Darian started to stand, his face pale and violet eyes wide. "Sabina, I can never apologize enough for the words that were said."

She placed a hand on his shoulder and gently pushed his body back into the tub and, aware of his lack of clothing, withdrew several feet.

"Sabina." His eyes now looked amused as he watched her focus her gaze anywhere but on his body. "Only months ago you were yelling at me because I would not let you inspect my body on a daily basis."

Her mouth opened and she sat in the chair next to the tub with a plop. "That was different, and you know it."

"How is this any different?" Darian badgered her, encouraged by the exasperated, sarcastic touch that her voice had once again acquired.

Sabina forced her eyes to meet his and they narrowed as she sensed his amusement. "Because then you were my patient, and it was necessary for me to look at your wounds. Your entire body had been badly wounded and you needed treatment." She had leaned forward slightly as she spoke and her hand rested upon the rim of the soaking tub.

"This does not count as wounded?" He gestured with his left hand toward his shoulder, and then let his hand fall lightly on top of Sabina's.

"Well, yes, but Lianna already treated those wounds. Besides," her voice trailed off and she averted her gaze.

"Besides?" He pushed, aware that her cheeks were becoming a bright shade of pink and her eyes darted to the door.

"That was before …" Her lips twitched into a smile despite her best efforts as stoicism. "That was before I knew how creative your mind was in regards to the uses of your body."

"Ah." Darian let himself slide deeper into the water as his blood rushed with the tales he spun for Cademar regarding his fictional clandestine meetings with the princess of the realm. He had pieced together a story based on stories and boasts heard from Cademar's group, but had little idea of what he was actually saying.

The last bit of sand dropped from the hourglass timer that Lianna had placed on the small table beside the tub. Sabina glanced at it, then at the thick, cotton robe that hung upon the back of her chair. "Time's up. Let's get you out of the tub. Lianna should be down soon with some warm clothes you can wear while you regain your strength, and then Savin will help you back up to the family suite."

"Am I welcome in the family suite?" His eyes held the barely contained, cautious joy that he may have been forgiven for his words and deeds.

"It would seem so." Sabina stood up beside the tub and took the thick robe into her hands. "Can you stand on your own? I'll close my eyes."

He winced and a low groan escaped his lips as he stood, his wounds pulling open slightly by the effort and muscles screaming as they immediately began to stiffen. Darian carefully stepped from the tub onto a plush mat and slid into the thick, brown robe. "You can open them now," he said, after carefully tying the cotton belt around his waist.

Sabina did so, and her pulse quickened at the expression in his eyes as he smiled at her. "Do you think you can make it to the other room?"

Darian nodded, but the first step was shaky. "I think I must have lost more blood than I thought."

"Here, lean on me." Sabina ducked under his arm, wrapping her own around his waist to help support his weight as they crossed out of the bathing room, through the receiving chamber, and into the small bedroom.

They stopped in the bedroom, Darian's breath rasping with the effort of making muscles move that had been greatly taxed from the earlier events. Sabina shifted her body so that she was standing in front of him, and wrapped her other arm around his body for support. He winced, and she shifted her arms so that they did not put any pressure on his back or shoulder.

He let out a long sigh and rested his head on her shoulder. "I hate to admit it, but I may need Savin's help to move through the castle more than I anticipated. Thank you, Sabina, for helping me."

Sabina smiled and tentatively laid her cheek against his chest. His body still radiated warmth from the bath, and his skin was slightly damp, smelling of earth and lavender. She suddenly found herself very aware that the only thing separating them was the thick robe, and that they were alone in a bedroom.

As if he could read her thoughts, his lips gently brushed against her ear, and then her temple. "One day," he whispered, "I hope to be able to hold you without either one of us being too severely injured to enjoy it."

Sabina laughed and pulled back just as Lianna entered the room with an armful of clothes. Her aunt's mouth twitched as she fought back mirth. "I was going to ask if you were feeling better, but judging by the guilty looks on both of your faces, you must be."

Her husband walked in just after her, his large body filling the space within the doorframe. His expression was grave, for he was less forgiving of Darian's prior words and actions. "Come on, Darian. I will help you change and we will get you up to your room to rest. Alcine wants to leave for Asimina as soon as you are physically able, and the sooner the better."

Hazel eyes twinkled mischievously as Sabina carefully unwrapped her arms from around Darian's body, mindful of the weight she was shifting back to his legs. On impulse and in slight defiance to a lifetime of self-imposed discretion, she gently caressed Darian's cheek and touched her lips to his before moving away.

The women walked in silence down the corridor, their slippered feet swishing slightly upon the stone floor. As they reached the section of the castle where the family rooms were located, Lianna placed a soft hand on Sabina's arm.

"Sabina, you have always been a responsible and mature woman, so I will not do you the insult of asking if you know what you are doing. But I do want to give you a word of caution. You have grown up in a family where love is given freely, and support is unconditional. Darian did not. Remember that, and it may save you some heartache."

She looked over at her aunt and nodded, not quite understanding. "I know of his past, and have made my own peace with it."

"I know, but you also need to make peace with the way his past may affect the future. In all likelihood, you will need to take the lead on all matters of the relationship. He has no experience of his own, or of others, to guide him in knowing what is appropriate. You will likely not find him to be as physically affectionate as you may desire, because he has had a lifetime of training to stand apart from personal wants."

Sabina's blinked in confusion. "I do not understand, are you telling me I should love him or warning me away?"

"Both, I suppose." Lianna sighed and looked down the hallway. The slow, unsteady footsteps of Darian and Savin echoed as they approached, though they were still out of sight. "Seb, all I am saying is do not set your expectations so highly that he cannot reach them, and understand that it will take some time for him to feel easy showing his feelings."

The younger woman stared down the hallway thoughtfully. "Is this warning coming from personal experience?"

Lianna gave a soft smile. "Perhaps. But then, that should serve as proof that anything is possible."

"Now that I think of it, I do not know if I have seen Uncle Savin show his affection for you, at least not in an environment where there are more people than just the family. I guess I always assumed you were both the type of people who did not want to touch often."

"Oh, no." Her aunt blushed delicately and lowered her voice as the men's steps became louder. "Your uncle can be two very different people in private and in public, and I suspect that Darian will be cut from the same mold." Her gaze sharpened and she raised an eyebrow. "That is another thing. I am assuming the two of you have limited experience with physical affection beyond kissing?"

"Um, that would be correct." Sabina squirmed under her aunt's gaze.

Lianna raised her hand and gently cupped the side of Sabina's face. "Do not rush it, love. Give yourself the time that you both need so that when you do cross that threshold, you hold no regrets." Her eyes twinkled as she glanced at the men who finally came into view. "You just might not want to tell your father when you do make that decision, okay?"

Chapter 41

The Court

"So you two did not have sex?"

Sabina groaned as Katrina asked the question for the third time in an hour. "No, we did not actually have sex. That was a fabrication made up to convince Cademar that Darian was on his side."

Her younger sister looked at the beginning of the line of riders thoughtfully. Her head cocked to one side as she studied Darian. "Well, maybe you should."

The clopping of the horse's hooves as they walked down the dirt path toward Asimina masked the low growl of irritation that escaped from Sabina. "I am not discussing this anymore."

She was used to defending her virginal status with friends of her own age, such as Mya or Gia, but found her patience touchier when the ribbing was coming from her younger sister. Granted, her younger sister also remained untouched, though that was more due to the watchful eye of the family and less with her sister's sense of propriety.

Yet, being around Darian made her wonder if it would not be good to finally give in and experience the act that all of her friends had committed many years past. Sabina had found plenty of time to think about it in the week between her talk with her Aunt Lianna and their departure for Asimina.

Darian had once again withdrawn, spending the majority of his time with her father and uncle. On the one occasion when Alcine had helped Darian come to the garden for a bit of fresh air, he did not respond to her subtle invitations for a private moment.

As she watched him, with his chest bare and tattoos exposed to the chilly early Spring air, a warm glow started in her heart and moved through her body. Alcine said something that made Darian laugh, and it made Sabina's heart do a little pitter-patter in her chest. Darian responded, then turned slightly in his saddle to look back before moving his horse out of the line to halt.

Katrina grinned as his horse fell in beside them on the path. "How are you not freezing without a shirt on?"

He gave a shy smile in return. "I actually am quite cold, but Lianna insists that my wounds need to breathe, and that a shirt rubbing against them would only make them worse."

Katrina winked at Darian. "At least this way Sabina gets to enjoy the view for the ride." Giggling, she heeled her horse into a canter and caught up with Alcine at the beginning of the line.

Darian shifted in the saddle as he noticed the tension in Sabina's body. "Your sister is a bit more outspoken than you."

"That's one way to put it."

His fingers fidgeted on the reins and his eyes shifted toward her. "I realize that I have been distant this past week. I want you to know that it was not by my choice. I have wanted to spend time with you, but have been rebuffed and distracted whenever the opportunity would arise."

Suddenly shy, Sabina glanced at him through her lashes. "Really?"

"Yes. It would seem your father and your uncle had other plans for me. It took an effort, but I think I have finally helped them to understand that I would never, ever hurt you again."

"Oh. I had thought you were having second thoughts about …us." She paused before the last word, unsure if she wanted to hear the answer.

His horse moved closer, so that their legs were brushing with each stride. "Never." Darian held out his hand, palm up, and smiled softly when Sabina hesitantly did the same. He entwined their fingers and stared at her a moment.

"I do not know how to be affectionate, but I want to try. I do not know if I can be what you need, but I will give you all I have."

"Where will you stay when we get to Asimina?" She felt a part of her body melting in pleasure as his thumb stroked her hand.

"I do not know," he responded slowly. "I had planned on staying with Alcine, because after our last discussion about inviting men into houses, I was not sure if I would be welcomed into your house."

Sabina felt the tingle of nervousness trickle down her spine and pushed it back. "I will always welcome you into my house." She glanced forward in the line where her father was giving them an odd look. "Although it may be best if we wait until my family continues on to Kylassame. They will be leaving tomorrow morning."

294

"I am unsure if your father approves of my affection toward you." Darian spoke carefully, aware he ran the risk of giving an unintended insult to Rowan.

Her fingers tightened on his and gave a gentle squeeze. "My father would not approve of anyone's affections toward me. My mom likes you though, and so does my aunt."

"They do?" Darian sounded genuinely baffled. "After ... everything?"

"Mhm," Sabina answered. "It would seem they have some experience dealing with stoic men who find it hard to show their affection."

That statement resulted in Darian giving the half-smile that Sabina found she treasured. His face grew serious a moment and he hesitated before asking, "What about Eric?"

She had thought about that very question over the last week, as well. "I still care for him, and perhaps Mom is right, and I will always care about people that I heal, but it's not the same. I think about him and it's a quiet thing. Maybe there was potential for it to turn into a big thing once, but life had other plans for us. If he and Yasmina are happy together, then that is a very good thing. If you and I are happy together," she glanced at him, encouraged by the small smile on his face, "then it is a wonderful thing."

Happy shouts of homecoming could be heard as they approached the village, and Alcine reined his horse in at the front of the line to wait for Sabina and Darian.

Darian glanced at the waiting man before reluctantly releasing Sabina's hand. "May I come to your house tomorrow night, Seb?"

She was too filled with emotion to speak, so she simply nodded.

Chapter 42

Asimina

The youth of the village gathered in the bathing house once more while their parents met in the comfort of Rowan's large hut to catch up with old friends. Spring was in the air and fewer fires were needed to provide heat for the large chamber, causing the room to be darker, with a more secretive aura, than it was in the months prior.

Rafael had returned to Asimina, along with his mother, staying the night before moving on to assist at one of the refugee camps. He had propped himself up on the edge of the pool with his shoulders, and was delighted to repeat the story of the near-mutiny to the residents of Asimina.

Sabina stood waist deep in the pool, still aware of how uncomfortable she was to have her body exposed. Her scars had fully healed and were nothing more than slim, white lines across her body, but she still felt vulnerable. She heard a collective gasp from the women in the pool and followed their attention to the door from the male's dressing room.

"He must be in so much pain. I should go comfort him!" Keri crooned as she moved through the water toward the edge of the pool where Darian stood. She had renewed her will to gain his affections and dressed in accordance to that will. The bright pink bikini left little to the imagination, and she had taken care to tie her hair in such a manner that it accentuated the near-nakedness of her body.

Sabina started forward, anger and jealousy churning in her gut. Then Gia's hand tugged lightly at her arm and Sabina forced herself to remain still at her friend's furtive headshake.

Gia slid next to Sabina as Keri continued across the pool, heading over to the steps where Darian would enter. "Don't let her see your jealousy, Seb. He needs to choose you over her, publicly, or else she will never leave him alone."

She felt her teeth grinding together as Darian entered the pool and spoke a few words to Keri. Keri's hand raised as if it were going to caress his shoulder on the pretense of inspecting his wound, but Darian shook his head. They moved down the steps, Keri being sure to move her body through the water so that her hips and chest was accentuated, and smiled seductively while she talked.

Darian moved silently, his eyes focusing on Sabina. She gave a self-conscience smile when she saw his gaze move to slowly travel over her body, and was suddenly flooded with self-doubt.

"Hello, beautiful." His arms came around Sabina's shoulders as he lowered his lips to hers, publicly attaching himself to her in a way that left no doubt of his affections. She moved her hands to rest on his hips, shivering in delight at the warmth of his body in contrast with the cool water.

Keri stalked out of the bathing house, followed by her friends. Alcine and Henry both gave the couple a splash. "Calm it down, you two. You made your point. They're gone." They laughed to take the censorship out of the words.

"Do I want to know what she was telling you?" Sabina asked from within the security of his arms.

"She was telling me about all of the wonderful things that she was willing to do to help me feel better," he answered in a low tone, slowly lowering his arms to his sides.

"Like making you chicken soup?" Sabina asked hopefully.

"Not quite," he admitted. "She was thinking of more physical means to take my mind off the pain."

Sabina forced the jealousy trying to escape back into a cage. "I take it you did not accept the offer?"

"No, of course not." He gently kissed her forehead and whispered, "But if you want to make me feel better in a similar manner, I would welcome it."

She found herself speechless and surprised by the rush of energy that coursed through her veins at the suggestion. They moved to join the group, who had tactfully moved across the pool to give the couple privacy.

Darian glanced at Sabina, and then looked around the group as they joined the circle, unsure of how to conduct himself in this new role. Eric and Yasmina were standing in the chest deep water, hands clasped underneath as they talked to Rafael and Katrina. Henri stood behind Gia, his hands wrapped around her waist and clasped at her stomach, her head resting against his bare chest.

Sabina slid her arm around Darian's waist, and he mirrored the movement. "So," she said, "what did we miss while we were gone?"

Yasmina smiled tentatively, still unconvinced that the feelings Eric and Sabina had were extinguished, though she was encouraged by the night's current actions. "There is talk about starting another refugee village, closer to Kylassame. The camps are getting too full, and the current residents of the village are afraid that the new people will not be able to adjust to such a different life, especially after such an upheaval."

Eric looked at Alcine uncertainly. "They came while you were all at court. I was going to send a message but they wanted an immediate answer. They were told I was in charge while you were gone, and I told them we would do what we could to help, but that they needed to come back to speak with you before any firm decisions were made."

Alcine waived off the white lie. "I am sure that you only did what was necessary. Don't think twice about it. I appreciate you stepping up to run Asimina while I was gone. It is somewhat of a relief to have my own heir to the village."

Sabina tilted her head slightly in curiosity as Eric's face paled. Once again her eyes trailed down to the scars that crossed his shoulders and torso, and felt a nagging feeling that she was missing something life-altering.

"Who will go there to assist in building and teaching the refugees about the realm?" Alcine questioned.

Henri rested his chin on Gia's shoulder. "Gia and I will be willing to move there in order to help out, at least for a year. There is also a small group from Kylassame who would like to go, including Philip and Mya. However, the group of children who were burned by the Oprimata will be moving there, so he was unsure if it would be too much for them."

The group all looked to Darian, who slowly ran his thumb up and down Sabina's hip as he considered the situation. "I think it could work. I think it would help if I was there in the beginning to assure them of Philip's honor, and that he was able to be trusted. I do not think they would trust him for quite some time, but they would be able to live together as long as they had some adult acting to guard them."

Alcine leaned against the pool wall nonchalantly. "What about you, Eric? This new place would certainly be closer to home than here."

Eric smiled, though Yasmina tensed and lowered her eyes. He lifted her hand from the water and kissed it, the action bringing a deep blush to her cheeks. "We have discussed it, but Asimina is Yas's home, and she belongs here. I want to stay wherever she is, so I will remain here as well, as long as it is okay with you."

Alcine nodded his blessing and smiled. "You are welcome to stay here as long as you like. Although, if you try to overthrow me, I'm going to be really pissed."

Eric placed a hand across his heart. "Never."

~ * ~ * ~

"Psst, Seb."

Sabina ignored the call once, but rolled over in her small bed when she heard it the second time. She had been trying to sleep for the previous hour, but had found herself too full of anticipation and anxiety for her future to relax.

"Alcine, what are you doing?" She slipped out of the front door to the hut, carefully moving through the tapestry door so that no stray gust of wind would sneak inside and awaken her parents or siblings.

"Doing you a favor. Come on." He took her hand and led the way as they snuck across the village toward the unoccupied solitary hut where newcomers were often taken. Once there, he gave her a smacking kiss on the cheek, whispered, "Have fun," and then moved off into the darkness.

She pulled back the door and stepped inside, wary, but sure of Alcine's good will and knowing he would never lead her to harm. Darian smiled at her from behind the solitary lantern in the hut.

"Alcine was under the impression that we would be useless tomorrow if we resisted another day."

"Oh," she said softly, her heart hammering in her chest.

Darian moved forward and slowly wrapped his arms around her. She breathed in his strong scent and felt the flutters move from her belly to encompass her entire body. "I do not know what to do, Seb, but I promise you that I will never, ever hurt you. All you need to do is say the word and we will stop."

She shook her head, then gently ran her hands over his broad shoulders. "No, I want to." Her fingers traced the intricate whorls and lines of his markings, beginning at his shoulder. They ended at his hips, just below his belt line, and his body shuddered at her touch.

He bent down and kissed her, sliding his hands within her shirt and reveling at the feel of her soft, warm skin. "Sabina, you are so beautiful, and so perfect."

Her response came out as a purr, her entire body quivering with the sensation of floating as his fingers brushed against her skin.

~ * ~ * ~

The creature stood a moment in the orchard, beady red eyes searching the surrounding darkness as his delicate nostrils scented the air. The pull had never taken him to this part of the realm before; the people of this village had always lived with pure intentions. He approved of this landscape, felt oddly at home within the rows upon rows of barely-budding pear trees. His muzzle tilted up as a familiar scent traveled the breeze and the moon shined down upon the creature.

Four lean legs carried him across the orchard and to the edge of the village. He moved silently, a dark shadow in the blackness, his claws retracted and fangs hidden within his closed mouth. The creatures of the night fell silent as he moved through the village, thin whiskers twitching as he passed each silent structure.

The pull strengthened as he approached a group of huts, the dens created by the people of this village. He hissed in frustration as the pull of his soul split, tugging him in two directions with equal measures. The deception smelled heavily of male, but this village was filled with men, it was both familiar and strange, and unsettling.

Murmurs floated through the night, and one of the tugs increased. He padded across the ground between him and one of the huts, then slowly slipped inside and melted into the shadows.

~ * ~ * ~

"Are you still sure?" Darian asked, his voice husky with desire and longing.

Sabina hesitated. Her body cried out for more, but her mind was filling with doubt. *How will he feel in the morning when he realizes he has violated his oaths for someone he barely knows? How will I feel in the morning? What if this is all a mistake?* The words and actions of the past month flooded her memory, and she found herself torn between doubt and desire.

"Seb?" His eyes traveled over her un-clothed body as he waited for her answer, holding his taunt body near hers, feeling his restraint growing thin with need.

"I can't do this," she whispered, eyes filling with tears. "I'm sorry. I thought I could but I don't think I can, and I understand if you don't …" she trailed off, certain that he was going to hate her for leading him on and then denying him the final act.

He closed his eyes and took a deep breath in an effort to regain control of his desire. When they opened he saw tears streaming down Sabina' cheeks and gently lowered his head to kiss her. "Sabina," he whispered as he shifted his body so that he was safely beside her. "I told you that I would never hurt you, and I will always hold true to that promise. We have a lifetime for this, and can wait as long as we need. All I ask is that you let me hold you a minute until I settle down."

She smiled through the tears and moved so that her shoulder touched his chest. His strong arms wrapped around her and she gently kissed his bicep in thanks. After a moment, his breathing slowed and his lips gently touched her neck. Her pulse beat in time with his and she felt her body melting within his arms, relaxed and tranquil.

"Darian, I lo-" Suddenly her words stuck in her throat as she noticed the wooden door move. "Did you see that?"

He raised his head as he felt her body go rigid in front of him. "See what?" His eyes fell upon the door which lay slightly open. "I thought we closed the door."

"We did." Sabina was grateful that the solitary hut was built with no curtained sections. A quick glance confirmed that they were still alone within the structure.

Darian carefully stood and moved along the edges of the hut, keeping to the shadows. He nudged the door open farther with his toe, body poised for action as he carefully inspected the darkness outside. He shrugged and moved the stiff door back into place before moving back toward Sabina.

She held up the thick quilt they had been lying under so that he could slide in beside her. He lay on his back, tucking her securely under his arm. "We still have a little time until sun-up. If it would help ease your mind, you can ask me any question and I will answer truthfully."

Sabina snuggled in tightly to the side of his body, taking care to avoid the puncture wound on his shoulder as she rested her cheek on his chest. "What are your real feelings about Philip? We will have to go to Kylassame, or this new village, at some point and be around him."

His hand stroked her side as he answered. "It goes against my nature to trust him, but it also goes against my nature to be lying next to a beautiful, naked woman. I will work to accept that if I can change so greatly in just a few months, it is not so unbelievable that he changed greatly as well." He glanced down at her. "What about you? Do you think you can be around Caela and Irena when we go back to the court?"

She tensed as she remembered their attempts to bed Darian while he was a member of Cademar's group. "Tell me truthfully; did you do anything with either one of them?"

"Nothing more than what you saw when we were all in the same public space," he answered. His arms wrapped around Sabina tightly in reassurance. "You are the only one I have ever desired, the only one I have ever touched in this manner, and the only one I ever will. You still did not answer the question."

Silence answered his question, and he glanced down to see Sabina's eyes flutter as her body fell into a deep sleep. He settled her head more comfortably on his chest and closed his eyes. *Just for a minute*, he told himself. *Just for one ...*

Chapter 43

Asimina

A panicked scream filled the near-dawn air, causing the residents of Asimina leap from their beds. Darian and Sabina scrambled to pull on their clothing from the night before, both having fallen into a deep slumber that prevented them from sneaking back into their former beds.

They darted out of the solitary hut, looking around wildly for the source of the scream. Two huts away, a child's shriek pierced the morning as Asli darted out from her home and ran, instinctively making a line for Sabina. With a hiccupping sob, Asli wrapped her small arms around Sabina's knees, tears rolling down her face.

Sabina dropped to her knees and encircled the child in her arms as Darian moved toward the hut, knife in hand. He covered half of the distance when Yasmina was shoved out of the front door from within, the momentum throwing her off-balance. He caught her, held her a second to steady her course, then nudged her toward Sabina as he crossed the final steps to the door.

Yasmina sank into a ball beside Sabina, wrapping her arms around Asli and sobbing frantically. "Help him, please, help him!"

By this time, the entire village had approached the hut. They were all dressed in night clothing, with only Rowan and Rhea fully awake, having roused much earlier in preparation for their journey. As one, they watched in silent horror as Darian backed out of the hut slowly, followed by a shirtless Eric.

Rowan and Rhea moved to stand next to Sabina, so she heard her mother's gasp of terror as a small, black creature emerged to slowly circle Darian and Eric. "Not again, I cannot endure this again," Rhea whispered, as the creature drew his circles smaller, stopping only when the two men were standing shoulder to shoulder.

The people of the village froze as the feline-like creature nimbly jumped upon Darian's shoulder and hissed. Sabina felt a sob catch in her throat as the creature bared its bright, white fangs and slid out long, devastatingly sharp claws.

"Do you remember me, Lady of Steinbrekka?" the creature asked, his voice sibilant and smooth. A red, forked tongue flicked out to touch Darian's cheek as the beady red eyes focused on Rhea.

"I do, venerable Gormellyn." Rhea bowed her head in respect without removing her eyes from the creature. "Why have you been awoken from your slumber?"

"Were you aware that you had a deceiver in your midst?" He crossed over to perch upon Eric's shoulders, the man barely breathing in his terror.

Rowan bowed his head. "We were not, venerable Gormellyn. What have these men done? Darian's actions in court have already been accounted for, and his duplicity necessary for the end result." Shadows flashed in his eyes as he remembered his conversation with Eric months ago in the bathhouse, his knowing that Eric had once gone by two other names, and the Gormellyn grinned.

"Ah, yes, you now realize. As far as this man," he paused, then crossed over to Darian and slowly sunk his claws in with just enough pressure to dimple the skin. "Are you aware, Lord Rowan, that your daughter lay with this man last night? Were you aware that he made a promise to never hurt her? Aware that she did not wish to continue the course of action begun by the hot blood of youthful passions?"

Sabina felt the anger radiated from her father and slowly stood, putting herself in front of Asli and Yasmina. "It was you who I saw in the darkness. I thought I saw something in the doorway ..."

"Sabina, is this true?" Her father's voice rumbled dangerously through the air.

She saw tiny, red dots began to well on Darian's shirt as the claws dug in deeper. "No!" Her mind cleared of her terror and she strode over to stand in front of the man. "He asked me if I wanted to continue. I said no, and he stopped. He never hurt me! He kept his promise."

Her bowels turned to water as the creature slipped onto her own shoulders. Though retracted, the long claws still pricked at her skin through her thin shirt and his soft fur brushed against her cheek. He tilted his black, furry head far to the side as he regarded her.

"You trust this man?"

"I do. I trust him with all that I am." She nodded slightly, careful to keep her movements to a minimum.

The Gormellyn's face moved until his muzzle touched Sabina's ear. "You have made a good choice in this man, daughter of Rhea. He is lucky that he kept his promise. Only because of that, shall I allow him to live."

She visibly shuddered when the creature lightly leapt from her shoulder to find purchase once again on Eric. The Gormellyn extended his claws and crimson drops highlighted the white scars that streaked down the man's shoulders.

Darian moved quickly, placing his body between the Gormellyn and Sabina. "I promise you anything I have done; I have done for the good of this place and its people. I would never allow Sabina to come to harm's way, and have done much to prevent that very thing."

The creature gave a dismissive wave with one of its paws. "That is why I allow you to live. Move away before my mind is changed." His attention focused back onto the face that was positioned perilously close to his sharp fangs. "You, however, do not have such pure intentions."

Eric's mouth barely moved as he croaked, "I have never wanted to harm these people."

Shrill, sibilant laughter bubbled from the Gormellyn. "Your desires and your sword *harmed* these people until they were nearly extinct. Tell them, imposter, deceiver, liar, who you used to be."

"No," Eric whispered in terror. "That wasn't me. I never wanted to hurt anyone." His eyes fell upon Yasmina, still curled in a ball with Asli, fear-driven tears streaking her face. "That wasn't my fault. I didn't know what I was doing."

"Tell them who you are, or I will destroy you as I should have done twenty-three years ago." Blood began to drip into flowing streams as the claws traced the path of the scars, opening the wounds anew.

"Please," Eric pleaded. "I have found a new life, a good life. Don't make me throw it away."

"You have lived as an imposter and lied to the people of this village, and this realm. You have five seconds to choose, and should do so wisely."

"My name is not Eric," he blurted out as the claws dug in deeper. Tears welled and spilled from his blue eyes as he looked out over the people he had come to love. Finally his gaze fell on Rhea, looking at him with narrowed eyes, confusion and disbelief writ upon her face. "My name was, is, Matt. I was kidnapped before and brought to this realm. I was brainwashed into thinking I was the High Prince Mateo, and heir to the realm. I didn't know until it was over. I swear, I didn't know what I was doing."

The crowd hissed, the older generation turning cold and forbidding. They remembered the past well, those few survivors. The memories rushed back as they recalled the terror, the pain, and the decimation their village sustained at the hands of the High Prince Mateo.

"No," whispered Rhea, as she stared at the face she had all but forgotten in the twenty-three years since her friend stepped through the portal to Virginia. She could see it now, though she had missed it when she first saw him, weakened by shock and hunger.

The Gormellyn fixed hard eyes on Rowan. "Ask your husband if these are truths."

"You knew?" There were equal measures of shock and venom in her voice as Rhea turned toward Rowan.

He nodded curtly. "I saw the scars, and I knew. He told me that he did not remember that time, and that he would never harm this realm or lie to those within it, again." His green eyes flickered to his daughter before returning to his wife. "That is why I wanted him away from Sabina. I did not want the man who beat, and nearly raped my wife, anywhere near my daughter. I did not tell you for your protection, and to allow him a second chance."

Sabina felt sick to her stomach as she absorbed the full impact of his words. From the corner of her eye she saw Rafael's body jerk stiffly as Agrafina lifted a shaking hand to her mouth.

"I never had ill will toward Sabina," Eric, who was once Matt, spoke desperately. "My words and my actions and my feelings since I arrived in this village have never been false, ever." His blue eyes filled with desperation as he looked at Yasmina and Asli. "The love I have for you all is true, and without reserve."

The Gormellyn tapped a claw in consideration. "And yet, you have never said why you came here. Will these people have love for you when you tell them that truth?"

"I came back for Rhea, to take her back to our world." Eric's voice was barely more than a whisper, yet every member of the community heard the words clearly. "But then," he raised his voice, panic setting in as members of the community turned their back to him and began to walk away, sealing his fate. "But when I realized that so much time had passed, I decided to commit myself to this village, and its people. I made up a new identity because I thought, I knew, that my past would never be forgiven. All I wanted was a second chance to prove myself, to show that I am a good person. I was brainwashed before, I didn't know what I was doing back then."

Fangs exposed, the Gormellyn asked, "Would you like me to dispose of this pretender, King Rowan?"

"No!" Alcine and Sabina shouted simultaneously. Alcine strode forward until he stood a foot away from Eric. "Venerable Gormellyn, I mean no disrespect, but the only deception of which this man claims guilt was why he came here, and who he was. It should fall upon the people of Asimina to decide his fate. He has been a valuable member of the community and we deserve the right to do our own justice."

Eric stood frozen as the eyes of the Gormellyn passed over the crowd. Finally, the creature tipped his long snout in agreement as Rowan, Rhea, Sabina, and even Agrafina echoed Alcine's plea.

The Gormellyn looked into Eric's eyes carefully, hissed, "Do not wake me again!" and then disappeared.

Chapter 44

Asimina

The DamaTalous called a council, all members present, save Nyssa and Sebast who were still smoothing over the Patrons of the court from the brief uprising. Sabina took her seat in the circle, grateful for the quiet support of Darian's body beside her. To her right, Rafael sat with his parents, Agrafina and Brokkan. Rowan sat with Rhea, and Eric was placed between Rowan and Alcine. Katrina sat quietly by herself several feet away from the circle, unwilling to be part of the judgment but her presence still required during the trial.

A slight breeze floated through the air of the orchard, where they sat in heavy silence. Sabina lifted her face to it, unable to hazard a guess at how this day would end. She could hardly belief that events could turn so suddenly, that a cherished friend had once been her family's mortal enemy.

"When I got back," Eric began, "only a few weeks had passed in my world. I missed Rhea, and I thought that she would have been regretting her decision. I searched for months to find a way back to this world, knowing that if I just saw her again, I could convince her to return with me."

"Then," he glanced at Sabina, "I found a way here, and met a young woman in the orchard who was like Rhea, but not. I learned that over twenty years had passed here, and decided to do it right this time. Since making that decision, I have never acted without honest intent."

Alcine began the questioning. "What do you remember from your previous time in the realm?"

Eric shrugged carefully, pain from the encounter with the Gormellyn flooding his shoulder. "Not much. I remember snippets, like remembering a dream. Unless it's prompted, I only seem to remember little bits of happiness from before, like when ..." his voice trailed off as his eyes drifted toward Agrafina.

"Why did you lie to us?" Sabina found her voice hoarse with distress and anger.

"I wanted a second chance, and for you to like me." Eric picked at a loose string on his pants. "It shocked me when I developed feelings for you, but they were true feelings, Seb. It was the same with Yasmina. I have never lied about my loyalty to anyone in this room, and would never willingly harm anyone in this village or this realm."

Rafael leaned forward, one eyebrow raised, his elbows resting on his knees. "I don't look at all like you. I'm not sure if that is a comfort or not."

Agrafina shot a dark look toward Eric. "Brokkan is Rafael's father, none other. You walked out of my life twenty-three years; do not expect a welcome return."

Eric held up a hand in supplication. "I have enjoyed the time I have spent with Rafael during his visits to Asimina. I want nothing more than to be his friend. I am glad that you found love, and would never want to take that away from you. I'm sorry, Agrafina, for everything."

Alcine stood up smoothly, his jaw set as he stared off to the horizon. "I am going to have to present this to the villagers as well. I will come back with their answer."

The group watched in tense silence as Alcine walked out of the circle and back toward the village. The rest of them stood, one by one, and walked away as well.

Rhea looked at Eric, eyes heavy with tears, and shook her head slowly. "After everything is decided, maybe then we can talk. I don't know how to handle this. I don't know if I can lose you a third time. I'm sorry." Head bowed, she walked away, lost in confusion and misery.

Finally it was only Darian, Sabina, and Eric left in the circle.

"Seb, could you give us a moment?" Darian gave her leg a comforting caress and she nodded and stood, then walked just out of earshot.

"Darian, I know you barely know me, and you probably hate me for causing Sabina heartache, but," Eric's frantic plea was stalled by Darian's raised hand.

"I too, know what it is like to have a dark past and need forgiveness. I have probably killed as many people as you, and the only difference between us is the location of the crime. It is far easier for my sins to be forgiven since they were not committed to people still here, or their families."

"I would never, ever hurt these people."

"Now? No." Darian shrugged as he watched Alcine and Sabina standing in the large group of assembled villagers. "But most of these people lost loved ones because of you; this very village was almost wiped off this world, because of you. That will be a difficult thing to get around."

"You and I do not have a history to dance around. What do you think will happen to me?" Eric saw Yasmina looking at him across the distance and felt a tear hover on his eyelid.

Darian hesitated. "I do not know their ways, but at the very least, I think they will ask that you never return to this village. That is what I would suggest if I were a survivor of genocide. I do not know if they would wish to add further security."

"Do you think they would try to kill me?" Eric's face had lost all color as he realized a possible fate that waited. While he had been a ruthless killer as Mateo, his perchance for violence disappeared when he was attacked by the Gormellyn two decades ago.

"I think some would try. Some of these women saw their husbands, brothers, sisters, and children killed under your hand. It would take a strong order from Alcine, or some way to prove your repentance, for you to be truly safe."

"Why did the Gormellyn go after *you* today?" Eric asked in an attempt to sway his mind from spiraling into terrified oblivion. The voices coming from the village did not sound as if things were going in his favor, and he felt his panic rise.

Darian hesitated, and then decided to trust in the man. "There was a plot at the court to overthrow the throne. A group of people who were discontent began a rumor that Rafael was the proper heir. As asked by the DamaTalous, I threw in with those people and said some horrible things about Sabina and the royal family to gain the usurpers trust."

Eric's eyes clouded in confusion. "But how could Rafael have a claim to the throne? He's Agrafina and Brokkan's son."

"Through one of his possible sires, the High Prince Mateo," Darian said dryly. "You may not realize, but you may have been responsible for the creation of Rafael, and you have an intimate past with Rhea and her daughter, as well as Agrafina. That is going to be difficult for others to work around."

Darian watched as Eric stood up quickly, stumbled a few steps away, and then was quietly but thoroughly sick in the grass. "Which persona will you keep now that your secret is out? Matt, or Eric?"

Eric spat the taste of sickness from his mouth and wiped his lips with the back of his hand. "I gave up who I was when I realized that there was no turning back. Matt belongs in my old world, Eric belongs here." His mouth went dry as Alcine, Rowan, Rhea, and Sabina headed back their way. "They don't look encouraging."

Alcine spoke, his eyes filled with regret and concern. "The people of Asimina have spoken. They do not wish for you to remain in this village; there are too many memories. The elder generation does not believe in the goodness of your heart, or the truth of your transformation. They worry that this is just part of a lengthy plan to destroy them from within, since you could not destroy them from without."

Rhea continued the discussion, her voice heavy. "We do not believe that you will be safe in this realm if you simply move out of Asimina. You were responsible for the thoughtless killing of people in two villages, Asimina and Albadarl, along with terrorizing the people in the court. Kylassame, too, holds too many survivors of your actions, and would not welcome you among their community."

"What must I do? Where can I go?" Eric fought down the panic that welled up.

Rowan looked at Rhea for confirmation, then spoke. "There is one way to prove your worth to the entire realm, in a manner that will not be disputed. However, even if you succeed, I do not think you will be welcome in any of the established villages."

"But?" Eric asked, a tiny grain of hope forming in his heart.

"But," Rhea softly spoke, "you will be able to join a refugee village, and have the second chance you desire."

"I'll do it," he agreed. "Whatever it takes, I will do it." His voice faltered. "Can I see Yasmina and Asli before I leave, just to tell them I love them?"

"No," Alcine said gently. "The village has said you will have no contact with them until after the test. You are to remain in the solitary hut until tomorrow morning, at which time we will depart for the Wilderness."

Eric bowed his head in acceptance as his heart cracked and splintered.

~ * ~ * ~

The fire pit in the center of Yasmina's hut was cold when Sabina entered, both mother and child curled in a ball on the large bed where the adults slept. They were still dressed in their night clothing, Asli wearing a long cotton nightgown and Yasmina wearing one of Eric's shirts. He was taller than her, and his shoulders larger, so the hem of his shirt fell to her mid-thighs. Her fingers were twisted in the hem, as if clinging to the memory of the man as he was before the Gormellyn intervened and turned her world sideways.

Yasmina's eyelids slowly lifted as Sabina sat down on the bed beside them. "Tell me this is all a nightmare. Please, don't let this be real."

"I wish I could, but I am afraid it is truly happening." Sabina lightly stroked Yasmina's hair, the black locks still tangled from the night before.

"I trusted him, Seb. I trusted him with me and with my daughter. He is a ruthless killer and I left her alone with him. We have all heard stories about what the High Prince did, about the evilness he spread across the realm. I let him into my house. I let him into my heart!" Yasmina's voice broke and tears began to flow.

"Momma, when is Eric coming home? He will protect us from the bad man." Asli's tiny voice broke Sabina's heart. The child could not understand how the man who played with her and gave her mother such joy could be the same person the adults all feared. For her, there was no connecting the High Prince with the man she had begun to love as a father.

"Asli, why don't you run over to Lady Rhea's house for breakfast?" Sabina suggested. She stood by the door until Asli was safely in Rhea's arms and led inside the house. After building a small fire and slicing some cheese, she sat next to Yasmina once again.

"Yas, I believe him when he says that he did not know the full truth about his past in the realm. He loves you, and he loves Asli. The first thing he asked about was whether he could just have one more chance to tell you that he loves you."

"I do not know what to believe." The tears fell faster as Yasmina huddled deeply within the cage that had snapped up over her heart, initially formed by the death of her first husband.

"He has shared my home for months now and I never would have thought him a man capable of any violence. But the other women, the elders, they tell me he is dangerous. They tell me that if I cannot see through his lies I am endangering my child. The men here who were once Patrons or servants at court, they tell me that even when he was here before, he convinced your mother that he was not an evil man. The entire time she thought he was a good person, he was slaughtering women and children."

Sabina encouraged her to nibble a piece of the cheese. "We are taking him to the Wilderness, so that the powers of the realm can decide his fate. There is no deceiving the forces that live within those woods."

"I know." Yasmina sounded miserable. "But my entire life is here, this is where I belong. Even if he comes out of the Wilderness, I will be shunned if I go back to him. I cannot survive without the help of the community, I am still repaying my debt. He ..." she fell into silence as the silent sobs stole her breath.

"He would have the option of going to a refugee village. You could always go with him."

"I cannot," she gasped out, her chest tightening as she began to panic. "I cannot. He has done so much for me, but if I even hint that I will go with him, I will never be welcome in this village. The others, they say that he will not survive this trial, and then where would I be? How could I take care of Asli if I am shunned by the community?

Every step forward I have made will be for nothing. I can't condemn her to a life of nothing because of my error in judgment, because I fell in love with a monster."

Sabina hugged her close. "Then make no commitments, no hints at the future. Hold Asli close and put the pieces of your heart back together while the forces of the Wilderness determine his character. Then, hopefully, the path forward will become clear."

Chapter 45

The Wilderness

They stood at the edge of The Wilderness, a vast forest left untouched by the inhabitants of the realm. A large swath of grassland surrounded the forest, and it had taken them nearly an hour to cross the waist-high grasses, eyes alert for snakes or other creatures. This land stretched over a wide expanse, its boundaries able to be crossed near both the village of Kylassame and the village of Asimina.

Eric took a deep breath as they stood at the tree-line, staring into the blackness that descended like a curtain only a few feet from where they stood. He was dressed only in a pair of linen trousers and cotton shirt, with sturdy leather boots to protect his feet. No weapons of any kind could be taken into The Wilderness, an area where people of the realm were taken to be judged for serious transgressions.

A series of tremors shook Sabina's body, a build-up of fear and anxiety. She had only seen a person be taken to the Wilderness once, and that was for the crime of purposefully killing a child from a refugee village. There was a legend about how her father once took two men to this place, and the Malakhor, a giant tiger she had never seen, served as jury and executioner.

She stepped up to Eric and wrapped her arms around him. While the passion between them had dissolved, she still considered him a close friend and was terrified for him. He returned the embrace, hoping it would not be the last time he would see her.

"It's okay, Seb. It will be okay." He drew back and tried to give her a brave smile, failing miserably. "Thank you for your kindness. Please tell Yasmina and Asli ..." His voice choked as he realized, no matter the outcome, he was probably never going to see Yasmina or little Asli again.

Sabina nodded as tears trickled down her cheeks. "I will tell them."

Darian stepped forward then and clasped hands with Eric. "Watch your back, and step lightly in there. Use all of your senses. Remember everything Alcine has taught you about defense and survival."

He nodded. "Take care of Seb, and Rhea. They are special and deserve their world to be at peace, and filled with love."

As Darian moved to wrap a supportive arm around Sabina, Rhea approached Eric. They stood for a moment, just staring at one another. They had been best friends, and almost lovers, twenty years ago. Then he was kidnapped and turned into the High Prince Mateo, and life had spun out of their control.

A tear slipped from her bright green eyes, and Eric automatically moved his finger to gently wipe it from her cheek. "It was worth it, to see that you are truly happy here. You have a wonderful daughter. Thank you for being my friend."

She wrapped her arms around him, holding tightly as twenty-year-old memories and emotions flooded into her mind. *Please, don't take him like this,* she pleaded with the world. *Let him have his chance for redemption, and life.*

The steady hand of her husband encouraged Rhea to move back to where Sabina and Darian stood, and then Eric was face to face with Rowan.

"Eric, Matt. It would be a lie for me to say that I have forgiven you of your past. The crimes you committed against me, and my world, are too deep to truly be absolved. However, I am not blind to what good you have done during this time in the realm." His hand came down with a hesitant pat on Eric's shoulder. "Stay true to yourself in there, no matter what happens."

Eric gave a weak smile of acknowledgement before turning to face the forest. His entire body trembled as he took the first step into the darkness, and his teeth sank into his lip hard enough to draw blood when he turned back and saw only a curtain of black where the grassland was once.

The air was eerily silent, the vegetation varying shades of green from near-black to fluorescent green and the only sound a light breeze rustling the leaves that carpeted the forest floor. As he carefully picked his way through thorny underbrush, stepped over gnarled tree roots, and edged around deep pits, Eric felt his breath quicken until his chest muscles ached. The forest had morphed into a dense jungle, with thick, twisting vines and ominously shadowed undergrowth that slid and pooled at his feet.

His legs shook as he fought for control, gently placing his palm upon a smooth tree trunk for support. Composure regained, he lifted a hand to rub his face and gasped to see it dripping with blood, though there were no visible wounds and no blood upon the tree.

Suddenly, the air filled with shrill cries and guttural screams, bird-like and deafening as an unknown creature came closer to his position in the forest. Eric crouched down, hiding himself as best he could in the dense undergrowth as his eyes frantically searched the black canopy sky.

The mass of tiny birds blotted out the little light that came through the trees as they gathered on a branch above his head. Blood-red, needle-like beaks opened and shut rapidly as the birds chattered with one another, their small, glittering green eyes searching the ground below for their prey. Crimson heads dipped and darted, and they ruffled their black body feathers in agitation as a breeze suddenly blew from behind Eric's position.

A leaf below his heel crunched as his weight involuntarily shifted, and as one, the birds spread their black-and-red feathered wings and shot into the air. The mass swooped down from the branch, wings tucked in so that their bodies shot like missiles toward the man below. His eyes closed in defense, his heart beating painfully against his chest, and then they snapped open at the sensation of hot air fanning upon his face.

They surrounded him, forming a living, and breathing, impenetrable column of red and black as they circled around him, wings buzzing and voices shrieking. One of the birds back-winged in front of his face, the pointed, red tips of its wings blurring with the rapid movement needed to keep the small body in the air. Shining emerald eyes regarded the man carefully, and the beak dipped and jerked, as if the bird were wielding a sword, as Eric watched in terrified silence.

"I mean this place no harm," he whispered, voice tight with horror. The creature's miniscule eyes blinked once and then it darted forward to prick its beak against Eric's brow. A trickle of blood ran from the wound, forming a thin, straight line as it dripped down beside his eye. With an ear-piercing trill, it launched itself into the air, the flock following in a tight spiral until they disappeared over the shadowed canopy above.

Eric crept forward again, unsure of where he needed to go, or why he needed to get there, but driven by a deep need for motion. The shadows deepened as he pushed farther into the jungle, forcing the man to rely on the feel of the ground beneath his feet as visibility slowly closed in to become a small bubble around his body. He tripped on an uprooted branch and gave a hiss of pain as he toppled into the undergrowth, bloody palms further damaged by the thorny-edged leaves on the bushes.

His blonde hair fell into his eyes, and when he shook it free, a pair of narrowed, amber eyes stared back at him. He carefully shifted so that his weight was over his hips, crouched down, lungs frozen in fear as the black and gold jaguar circled him in the dimness. Powerful muscles rippled as the cat melted out of the underbrush, those golden eyes never leaving Eric's face. Paralyzed by fear, Eric realized that not only was the cat bigger and stronger than he, but it was willing to patiently circle until Eric made the first move.

"I just want a chance to help. I want to be good, again." His voice barely more than a whisper, Eric's eyes stayed trained upon the circling feline. Already he could feel his legs protesting at the deep crouch, the blood still slowly trickling from the wound inflicted by the small bird.

The jaguar moved closer, its coarse whiskers coming close enough to graze Eric's cheek. The man tried to suppress a muscle spasm as the cat rubbed his jaw against his shoulder, the edge of the yellowed fangs scraping Eric's skin through the cotton shirt. Moving forward, the cat then melted back into the surrounding foliage as quietly as it arrived.

Eric lowered himself to the ground below, heedless of the myriad of thorny twigs and spiked leaves that punctured his legs by the dozens. Nostrils flaring, his eyes clenched shut tightly as he fought to get his fear under control, knowing that, in his current condition, the terror would kill him before anything else had the opportunity.

After a few moments, he stood and began to journey through the harrowing jungle once more.

~ * ~ * ~

"How long are you going to sit here and wait?" Rowan crouched down uneasily beside his wife and daughter. He had left them under Darian's guard so that he could return to Asimina and gather thick blankets and food baskets for his family.

"As long as it takes for us to know the outcome." Rhea took the basket and pulled out a wheel of cheese, breaking off several pieces and passing them around.

Rowan closed his eyes in frustration. He stood up and gazed toward the edge of the woods. The sun was beginning to set and there had been no sound from the tree-line, no indication of what was occurring in the depths of the Wilderness.

When people had been taken there in the past to atone for their crimes, the result was immediate, and the sounds unable to be misinterpreted. Yet, today, there was only ominous silence as the day passed into night. Whether that was a sign of condemnation or forgiveness, he did not know, and the unknowing left him unsettled and skittish.

Sabina looked up as Darian settled on the flattened grass beside her. "Thank you for staying with me."

His hand gently closed on top of hers. "I will stay here as long as you need." Hesitantly, he gently kissed her temple, the gesture still frightening and alien to a person who had been trained to display no emotion.

With a heavy sigh, Sabina lay her head upon his shoulder, needing the comfort of his closeness. "Do you think he will come out?"

"Love is a great incentive, so it is a possibility. All we can do is hope, the rest is on him."

~ * ~ * ~

The night air was thick, causing Eric's lungs to heave as they tried to filter oxygen from water in the humid air. His clothing stuck to his body, plastered to his skin with sweat, blood, and dirt. Darkness fell around him, forcing his progress through the jungle to an antagonizing crawl.

Something thick crunched beneath his foot and toppled him to the ground. Eric let himself lay on the ground a moment to catch his breath. He had lost track of how many times he had fallen, as if the ground itself were trying to prevent him from continuing his journey

329

to an unknown destination. *What is it this time?* He gave out a low growl of frustration as he twisted his head to look.

At first, he thought it was a gleaming white tree root that his foot had slipped upon. Closer inspection had him scrambling backward as he realized he was staring at a human skeleton. Several rib bones had snapped where his foot sank into the torso, and the jaw of the skeleton was open in a silent scream.

This death had been far from natural, or painless. Deep gouges created long canals in the bones, evidence of an attack from a creature with claws large enough to slice through flesh and sink into the bone below. The top of the skull was crushed, and several vertebrae had been knocked loose. While the left side of the skeleton was intact, the right side was missing the entire hand and lower arm.

Leaves rustled to his right, and Eric whipped around. The first thing that caught his eye was the creamy-white hand bones that were laying several feet from the body. Then his brain processed the creature glowing as it sedately walked out of the jungle toward him.

This is not real. There is no way this is real. "I did not do that." Panic pitched his voice as he slowly gestured toward the body.

Cloven hooves lightly moved across the underbrush as the black creature stepped out of the shadows and into a small patch of light. Large, gray eyes stared at the man as graceful legs brought the creature close enough to touch. Dappled-black fur covered the lithe equine body, powerful muscles rippling beneath the skin as it moved. It tossed its head and snorted, warm, metallic breath blasting Eric's face as his body froze and his limbs began to shake.

One long, spiraling horn glistened as the creature dipped its head, the deadly point aimed at Eric's heart. In the space of a few seconds, Eric realized the glistening was caused by thick blood, and felt certain this animal would be the one to end his terror.

His arms spread wide; he stood his ground as the unicorn advanced, and the horn began to puncture his chest. "I accept the judgment. I know that I did wrong, though my memories of the actions are limited. I know I came back here for the wrong reasons, but have found so much to love in this realm. At least, I have loved, though not nearly long enough." Eric closed his eyes tightly, body braced against the pain, waiting for the final thrust.

Instead, light fingertips trailed from his throat down his chest. Slight pressure was placed on his chest, just above his heart, and a sickly-sweet, metallic odor filled his nostrils.

Eric slowly opened his eyes, his body rigid as he took in the woman now standing in front of him. Her tangled, wind-blown hair was so red it shone against the blackness of the forest, and the length of it wrapped around her naked body, concealing herself from his view. Gray eyes shone in a face so pale that he could see the blue veins that pumped blood beneath the flawless skin. A single tattoo adorned her body, a red, tight, barbed spiral just above the space between her eyes.

"Why are you here, man of the other world?" Her voice was smooth, seductive, and Eric felt his body lean into her touch of its own accord.

"To make amends, and receive judgment." He blinked hard, trying to shake her presence as it coiled around his soul.

Blood-red nails dug into the fabric of his shirt and her lips curved into a sensual, yet terrifying grin. She leaned in closely, her lips lightly brushing his collarbone as she inhaled his scent. "For some acts, there can be no amends made. The judgment may be harsh, everlasting, and beyond the scope of mortal pain."

Shaking with the effort, he resisted the urge to wrap his arms around her, too aware of her naked body pressing against the thin cotton he wore. "I never wanted to come here, back then. I did not realize what I was doing. Now, I do. Now, I want a chance to make amends for that time when I was not myself. My heart is good, but they don't know that yet. I need that chance, to let them see what is truly within my heart."

A red tongue darted out, tasting the fear on his skin as it traced the edge of his ear. She pulled back, putting no more than an inch between their bodies and tilting her delicate face up so that she could meet his eyes. Thick, black lashes framed her shining orbs, fluttering enticingly as she blinked. "You could always stay here with me. There would be no pain, only eternal pleasure."

His blood surged at her voice and he choked back the affirmative response. Instead, he closed his eyes tightly and pictured Yasmina, remembered the feel of her soft skin under his hands, the way her thick, stick-straight hair would fall upon his chest as they slept. "My heart already belongs to another."

The fingers trailed downward, their touch feathery as she leaned close again, her lips brushing the corner of his mouth. "I am not interested in your heart, man who trembles beneath my fingers."

Fighting against every instinct, he remained still, with heightened awareness of her touch, her scent, and the affects they were having upon his body. "My heart, body, and soul belong to another. Please, let me go back to her."

At that, she drew away, long nails lightly scraping his arm. "Do not cross us again, man who is reborn. You provide far too much temptation for me to release you should another transgression occur." She turned, the long, red waves falling like a curtain across her back. It brushed her thighs and she took two steps forward, halting and turning to fix those eyes once again upon him.

"Well? If you can resist me long enough to follow me, I shall guide you out. Are you coming?"

~ * ~ * ~

"Seb!" Darian's voice was a low, urgent whisper as he shook her. Sabina had fallen asleep hours earlier, her head cushioned on his solid thigh. He had spent the time gently running his fingers through her hair, marveling at the power of emotions that surged through his blood after being denied for so long.

"What is it?" She sat up, looking around in the pre-dawn dimness

He pointed toward the edge of the woods, where a shadow moved clumsily through the dense brush. "Wake up your mother."

Sabina quickly shook Rhea awake as Darian stood, warily drawing out his long knife and holding it loosely at his side. Her breath caught in her throat as the shadow turned into a man, and she saw familiar blue eyes staring at her from the darkness.

Rhea moved first, taking a few tentative steps toward him. "Matt? Eric? Is that really you?"

The man nodded and moved forward again. His face was covered with small lacerations, his palms and exposed skin on his arms no better. Yet, his eyes were peaceful, and his lips curved in a soft smile. "It's really me. Please, take me home."

Chapter 46

Selo Natali

Loud pounding filled the air as Eric's steel hammer drove another nail into the board. A bell clanged and he lightly dropped the mallet onto a nearby bench, rolling his shoulders to ease the tension and strain.

"Hey, Eric, give me a hand?"

He turned and grinned as he saw Philip waving from the next house. The pieces for a sturdy, large, wooden bed frame stood in front of Philip's house, ready for transport. "You got it."

Philip grunted as he hefted the piece onto his shoulder. "I figured I would build this in pieces so we don't have to maneuver it through the door. We just need to put in a few bolts once we're in the house and you will be all set."

Eric steadied the second half of the frame on his shoulder and trudged back to his house. The frame fit perfectly through his front door, and he led the way into the master bedroom. "Not a bad idea at all."

The frames dropped to the wooden-plank flooring with a soft thud and within moments the two men had the frame bolted together.

Philip helped Eric to slide the thick, wool-filled mattress onto the frame and gave it a quick test.

"Sturdy and comfortable." Philip hopped back up and shook Eric's hand. "Will we be seeing you for dinner tonight?"

"Of course, if it's not an imposition."

"Not at all!" Philip grinned as Eric followed him to the front door. "Mya and I love having you over and it's easier for her to cook for three than you to cook for one."

Eric walked back into his house and stood in thought for a moment, surveying his domain. His deep connection with Philip had come as a surprise to him, although he later realized that they were well suited to one another. Both from a different world and both having committed crimes that were unforgivable; the men understood one another and the constant quest to be virtuous and make amends for the past.

His eyes glanced around the room and he allowed himself a small grin. They had decided to clear a small portion of the forest that surrounded this new village, Selo Natali, so that the houses could be built in a style that emulated the old home of the refugees. Thick plank walls gave shelter from the winds of the valley, and the tiles imported from Kylassame made for sturdy roofs. One of the refugees had immediately begun working on glass windows, while another set about constructing sturdy wooden doors for each of the dozen homes.

Philip had turned his hand to furniture making, and had taken Eric under his wing as an apprentice. Eric ran his fingers over the sanded and polished kitchen table and the set of four chairs, then rested his hands upon the rocking chair he had placed in front of the fire.

The refugees had adopted a new way of cooking in their old world, similar to a pizza oven, but with a flat stone top so that food could be cooked on top of the space as well as within the heated interior. Sink basins had been carefully carved of soapstone and set within a polished, wooden counter. One of the refugees had come up with the idea to create a drain by carefully drilling a small hole in the bottom of the sink, then using the local bamboo supply to create a series of tubes that led outside of the house to irrigate a vegetable garden.

Toward the back of the house were the bedrooms, modest chambers that housed a bed, dresser, and cushioned chair for reading. While he had not heard from Yasmina since the announcement of his past life by the Gormellyn, he still held on to the hope that they would one day be together. His heart bruised but determined, he asked Philip to make one bed large enough for two, and the second bed big enough for a young girl.

Philip had not been able to conceal the pity that filled his eyes for the man who held onto hope with no indication of reward, but did as Eric asked without comment. If Eric was going to continue hoping for a reunion with the woman who never came, far be it for Philip to dash his spirit into the ground.

This truly was a "village of birth" for the residents, most of whom were refugees from the other realm, but some were people who just needed a change of scenery. It lifted his heart to see the children who had been so near death in their old world receive a second chance at childhood, a chance to regain some of the lost innocence.

It had been months since he left the darkness of the Wilderness, and he was hard-pressed not to give in to despair. For a foolish moment, he had thought himself forgiven when he left the woods and found himself tightly embraced by both Rhea and Sabina. Then, they had dropped him off at the refugee camp, wished him luck, and disappeared from his life, pulled back into their necessary travels.

Darian had come to see him, once. He found out then that both women were busy both at Asimina and in court, as the knowledge of his past spread through the realm. While it hurt him, he understood Yasmina's absence, and in the bleakest parts of the night he wondered if it would have been better to succumb to the charms of the woman in the woods.

You're still alive. That means there is still a chance. He clapped his hands in an effort to shake the grim thoughts, the sound bouncing off the walls of the house. His feet moved him into the bedroom, where he mechanically removed the simple blanket from the corner and spread it over the bed.

A glance out of the window confirmed that it was nearly dinner time, so he walked out of the house, carefully latching the door behind him. Voices drifted over the breeze from the path that led into the village, and his head turned toward the dirt pathway in curiosity. The setting sun shone directly into his eyes, momentarily blinding him as he glimpsed four silhouettes cresting the rise.

His heart twisted and his stomach leaped as the smallest of the silhouettes suddenly dashed forward, long hair streaming behind as small feet propelled the shadow forward. Her body crashed into his and he spun in a circle, arms tightly wrapped around the lean body to keep them both from falling backward.

"Eric! Eric!" Asli's cries of joy brought tears to his eyes as he held her close, hardly daring to believe this was not a dream, the weight of her presence upon his heart bringing him to his knees.

He looked over her head and saw Yasmina standing several yards away, her body tense and eyes bright with tears. Behind her, Sabina and Darian lowered a small trunk to the ground, waved, and then moved off toward Philip's house to give him privacy.

Eric stood slowly, Asli clinging to his leg. "I didn't think you would come."

Yasmina flinched, but moved forward until they were close enough to touch. "I did not know if you would want us here."

His fingers tenderly caressed her hair, then she was in his arms in a tight, desperate embrace. Asli adjusted so that she had one arm wrapped around his leg, and one around her mother's. Both of the adults dropped to their knees, and tears of pain and joy rained upon the earth as the three of them held tight to one another.

"Are you sure?" Eric's voice was barely a whisper. His thumb gently wiped away a tear that fell from Yasmina's face.

She nodded. "I am sure. No matter where we go, no matter what we do, I want to do it by your side."

A grin spread across his face as he took them inside to show them their new home, and begin their new life.

~ * ~ * ~

"That ended well, at least." Sabina leaned against the outer wall of Philip's house and smiled as Eric guided his family into their new home.

"It did," Darian agreed, as he laced his fingers with hers and gave her a rare, unguarded smile. "Now we just have to decide where we will settle down."

Sabina laughed, the sound rich and vibrant and her green eyes twinkled as he winked in response. "How could we settle down with so much left to explore? Next you are going to suggest we go live at the court."

His purple eyes flashed with equal measures humor and alarm. "Ah no, not us. We belong with the wind and the rain, the court belongs to your sister; besides," he added, his eyes focused on the horizon, "that would not be nearly the life we have chosen as our destiny."

Novels by Kristi Strong

Land of Kaldalangra series

The Lady of Steinbrekka

Heart of Kylassame

Soul of Asimina

Standalone Novels

Finding Keepers

Author Biography

Fixing broken computers, wrangling a very spirited little toddler, and creating a world with mysterious people are all parts of the average day for Kristi Strong. A graduate of James Madison University, she uses her degree in anthropology and fascination of cultures to draw inspiration for her fantasy novels.

Connect with Kristi

StrongNovels.Blogspot.com

StrongNovels@live.com

Facebook.com/StrongNovels

Twitter.com/StrongNovels

www.ingramcontent.com/pod-product-compliance
Lightning Source LLC
Chambersburg PA
CBHW030406180626
46812CB00005B/1940